Moonlight Reverie

Robert had almost given up on his Miss Lindquist when he heard the quiet closing of a door and rapid footfalls. His heart lightened at the sound of her approach.

"Good evening, Miss Lindquist. I hoped this sky would draw you outside."

"Good evening, Lord Elston." As she turned her face heavenward, the hood of her cloak slipped back a bit. He managed to glimpse her delicate features, a petite frame, and a swath of pale hair before she turned toward him. She stared up at him for a moment, as if to study his features, then retreated to the same shadowy corner she had occupied the night before.

Silence reigned for several minutes, but Karla, or *Miss Lindquist*, did not find it uncomfortable. Theirs was like the silence between old friends. Then they spoke simultaneously.

"Lord Elston—"

"Miss Lindquist—" The marquess deferred to her.

"Society has rules for everything, doesn't it?"

"So it seems." A wry smile accompanied his words.

Oh, how she regretted deceiving him! Karla want to speak to him, but she still feared his scorn, should she confess her lie. She watched as he leaned back against the stone baluster of the terrace and crossed one booted ankle over the other. . . .

The Marriage Campaign

Susannah Carleton

A SIGNET BOOK

SIGNET
Published by New American Library, a division of
Penguin Putnam Inc., 375 Hudson Street,
New York, New York 10014, U.S.A.
Penguin Books Ltd, 80 Strand,
London WC2R 0RL, England
Penguin Books Australia Ltd, 250 Camberwell Road,
Camberwell, Victoria 3124, Australia
Penguin Books Canada Ltd, 10 Alcorn Avenue,
Toronto, Ontario, Canada M4V 3B2
Penguin Books (N.Z.) Ltd, Cnr Rosedale and Airborne Roads,
Albany, Auckland 1310, New Zealand

Penguin Books Ltd, Registered Offices:
Harmondsworth, Middlesex, England

First published by Signet, an imprint of New American Library,
a division of Penguin Putnam Inc.

First Printing, February 2003
10 9 8 7 6 5 4 3 2 1

 REGISTERED TRADEMARK—MARCA REGISTRADA

Printed in the United States of America

PUBLISHER'S NOTE
This is a work of fiction. Names, characters, places, and incidents either are
the product of the author's imagination or are used fictitiously, and any
resemblance to actual persons, living or dead, business establishments, events,
or locales is entirely coincidental.

BOOKS ARE AVAILABLE AT QUANTITY DISCOUNTS WHEN USED TO PROMOTE
PRODUCTS OR SERVICES. FOR INFORMATION PLEASE WRITE TO PREMIUM
MARKETING DIVISION, PENGUIN PUTNAM INC., 375 HUDSON STREET, NEW YORK,
NEW YORK 10014.

To Carla Arpin and Jane Bowers, for inspiring such interesting characters.

To Melissa Jensen, Dee Hendrickson, and Sandra Heath, for their advice and encouragement.

To Tim and Andrew Jones, for their love and support.

Prologue

27 December 1812

*H*e fled for the border. Like a thief in the night, or a fox pursued by a tenacious pack of hounds, he raced along the back roads of Gloucestershire through the deepening dusk, hoping to elude his pursuers.

No one chasing him would expect him to make a run for it tonight. Or any night, for that matter. Yet here he was, skulking in the shadows like some highwayman of yore, hoping that no one would see him.

With the collar of his greatcoat pulled high, the brim of his hat tugged low over his brow, and a muffler protecting his ears and the lower part of his face from the biting cold, he looked more like a knight of the road than a leader of the *ton*. No travelers need fear being robbed of their money and jewels, however; his mission was quite different.

This was not how Robert had expected to spend the holidays. But death has a way of destroying even the best-laid plans.

A fortnight ago he'd been in London, searching the shops on Oxford and Bond Streets for Christmas gifts for his father and his great-aunt Lavinia. His father had been in the country, riding a new gelding in the squire's hunt. No one knew for certain what happened at the second fence, but horse and rider had parted company going over it. The horse had broken a leg; the marquess, his neck.

Now Robert was the marquess—and the most persecuted man in Gloucestershire.

The marriage-minded misses and matchmaking mamas had made his life a misery. He'd been fawned over, flirted with, and fondled—and that was just in church on Christmas Eve! There had been more lady callers at Elston Abbey in the past ten days than in the last decade. Young ladies who never misstepped on the dance floor had fallen down the front stairs and injured their ankles. Perfectly serviceable carriages had broken down outside the gates. He'd borne all that with false smiles—and gritted teeth.

But today, while escorting his great-aunt to her room after tea, he'd caught Squire Dinwoody's platter-faced daughter sneaking into his bedchamber. Tonight Robert was fleeing to his most remote property to avoid being compromised into marriage by some conniving chit more interested in his title and fortune than in him. When the time came, he would choose his bride.

Reaching the main road, he turned north and set his horse to a gallop. Yet even at that pace, he couldn't outrun his thoughts.

According to the codicil in his father's will, the time had arrived. Robert had a year in which to wed, and his choice was limited to the ladies his parent had listed. Of the twenty, fourteen were still unwed, but three were in the schoolroom. He knew four of the remaining eleven—and thought it highly unlikely he'd find wedded bliss with any of them.

Seven unknown women from which to choose a bride. Who would believe that Robert Edmond Alexander Symington, Marquess of Elston, one of the most eligible bachelors in the realm, would find himself in such straits?

Chapter One

*R*obert Symington, fifth Marquess of Elston, glanced at the guests with whom he was enjoying a convivial dinner at Hallack Grange, the smallest of his estates, then did something he rarely ever did. He acted on impulse.

"I have problem, and I hope the two of you will assist me in resolving it."

Despite the fact that impulsive behavior was not Robert's wont, his decision was not a reckless one. The man on his left, George Winterbrook, Earl of Weymouth, was his closest friend, and had been for nearly twenty years—since the day they'd arrived at Eton as ten-year-olds, both feeling lost and alone, and more than a bit surprised to discover that school did *not* possess all the comforts of home. Their friendship was so deep and so strong that the earl was the only person, aside from Robert's father and great-aunt, who called him by his Christian name.

George looked askance at him. "After all that we have been through over the years, Robert, I am offended that you feel the need to ask. Of course I will help you."

Robert turned to the lady on his right. Miss Beth Castleton had saved George from being forced into marriage with an unscrupulous woman, and had taken a pistol ball in the shoulder in the process. Robert had known her only a fortnight, but he was honored to count her—and be counted by her—as a friend.

"I will assist you in any way that I can, Lord Elston,"

she declared, her melodious accent betraying her American upbringing.

Robert released the breath he hadn't realized he was holding. "Thank you. Thank you both. But"—he smiled at her—"if you are friend enough to help solve my problem, there is no need for such formality between us. Please call me Elston."

She returned his smile. "And will you call me Beth?"

"Sometimes, perhaps, but not in public. Such informality might be misconstrued as impropriety."

Her smile dimmed slightly, but she nodded, acknowledging the constraints Society imposed upon unmarried men and women.

George returned the conversation to its original topic. "Is this problem the same one that was troubling you at Stranraer?" Robert knew his friend referred not to the Scottish town but to Robert's fishing lodge just outside it— Hawthorn Lodge, the place to which he'd fled when he left Gloucestershire. The earl had sought refuge there for himself, his niece Isabelle, Beth, and two servants after Beth was wounded.

"It is."

"Does it have something to do with your father's death?"

Robert started at the soft question, then turned to Beth. Her perspicacity would be alarming were she any other woman. But she was his friend, and his feelings for her were similar to the affection a man might feel for his sister—unencumbered by any romantical urges. "It does."

After a sip of wine and a deep breath, he told them of the codicil. Several seconds of shocked silence greeted his words.

"So he is still trying to control your life from beyond the grave, eh?" was George's comment.

Beth glanced at the earl as if surprised by his remark. "Was your father a controlling man, Elston?"

"Only in one area, until this." Seeing her perplexed frown, Robert explained, "My father inherited the title when he was at university and, as a result, never had the carefree years as a town buck most young men have. He gave me that freedom, but I yearned for responsibility. We were often at loggerheads because he couldn't understand my desire to manage one of the estates. Finally, in frustration, I bought a pair of colors."

"You wanted something to occupy your time and, I suspect, a chance to implement his lessons on estate management—"

"Exactly so."

"But," she continued, "he gave you leisure instead of occupation."

Robert nodded.

"He gave you the life he wanted as a young man—"

"I never thought of it in just that way, Beth, but you are quite right."

"Now you are in the same position he was, with estates to manage and no experience at doing so."

He sighed. "Yes."

After a moment's thought, she got to the heart of his dilemma with three questions. Not surprising, that; her intelligence was formidable. "Why did your father write the codicil? Do you intend to honor it? And what are the consequences if you don't?"

"Even after two months of thinking of little else, I am not certain why my father wrote it. Most days I can accept the codicil and believe it was written in love, not anger. But there are times when I deeply resent it and cannot see it as anything but a last attempt to dictate my life."

He paused for a moment to control his rising ire. "During my sojourn in Scotland, I resolved to try to accede to my father's wishes, but I refuse to shackle myself for life to a woman for whom I feel neither affection nor esteem."

"Very wise," said Beth. George nodded in agreement.

Robert drank from his wineglass. "I have no wish for what Society calls a 'marriage of convenience'—they seem damnably inconvenient to me—nor do I want a wife who is more interested in my title and fortune than in me."

"No man would. No sensible man," George clarified.

Robert wasn't certain if his friend's comment referred to marriages of convenience or to women who wed for a title and fortune. Probably both. It was well-known throughout the *beau monde* that Winterbrooks always married for love. Robert knew he was unlikely to be so fortunate. Mutual affection was probably the best he could achieve. He hoped it would be enough.

"I take it you are hoping that one or more of the ladies will earn your affection and esteem?" Beth's frankness was a trait Robert admired, but at times he found it disconcerting.

"Beth!" George remonstrated. "Such appalling directness shows your American upbringing."

Robert saw the hurt expression in her blue eyes before she lowered her gaze to her empty plate. "I beg your pardon, Elston."

"There is no reason for you to do so, Beth." His tone was gentle but the glare he directed at his old friend was not. "And you are quite right. I hope for exactly that."

George gazed for a moment at Beth's still downcast head, then took up the role of devil's advocate. "And if none of the ladies earns your regard?"

Robert shrugged. "Then I will not meet the terms of the codicil."

"What—" Beth interrupted her question to look at the man across the table.

The earl smiled—a peace offering—then asked the question she hadn't. "What are the consequences if you do not?"

"I don't know."

"You don't . . ." his interrogator sputtered. "How can you not know?"

"The consequences were not stated in the codicil. Even my solicitor doesn't know. He has a letter from my father to be given to me on the anniversary of his death. Presumably they are detailed in that missive."

"Good Lord!" Weymouth's exclamation was as much curse as prayer.

"So you must live with this sword of Damocles hanging over your head until December?" Beth's tone was hesitant, as if she feared she overstepped.

"It is not quite so bad as that. The title cannot be taken from me, nor the estates; they are all entailed. The worst that could happen is that my father's personal fortune would be bestowed elsewhere." Robert toyed with his wineglass, his eyes following the movement of its contents. "That would make life difficult, but not unbearably so. Not enough to sentence myself to certain unhappiness to avoid it."

After several moments of silence, Beth touched his hand

fleetingly, offering sympathy for his plight. "What can we do to help?"

Robert looked up, drawing comfort and strength from his friends' earnest desire to aid him. "First, you can tell me what you know of the ladies."

"I doubt that I know any of them," she demurred, "unless they live near Castleton Abbey."

"I sometimes forget that you have lived in England for only a year, Beth." He offered her a smile of apology, even as he berated himself for the lapse, for she had spent that year in mourning for her maternal grandparents, who raised her after the deaths of her parents and sisters.

"First," George said, chuckling, "you must tell us who the ladies are."

"Lud!" Robert propped his elbows on the table and dropped his head into his hands. "I thought I had already done so."

After a few moments spent collecting his thoughts, he raised his head. "Shall we adjourn to the drawing room?" He stood, then offered his arm to Beth.

"You aren't going to drink port and discuss . . . whatever it is that gentlemen discuss after ladies leave the table?"

He smiled down at her. "We will drink our port in the drawing room and talk with you instead."

"Thank you, kind sirs." She curtsied gracefully before seating herself on the blue-and-white-striped sofa. A rather frayed sofa, Robert noted, adding its re-covering to the mental list of repairs he would assign his steward on the morrow.

Crossing the room, he investigated the decanters on a side table in the corner. None contained port. "Brandy, George? Or would you prefer port?"

"Brandy, please."

Robert poured the dark amber liquid into two snifters. "Beth, would you like a glass of sherry?"

"No, thank you, Elston. I will wait for the tea tray."

"Shall I ask Hodge to bring it now?" He handed the earl a snifter, then strode toward the bellpull.

Beth shook her head, a soft smile twitching one corner of her mouth. "That isn't necessary. I will wait until later, in the unlikely event you or Weymouth eschew brandy and join me."

As he walked toward his friends, Robert caught George's

eye and received a slight nod. They would both drink tea with her.

After seating himself in one of the chairs facing the sofa, Robert crossed one pantalooned leg over the other. They had not dressed for dinner because his companions' choice of attire was extremely limited. Beth had been kidnapped while attempting to rescue a child—George's niece—from that fate, and had only the carriage dress she'd been wearing at the time and a simple round gown her new maid had sewn from an ancient bolt of cloth unearthed in the attics at Hawthorn Lodge. George, too, had been abducted, and, although he'd had a small portmanteau with him, its contents were limited and did not extend to evening attire. He was reduced to wearing combinations of the few garments he had and whatever items of Robert's clothing fit. Although they were very similar in stature, George was two inches taller, but his only complaint had been that the too-short sleeves of Robert's shirts made driving difficult.

"You were going to tell us the names of the ladies," his old friend prompted.

"So I was." Robert lifted his eyes from their contemplation of his Hessians. "There were twenty on my father's list, but six have wed and three are still in the schoolroom."

"How many of the remaining eleven do you know?" his companions inquired, almost in unison.

"I am acquainted with four, but I cannot imagine being married to any of them." Robert steeled his muscles against the shudder that always accompanied contemplation of a future with any of the four.

George's left eyebrow arced. "Who are they?"

"Greenwich's daughter, Winton's oldest daughter, Montrose's youngest, and Chesterfield's girl."

"Elston"—Beth's tone was apologetic—"if I am to be of any help, you will have to tell me the ladies' names. I know Lady Christina Fairchild is the Duke of Greenwich's daughter—she was presented at the Queen's Birthday Drawing Room, as I was—but I am unfamiliar with the other titles."

Damnation, he'd done it again. Beth was such a comfortable friend and companion that it seemed he had known her for years. It was often difficult to remember that she was less familiar with British Society than any green girl. "My apologies, Beth. The Earl of Winton's eldest daughter is Lady Sybil Chesterton, Viscount Montrose's youngest is Faith Monroe, and Lord Chesterfield's girl is Amelia Forbes-Symthe."

"Thank you." Beth's smile was a bit rueful. "I do not know any of them."

"All have been out in Society for a year or more, and none live near your uncle's estate," George explained, "so it would be surprising if you did. I know them all, and I agree with Robert's assessment."

Robert glanced at his friend, comforted that they agreed on the unsuitability of those four ladies to be his marchioness. "The final seven are: Ladies Deborah and Diana Woodhurst, daughters of the Marquess of Kesteven; Lady Mary Foster, the Earl of Foxton's middle daughter; Lady Sarah Mallory, the Earl of Tregaron's daughter; Karolina Lane, the eldest daughter of Viscount Padbury—"

"Of the late viscount," George corrected.

Robert's gaze slewed to his friend. "Are you certain? Padbury was one of my father's closest friends. If he died, Father would have said something to me."

The earl frowned, his eyes narrowing in concentration. "Not entirely certain, no. I seem to recall my father mentioning it in a letter, but I could be mistaken."

"I hope you are. I was looking forward to renewing my acquaintance with him."

After a moment's pause, Robert continued. "The final two unknowns are Clarissa Merrick, Lord Merrick's daughter, and Harriett Broughton, whose late father was an active member of the House of Commons."

"I have met only two of the ladies, but I will make every effort to get to know the others during the Season," Beth said.

Robert couldn't help but smile at her earnest promise. "Thank you. That will help a great deal."

"Which two?" George's tone was curt, more demand than question. "I also know two of them."

Robert looked askance at the earl, as did Beth before she answered. "Lady Sarah and Miss Broughton were presented at Court when Lady Christina and I were. Aunt Julia introduced me to them—and their mothers, of course—because all three girls are reputed to be very fine musicians."

"Are they indeed?" As a violist and music lover, Robert

found that tidbit extremely useful. "I hope you will introduce them to me when I arrive in Town."

Beth smiled. "Of course I will, Elston."

He drank the last of his brandy, then set the snifter on the table between his chair and the one George occupied. "Do you know if they are singers or instrumentalists?"

"Miss Broughton is a singer. I believe she also plays the pianoforte, but she prefers singing. Lady Sarah is a harpist. Lady Christina plays the pianoforte."

"Thank you, Beth. That is very useful information."

As one, he and Beth turned to Weymouth, but it was Robert who queried, "With which ladies are you acquainted, George?"

"With Lady Mary and Miss Broughton, but I did not know the latter was musical. Nor that Lady Christina was a pianist." He lifted his snifter in salute. "Well done, Beth."

Robert was surprised that his old friend was unaware of the ladies' reputed skills. As a cellist, George knew most of the *ton*'s musicians, and his father, a violinist, was believed to know every single one—and the extent of their talent. Robert had spent many an hour playing trios with the pair and had often heard George's father animadvert on the skills—or lack thereof—of the *beau monde*'s musical members. Father and son were, in Robert's opinion, the most talented, but George, who had heard Beth—also a violinist—play, declared her skill superior to his father's.

Robert's attention returned to his guests when Beth stood, an apologetic smile on her rather pale face. "Forgive me for deserting you, but I am very tired and I know Weymouth will want to make an early start tomorrow."

Berating himself for not noticing her fatigue, Robert rose and offered his arm to escort her to the stairs. George lunged to his feet, bowed over Beth's hand as he bid her good night, and assured her she must sleep as late as she wished.

"I shall be ready to leave at nine o'clock, as usual. I can sleep in the carriage."

When he returned to the drawing room, Robert was not surprised to see George refilling both snifters, although his frown was unexpected. "What's amiss?"

"I am worried that Beth is not sufficiently recovered for this journey."

"I worry about her, too, but surely she is a better judge of her condition than you or I."

George shrugged, placed the decanter of brandy on the table between them, then resumed his seat. "What else can I do to help you?"

Robert accepted the change in topic. Although it was obvious to him that George was falling in love with Beth, his friend seemed unaware of his feelings. "Meet the ladies you don't know. When I arrive in Town, you can give me your impressions of them."

"Of course. What else?"

Robert pondered the question, but he could think of no other assistance his friend—or anyone else—might provide. "Naught. I must get to know them before I can make a decision."

George drained his snifter, then rose. "I, too, am for my bed. Good night, Robert."

"Good night, George. Thank you for your help."

"For whatever it is worth, I am of the opinion that Lady Mary would not be a suitable bride." After uttering that rather cryptic remark, the earl left the room.

"Well, hell." Robert drank the last of his brandy, then followed his friend upstairs.

After breakfast the next morning Robert escorted Beth outside. As they strolled down the front steps to join the rest of the party on the carriage drive, she thanked him very prettily for the assistance he had rendered. "I shall miss your conversation—and your friendship."

He bowed over her hand. "You shall always have my friendship, whether I am present or not, but further conversations will have to wait until I come to London later this spring. I hope you will save a dance for me at your come-out ball."

As he handed her into the carriage already occupied by her maid and George's three-year-old niece, Beth smiled shyly. "I would be honored, and delighted, to dance with you then."

As he waved his friends off, Robert's feelings were mixed. He understood their need to return to Town and reassure their families that they had survived their respective ordeals, but he knew he would miss their company. After a fortnight of companionable conversation and wor-

rying about other people's problems, now he would have
to deal with his own. And there was no time like the present
to start.

By noon the next day, after a series of meetings with his
steward, the housekeeper, and the butler, Robert completed
his business at Hallack Grange. It was time to get
on with the rest of his life—and to begin his search for a
bride. Thus resolved, he strode from the study into the hall.

"Higgins!" It was the voice that had commanded troops
on the Peninsula.

"Yes, Major—um, Lord Elston?" His former batman,
now his valet, appeared at the top of the stairs, a stack of
freshly laundered shirts in his hands.

"We leave for London in the morning."

"Lunnon, sir? Not Gloucestershire and the Abbey?"

Robert narrowed his eyes as an idea struck his mind with
the force and brilliance of lightning. "London is our ultimate
destination, but we will make several stops along the
way, including an extended one at the Abbey."

The beginning of a smile lifted a corner of the manservant's
mouth before he bowed his head. "I will begin packing
immediately, my lord. Er, what clothing will you need
for these 'stops'?"

"Riding clothes, afternoon attire, and evening dress."

"Very good, my lord."

When his valet bustled off, Robert returned to the study.
As the afternoon progressed, he mapped his journey to
London as carefully as e'er he'd prepared a battle strategy
for Wellington. By the time the dinner bell rang, Robert's
matrimonial intentions were still as murky as ditch water,
but he did have a plan of sorts.

The next morning Robert and the faithful Higgins left
Hallack Grange. It was a cold but sunny morning, hinting
of the approach of spring although it was only the third
day of March, and the roads were more dry than muddy.
Today's journey would be a relatively short one, to the
home of Lord Merrick. Robert did not know the baron
well, and had never met his daughter, but Miss Clarissa
Merrick was one of the unmarried ladies on his father's
list, so make her acquaintance he would.

After luncheon and a change of horses near Barnard Castle, Robert spelled Higgins on the box. As the only servant who had been entrusted with the marquess's destination when he'd left Gloucestershire, Higgins had driven the coach to Stranraer, served as butler there, and was now doing double-duty as coachman and valet. Tooling the carriage toward Darlington, Robert reviewed his plan and debated, again, the merits of arriving unexpectedly. The visits would appear casual, instead of contrived, and the young ladies would not be primped within an inch of their lives—definite advantages—but the families might leave for Town before he arrived.

Robert shrugged, then cracked the whip over the head of the lagging off leader. All the ladies would, undoubtedly, be in London for the Season. If he did not meet them on his way to Town, he would meet them there.

"Welcome, Lord Elston," Lady Merrick gushed when the butler ushered him into a cozily comfortable, if slightly shabby, parlor.

"Forgive me for arriving unexpectedly, but—"

"Nonsense. You are welcome anytime." Lord Merrick, a hearty man with a shock of grizzled hair, punctuated his greeting with a slap on the shoulder.

"Indeed." Lady Merrick asked the butler for tea—and her children's presence. "Please join us, my lord."

Robert sat in the chair his hostess indicated and accepted their condolences on his father's death. As the butler entered with the tea tray, the baron asked what brought him to County Durham.

"I have been visiting my estates and paying calls on people my father spoke of before he died, and I am now returning to Gloucestershire." No need for the baron to know that mention of his name had been in a codicil to the late marquess's will, Robert thought.

Merrick smiled, but his reply was overridden by another.

"Will you be in London for the Season?"

The strident voice brought Robert to his feet, even as his head turned toward the doorway. His interrogator was a blond miss of unexceptional looks, barely out of the schoolroom, dressed in a pink muslin round gown with lace trim at the neckline and a profusion of flounces adorning the hem. As the baron introduced his daughter, Robert wondered if the chit often asked total strangers impertinent questions. The baron's son and heir, a seemingly bookish lad of four-and-ten, shuffled into the room and was presented. Robert was not at all surprised when Miss Merrick took advantage of the distraction to usurp her father's chair—which was beside his.

After Robert resumed his seat and Lady Merrick served them all, Miss Merrick turned to him. "Will you be in London for the Season, Lord Elston?"

"For part of it. I expect I will arrive in Town in April."

"April?" Robert winced as Miss Merrick whacked his arm with her fan. "But that is too late. You will miss—"

"Hush, Clarissa." Lady Merrick's whispered reproof was accompanied by a mind-your-manners glower.

"I will miss the early social events, but I have other obligations." His hope that the baron's daughter would abandon the topic was only partially realized.

"Do tell us the latest *on dits,* my lord."

It took Robert several seconds to translate Miss Merrick's mangled pronunciation into a recognizable word. "I don't believe I have heard any."

"Oh. Then tell us what the most fashionable ladies are wearing this Season."

"I have not been in London since December, Miss Merrick."

"Oh."

Before she could quiz him about the weather, Robert turned the tables. "What are you looking forward to doing in Town?"

Miss Merrick's titter sounded like the braying of a donkey on the home farm at Elston Abbey—and was punctuated by another whack of her fan. "Shopping and parties and dancing and . . ."

Once launched on the topic, the young lady carried on a lengthy monologue about the delights in store during this, her first, Season. By the time tea was over, Robert's arm was sore from the many times she had hit it with her fan, and he was firmly convinced that Lady Merrick would do better to send her daughter back to the schoolroom than introduce her to Society. Miss Clarissa Merrick, with her questionable intelligence and rather ragged manners, would benefit from another year of study—with a good, firm governess.

Long before dinner was announced, Robert wished he had declined Merrick's invitation to stay overnight. By the time the evening finally dragged to a close, Robert feared Miss Merrick's shrill voice, musical butchering, and impertinent questions would haunt his nightmares.

If he dreamt amid all his tossing and turning, Robert did not remember his night visions in the morning. After an early breakfast with the baron, Robert made his escape and mentally crossed Miss Clarissa Merrick off his list of prospective brides.

Morning rain muddied the roads and slowed travel, but Robert arrived in Thirsk late in the afternoon. Twelve Oaks was one of his larger estates, part of the barony of Symington and Thirsk, one of his lesser titles. The three days he spent there, exploring the estate with his steward, a childhood playmate, were both instructive and relaxing. His old friend's explanations were lectures of a sort, practical demonstrations of how a well-managed estate was run. It was helpful to know that enlightening answers to his questions could be obtained at any time, via the post.

Robert left Thirsk in hopeful spirits, confident that he could handle the management of his estates. He would, no doubt, make mistakes along the way, but that was part of the learning process. Provided he learned from those mistakes and did not repeat them, he should do quite well. It was a comfort to know that one aspect of his life was under control.

His destination was Paddington Court near Selby, the home of Viscount Padbury, a friend of his father's from their days at Eton, and his daughter. Apparently Padbury had several daughters, for the codicil specified "Karolina Lane, the eldest daughter of Viscount Padbury." Although Robert had counted her among the unknown ladies, he had met Miss Lane previously, on more than one occasion, years ago. He remembered a silvery blond sprite with big blue eyes and a sunny smile and wondered if the young lady of the present—she must be three-and-twenty now—would elicit the same pleasant thoughts as the little girl of his memories.

As the coach rolled past farms and fields being prepared for planting, Robert pondered the significance of the exclusion of the younger daughters. If he remembered aright, the viscount had remarried several years after his first wife's death. The more he thought about it, the more certain Robert was: his last visit to Paddington Court—and his last meeting with Miss Lane—had been on the occasion of the viscount's second marriage. Karolina, called Karla by her father and the servants who doted upon her, was accustomed to being the center of her father's world and had not been happy when she realized that would no longer be the case. When the realization struck, she had not thrown a temper tantrum or sulked and pouted; instead she'd been unusually quiet for several days, her sunny disposition clouded by the impending changes in her life.

Though she'd been six and he twelve, he knew he would feel much the same if his father suddenly remarried, and so he had befriended her. On foot and on horseback they'd explored the estate. He'd taught her to fish—and to climb trees. The latter was not a skill of which her stepmother would have approved, but he'd known nothing of ladylike accomplishments and so had taught her the things he enjoyed.

He wondered if Karla remembered him. Wondered, too, if the exclusion of her half-sister or -sisters was due to the fact that his father had disliked the second Lady Padbury, almost on sight. He remembered his normally mild-mannered parent's scathing denunciation of the woman as "a grasping harpy who will destroy Padbury's career." The viscount was—or had been—a member of the diplomatic corps. Robert had not heard anything of the man in recent years, but that didn't necessarily mean the late marquess's prediction had come true. Nor Weymouth's, for that matter.

Robert knew those answers would be forthcoming. So, too, would he learn if Karla remembered him. At the time of his last visit, he'd been all arms and legs and coltish grace, with a voice that squeaked and dipped at the most awkward times. The scholarly, rather solemn lad had become a reserved, serious, dignified man, very much like his father. Robert's mother had provided the laughter in their lives, and although she'd been dead for almost twenty years, he still missed her; she had been the bright sun that centered his and his father's worlds.

Pondering that, Robert considered the importance of character and personality in a marriage and family. He wanted his bride, whoever she might be, to have the same bright spirit and gift for happiness his mother had. Otherwise, he feared he would become a curmudgeon.

Without realizing it, he had set some requirements for his bride-to-be. He ticked them off on his fingers. "She must be attractive. Well mannered. Reasonably intelligent. Possess some musical talent. Have a sunny disposition and the gift of laughter."

What other traits and talents did he wish his wife to have? "She should be a capable chatelaine and hostess." He tapped his fingertips together as he contemplated, but before he could add to his list, the coach slowed, then turned into the courtyard of a posting inn and halted.

He heard the ostler's shout although the words were indistinguishable. Higgins's reply was clear enough: they were stopping for a meal and did not require a quick change of horses. With a start, Robert realized it was well past midday. He hastily pulled on his gloves, donned his curly-brimmed beaver, and descended from the coach.

As he waited for his man to finish giving the ostlers their orders, Robert glanced around the innyard and was startled to recognize the George in York. He'd been so lost in his musings that he had not realized they'd traveled so far. Frowning, he recalled a change of horses earlier, perhaps two.

"What's amiss, my lord?"

"Naught, Higgins. I was just surprised at how far we have traveled."

"Sleepin', was ye?" His batman *tsk*ed, but merriment lit his eyes. "Whilst me and them horses was laboring so mightily?"

"No, I wasn't asleep. Just deep in thought, considering all the changes in my life now that I am the marquess."

"I reckon there's more in store."

"I know there are," Robert replied, his tone as grim as his thoughts.

Chapter Two

After a night spent at the posting inn between York and Selby and a leisurely breakfast, they continued on to Paddington Court. Robert delayed their departure from the inn so as to arrive at the viscount's estate shortly after two o'clock, the proper time for a morning call in Town and equally suitable in the country. As they came up the drive, he was both pleased and dismayed to see another carriage in front of the house. Pleased because there were other callers and his visit would not stand out so noticeably, dismayed because with others present it might be more difficult to speak to Miss Lane.

He had little time to ponder his feelings. Before the coach had drawn up in front of the house, the massive door opened and a footman ran out and stood ready to open the coach door and lower the steps. Robert stepped down, then gave the man one of his calling cards.

"Good afternoon. I am Elston. Are Lady Padbury and Miss Lane at home this afternoon?"

"Yes, my lord. If you will follow me, please."

Robert glanced around as he followed the footman. Paddington Court was much as he remembered it, more grange than manor, but well kept. The house dated, he supposed, from the reign of Elizabeth, although a number of additions had been made over the years, some of which did not blend harmoniously with the original dwelling.

Once inside, after doffing his greatcoat, gloves, and hat, he was passed from footman to butler and again requested to "Follow me, please." Which he did, to a large parlor on the east side of the house, furnished in crimson and dark wood.

The butler announced him without first presenting his

card. A stripling of about fifteen, a brunette miss of sixteen or so, and two older women were the only occupants of the room. Robert recognized Lady Padbury instantly. Her once-brown hair was liberally streaked with gray and she had grown considerably stouter over the years, but the narrow-set brown eyes and pursed mouth were unchanged. He crossed the room and bowed over her hand.

"Good afternoon, Lady Padbury."

"It is a pleasure to make your acquaintance, Lord Elston," she replied, a frown creasing her brow.

"Actually, my lady, we met many years ago, at your wedding. I was Viscount Wrexton then."

The blank look in her eyes indicated she did not remember him, despite her murmured "Ah, yes. You attended with your father, I believe." Then, recalling her duties as hostess, "My lord, allow me to introduce my friend and neighbor, Lady Blackburn. And my eldest daughter, Lydia, and my son, Charles, Viscount Padbury."

The Countess of Blackburn was an attractive lady in her early fifties, but she looked a decade younger despite the off-center silver streak in her mahogany hair. Robert, who knew her son, bowed over her hand and expressed his pleasure in making her acquaintance. He then greeted Miss Lydia, who strongly resembled her mother, and the young viscount, who was blessed with his father's good looks.

When, Robert wondered, had his father's friend died? "Lady Padbury, allow me to express my belated condolences on the death of your husband."

"Thank you, Lord Elston. It has been four years, but we miss him still." The viscountess bowed her head and touched a lace-trimmed handkerchief to dry eyes.

The entrance of the butler and a maid with refreshments brought a quick end to the false display of grief. Lady Padbury glanced up as she reached for the teapot—and nearly knocked it over when she realized her rudeness. "Oh, Lord Elston, please do sit down. That chair next to Lydia is particularly comfortable."

Since all the chairs were identical, Robert took the invitation for what it was: an opportunity for Miss Lydia to further her acquaintance with an eligible bachelor. He sat in the indicated spot, catching a glint of amusement in Lady Blackburn's eye as he did.

When all had been served, Robert inquired, "Will Miss Lane be joining us?"

The viscountess looked at him as if he had sprouted another head. "My daughter is here, sir."

"I was referring to your stepdaughter, ma'am."

"Caroline?" Lady Padbury's tone conveyed her startlement. "No, I don't believe Caroline will be joining us."

"How disappointing. I haven't seen Karolina in an age." Robert noticed Lady Blackburn's subtle emphasis on the correct pronunciation of Miss Lane's name, but the viscountess obviously did not.

"Caroline is . . . ah, visiting one of the tenants this afternoon."

"But I thought she was—"

Lady Padbury interrupted her daughter whilst glaring at her son. "Caroline is visiting a tenant this afternoon, isn't she, Charles?"

The viscount looked down at the cup in his hand. "Yes, Mama."

Lady Blackburn frowned. Robert, too, was certain both the viscountess and the boy lied, and he thought poorly of Lady Padbury for forcing her son to do so. "Perhaps if I call tomorrow she will be at home then."

"Why do you want to see Caroline, Lord Elston?" Miss Lydia inquired.

Why? Why not? Robert maintained his neutral expression with an effort. "Because I made Miss Lane's acquaintance many years ago and wished to greet an old friend."

Lady Blackburn nodded approvingly. "Very proper. Are you visiting in the neighborhood, my lord?"

"Not exactly, my lady, although it appears I will be staying for another day. I visited my estate at Thirsk, and since my travels took me through Selby, I called here to pay my respects to the family."

"You must stay with us, Elston." Robert recognized the viscountess's tone; it was pure "mother whose marriageable daughter has been granted an unexpected opportunity to charm an eligible peer."

"Indeed you must," chimed Miss Lydia.

"Oh, no. It is very kind of you to offer, but I would not want to impose." Robert did not want to be put in the uncomfortable position of creating expectations he had no intention of fulfilling in either Lady Padbury's mind or her daughter's heart. And he had no wish to be compromised into marriage with Miss Lydia, if that was the viscountess's intent. For one thing, Lydia was not on the list. For another, she had thus far behaved like a passably pretty doll; if she had a mind and personality of her own, she had not yet displayed it.

"It wouldn't be an imposition at all, my lord. We would be delighted to have you stay with us for a few days." Lady Padbury's assertion was belied by the slight frown creasing her forehead.

"Indeed we would." A vigorous nod accompanied Miss Lydia's words.

"Decent hunting hereabouts, if you enjoy that sort of thing," Charles added.

Quickly, Robert considered his options. If he stayed—and locked his bedchamber door—he should be safe enough from any schemes the ladies might be plotting, and he would have the opportunity to see and speak with Miss Lane at dinner and in the drawing room afterward. If he left, his chances of seeing her decreased significantly.

Lady Blackburn caught his eye and nodded slightly, so Robert allowed the Lanes to override his protest and accepted their invitation.

Had he known that tea would be the high point of the day, Robert would not have allowed himself to be persuaded to stay. From there the afternoon had careened downhill like a runaway cart, he mused as he stepped through the French doors in the dining room onto the terrace, a glass of port in hand. And like an errant cart, the afternoon had held equally dangerous obstacles for the unwary.

The first surprise had come when Lady Blackburn asked him to walk her out to her carriage. She had voiced her concern about Karolina, who had not been seen in the village for months, not even in church, and asked Robert to call before he left, so he might tell her if Karla was well.

Next, Miss Lydia, at her mother's suggestion, had shown him the gardens. Since it was not yet the middle of March, there had been little to see. He had been wary of such an obvious ploy to throw them together, but Miss Lydia had tripped along at his side, chattering about the joys of the coming Season. Robert did not think it would be the success she envisioned, but he said nothing to quell her enthusiasm. He was thoroughly bored by her nattering, but fighting ennui was far better than dealing with swoons or sprained ankles. Or fighting off unwelcome advances.

The dinner hour came; Miss Karolina did not appear. When he inquired if they would await her return, he was told she was dining at the vicarage.

He did not believe it for a moment.

Something havey-cavey was going on. He didn't know what—at least, not yet—but he was determined to ferret out the truth. He had to know it to carry out Lady Blackburn's commission. He had to know it for himself.

Reaching the end of the terrace, he placed his glass on the wide stone balustrade and lit a cheroot. When it was drawing properly, he turned, leaned back against the finial in the corner, crossed one booted ankle over the other, and gazed up at the stars, smoking contentedly.

A smothered gasp was Robert's first indication he was not alone on the terrace. Maintaining his casual pose with an effort, he darted a glance left, then right, but saw no one. Silently cursing the clouds that obscured nearly all of the moon's light and his stupidity in choosing this dark corner, he turned and searched the lawn but detected no movement. Nor had any of the shadows changed position. The prickling along his spine that had saved him several times in the Peninsula indicated the interloper was behind him. Robert could feel the watcher's eyes boring into his back. Abruptly he spun about, muscles coiled to spring, eyes narrowed to pierce the gloom. In the opposite corner, deep in the shadows, he spotted the dark, still figure of a woman seated on a bench against the wall of the house.

Karla rued the surprised exclamation that had escaped her lips when she'd recognized the tall, broad-shouldered, dark-haired man standing in the little bit of moonlight that penetrated this corner of the terrace. Well, she hadn't recognized him exactly—he had changed a great deal in seventeen years—but she'd instantly known his identity. Viscount Wrexton, the boy who'd befriended her during that difficult time so many years ago, and who had helped her understand that her father's remarriage did not mean he had stopped loving her.

Fascinated, she watched as he took a deep breath and released it slowly, the muscles in his arms and legs relaxing as he did. She must have scared him half to death.

"I beg your pardon, ma'am. I did not realize anyone else was out here. Forgive me for intruding." He bowed, then dropped his cheroot and crushed it beneath his heel.

"I apologize for startling you, sir. You are not intruding, nor did I find your tobacco offensive. On the contrary, the smell reminded me of my father."

He took a step forward and bowed. "Since there is no one to introduce us, we must do the honors ourselves. I am Elston, ma'am."

So he was no longer Wrexton. Or not solely. Now he was the Marquess of Elston, Viscount Wrexton, and Baron Symington of Symington and Thirsk. And she was on the horns of a dilemma.

Much as she wanted to know if he remembered her, she was equally loath to have him know of the unenviable position in which she dwelt. After a short, sharp struggle with her conscience, Karolina Ingrid Catherine Lane, daughter of the late Viscount Padbury and his first wife, Ingrid Lindquist, inclined her head in acknowledgment of the marquess's introduction and, for the first time in her twenty-three years, told a bald-faced lie. "I am honored to make your acquaintance, Lord Elston. I am Catherine Lindquist."

"Are you a relative of the late viscountess?"

"Indeed I am. Were you acquainted with the first Lady Padbury?"

"Yes." Elston smiled in reminiscence. "I remember her from visits here as a boy. A beautiful blonde who smelled of roses and always had time to listen to a child's tales."

"I do not remember her very well, but I have a . . . a memory, I suppose, of her rosewater scent."

"You have lived at Paddington Court a long time then."

Karla nodded. "More than twenty years."

"Yet you did not join the family for dinner." It was half question, half statement.

"No. I am a relative, but I am not considered a member of *this* family."

"That is their loss, ma'am, not yours."

Karla blinked back the tears that suddenly pooled in her eyes. "Perhaps."

"And mine as well. I feel certain you are a very pleasant dinner partner."

"Thank you, Lord Elston. You are most kind to say so." Drawing her handkerchief from the pocket of her hooded cloak, she leaned farther back in the corner and wiped her streaming eyes.

Apparently he recognized her actions for what they were for he attempted to divert her. "Kindness has nothing to do with it, ma'am. I have no doubt that your conversation would be far superior to Charles's complaints about the amount of schoolwork his tutor gives him and Miss Lydia's gossip about people with whom I am not acquainted."

"Oh dear. Surely Lady Padbury had something better to offer?"

"I daresay that depends upon whether one is the inquisitor or the one being questioned. She seemed to enjoy her role, but I did not much care for mine."

"I imagine not. I am sorry you had no lively conversation, my lord. If Pa—" Aghast at what she had almost said, Karla coughed harshly to cover her blunder. "Excuse me. If Padbury were still alive, the situation would have been quite different."

"Undoubtedly, ma'am. I imagine your situation would be different as well."

"Vastly different."

"Yet Lady Padbury allows you to stay on here. She must think highly of you."

Karla fought to keep the bitterness from her voice as she replied. "No, Lord Elston, she does not. I am allowed to stay only because the viscountess finds me useful. And because she fears she would be shunned by the neighborhood if she cast me out, as she would like to."

The marquess's eyebrows lowered, a muscle in his jaw clenched and unclenched repeatedly. He looked quite formidable, as well as furiously angry, but his tone was even when he spoke. "You said that Lady Padbury allows you to stay because she finds you useful. May I ask what you do?"

"I serve as governess to the younger children, my lord."

"Were you governess to Miss Karolina and Miss Lydia?"

"No, sir, I was not. I was a member of the family until Padbury's death and . . . tolerated by the viscountess afterward. It is only since Lydia lowered her hems and put up her hair that I have been forced to become useful."

"Ah!" Elston's exclamation was one of enlightenment. "Cast Miss Lydia in the shade, do you?"

"I don't know what you mean, my lord."

"From what you have said, Miss Lindquist, it sounds as if Lady Padbury fears your beauty outshines Miss Lydia's."

Karla shook her head. "Lydia and I are not at all alike, my lord. There is little basis for comparison."

"Comparisons are always made, ma'am, sometimes consciously, sometimes not. The fact that you are not like Miss Lydia is undoubtedly the source of Lady Padbury's concern."

Karla frowned, still not comprehending his point. "What do you mean, sir?"

"I have no idea what you look like, Miss Lindquist—the moon is too obscured by the clouds to cast much light tonight. But if you had been in the parlor this afternoon, I would have been drawn to you by your obvious intelligence and lively conversation. Any man of sense would."

"Hmm" was her only response as she thought back to the time before she had been banished. When Lydia left the schoolroom, the local swains had come calling, first with their mothers, then on their own. Initially, they'd divided their attention equally between her and her half-sister, but within a fortnight or so, Karla was receiving the lion's share. The final straw had been an assembly at which she had danced every dance while Lydia languished on the sidelines. The next morning, after summarily dismissing the governess, the viscountess had excoriated her stepdaughter for the "brash, forward behavior" she'd displayed, then exiled her to the schoolroom, where her "brazen ways" would not shame them all. Commanded to teach her younger half-brothers and -sisters their lessons or to leave the only home she'd ever known, Karla had chosen to take on the role of governess. That was preferable to taking on the world—alone.

Lost in her thoughts, she was unaware of the passage of

time until the marquess shifted restlessly. Glancing up at him with a smile he probably could not see, Karla said, "You may be right, my lord."

His arced eyebrow prompted her to elaborate. "Looking back, it seems possible your speculations are correct."

"Amazing, isn't it," he drawled, "how much clearer things are in retrospect?"

She laughed, as he'd undoubtedly intended. "Indeed it is." Then, gathering her cloak about her, she rose. "Thank you, Lord Elston. I have enjoyed our conversation."

"As have I," he responded, bowing.

She turned to walk back inside, but his next words stopped her. "Miss Lindquist, do you sit out here every evening?"

"Usually I do, unless it is pouring rain or very cold."

"Then I shall hope for fair weather tomorrow." He smiled and bowed again. "Good night, Miss Lindquist."

"Good night, Lord Elston."

After two steps, she swung back to face him. "May I ask a favor, my lord?"

"You may, but if your request is that I not mention our conversation to Lady Padbury and Miss Lydia, you need not voice it. I have no intention of sharing this enjoyable interlude with them."

Karla curtsied. "Thank you, my lord." Turning toward the side door she'd left unlatched, she called over her shoulder, "Good night, Lord Elston."

"I wonder if I might request a favor, ma'am."

His words stopped her just before she reached the portal. "You may, but there is little I can grant."

"Would you please convey my respects to Miss Karolina, and my hope that she will join the family for meals—or for tea—tomorrow? I remember her fondly from my last visit and I would like to see her again."

Oh, the folly of false pride! Ruing her deception, Karla bit her lip, wondering how best to answer him. "I will pass on your message, my lord, but I cannot guarantee the outcome you desire." Curious, she inquired, "Why did she not join the family for tea and dinner today?"

"She was visiting a tenant during tea and she dined at the vicarage." The marquess's voice was even, but something in his tone suggested he did not believe what he'd been told.

"Hmm" was the only comment she allowed herself. Then, "Karla will hear your request, Lord Elston, but—"

"Wrexton. She knew me as Viscount Wrexton."

Nodding, she reached for the doorknob. "Karla will receive your message, my lord, but I can promise no more than that."

"I understand, Miss Lindquist. Thank you." With another bow and a soft "Good night, ma'am," he turned and walked toward the French doors to the dining room.

Smiling, Karla entered the house and rapidly climbed the stairs, the joy in her heart lending wings to her feet. *He remembered her! Remembered her fondly.*

Robert woke early the next morning and hastened downstairs for breakfast, hoping Miss Karolina ate the meal in the dining room instead of her bedchamber. Through two helpings, a full pot of coffee, and a thorough reading of yesterday's *London Gazette* he waited, but she did not appear. No one did. After two hours, he finally rose from the table—only to encounter Charles entering the room. Ever polite, Robert resumed his seat and listened to the young viscount's rather disjointed conversation, which covered every topic from complaints about the amount of work his tutor required to his mother's determination to puff off Lydia this year to comprehensive descriptions of his two best friends and their plans for the summer holidays. With a few well-placed questions, Robert learned the ladies would not be seen belowstairs before noon and that there was at least one horse in the stables up to his weight, so he changed into riding clothes and hied himself off to the stable to work off the enormous breakfast he'd consumed.

Since he did not know the area, Robert asked that a groom accompany him and learned more about the family from the lad's artless chatter: the young viscount had a decent seat, Miss Lydia was afraid of horses, Miss Karolina was an excellent rider, and the "younguns" sat in the saddle like pudding bags. Much as he wanted to ask the boy about Karolina, Robert refrained. Not because he disdained questioning servants—his years in the Peninsula had taught him to accept information from any likely source—but because he feared the lad's indiscreetly flapping tongue would broadcast the Marquess of Elston's interest in the lady to the entire county within a sennight.

When he returned from his ride, the ladies were still abovestairs and Charles was with his tutor, so after changing clothes, Robert wrote a letter to his great-aunt Lavinia, then perused the shelves in the library for something lighter and wittier than the weighty agricultural treatise he had been reading. Finding *Sense and Sensibility* by A Lady, he settled in front of the fire to pass the time until luncheon. He was rather surprised when the gong sounded, so thoroughly was he engrossed in the tale.

Luncheon was much like dinner the previous night: Charles complained about "boring lessons"; Lydia told anecdotes about the neighboring gentry; Karolina did not appear. Nor did Miss Lindquist. Robert did not even have to inquire about Miss Lane. As soon as they were seated, Lady Padbury reported that her stepdaughter was visiting a friend in the village and would not be dining with them.

He did not believe her. Quite apart from the fact that it was the height of rudeness for a daughter of the house to ignore a guest and spend the day with neighbors she might visit anytime, Lady Blackburn had said Karolina hadn't been seen in the village for several months.

What he did not know was why. Why had Karolina not honored his request—conveyed to her family as well as to the governess—to speak with her? Why was Lady Padbury lying? Why hadn't Karolina been to the village? There were several possible answers to the first and last questions, from illness to a disfiguring accident, but none made sense in light of the viscountess's blatant lies. He was forced to conclude that she didn't want him to see her stepdaughter, but he could not imagine her reasons.

Robert found the afternoon a bit of a bore, although rather farcically entertaining. Several of the local bucks came to call—ostensibly to see Miss Lydia, although most spent more time in conversation with him. Which, of course, made her angry, until she got the idea to snub them and favor him. If her intention was to make her swains jealous, she failed dismally. Since they were, more or less, ignoring her, they did not notice she was doing the same to them. If her intention was to irritate him, however, she succeeded admirably. Simpering and cooing, she greeted his every word as if it were the Gospel. It was a wonder he hadn't caught a chill from the constant fluttering of her eyelashes. He was certain he had a bruise on his arm where she'd repeatedly rapped it with her fan.

Miss Karolina Lane did not make an appearance. Robert was disappointed but not surprised.

When the visitors departed, he inveigled Charles into a game of billiards. The young viscount released a huge sigh when they reached their refuge, and leaned back against the door after firmly closing it.

Robert suppressed a smile. "Do you not like those young men? Or do you dislike doing the pretty?"

"It isn't that I dislike it. I just wish I didn't have to do it so often. Usually I have to do it only during the holidays, but they closed school because of an outbreak of influenza, so I am stuck with the duty until the new term begins. I don't have to pay calls with Mama, though, so that's a bit of a break." Charles flashed a cheeky grin.

"As for Croyden, Willoughby, and that lot, I like them well enough. Admire some of them, too. But if there is a Young Lady in the room"—the boy rolled his eyes theatrically—"or a Corinthian such as yourself, I might as well be invisible.

"Of course," he added, starkly honest, "if I were a caller, I'd rather talk to you, too."

"Thank you." Robert sketched a bow. "Now, do you wish to break or shall I?"

The viscount opted to play second. After taking his shot, Robert asked, in the tone of one making idle conversation, "Your sister seems to enjoy entertaining visitors. Does Miss Karolina not like doing the pretty?"

"Karla likes callers and calling well enough, I suppose, but—" Charles broke off, looking a bit self-conscious, then squared his shoulders manfully. "Mama thinks gentlemen won't pay attention to Lydia if Karla is in the room. And maybe they won't. But it isn't fair to Karla! It's not her fault that Lydia is a wigeon."

The boy's voice had risen nearly to a shout. Robert placed a calming hand on Charles's shoulder. "I agree it seems unfair, but life sometimes is, you know."

"I know." The viscount's tone changed from morose to pugnacious as his chin jutted out and he crossed his arms over his chest. "But I don't have to like it."

"No, you don't, but I doubt there is anything you can do to change your mother's mind."

"Probably not," the boy agreed, then bent over to take his shot.

After his conversation with Charles, Robert felt certain Karolina would not appear in the dining room. And she did not. Nor was any explanation given for her absence until after the ladies had withdrawn, when Charles told him that the viscountess had expressly ordered her stepdaughter to remain abovestairs and to take her meals in the schoolroom with the younger children. Robert commended the viscount for his probity and for his outrage at the unfair treatment his half-sister was receiving. 'Twas obvious Charles loved and respected Karolina—perhaps more than he did his mother—and he was the only member of the family Robert had met who pronounced her name properly. Although he might not have expected it initially, Robert liked the boy. He would bring credit to his father's title when he was old enough to assume all its responsibilities.

Robert could not help but wonder at Lady Padbury's logic in ignoring the expressly stated wishes of a guest. Especially since she had an unmarried daughter about to make her bows in Society and the guest was a wealthy, titled, extremely eligible bachelor. Visits from a marquess could not be a common occurrence in this corner of Yorkshire; there were only fifteen or sixteen of them in the kingdom and none had seats in this part of the country. Given that the current viscount was only fifteen and had held the title for four years, visits of a wealthy, unmarried, eligible marquess to Paddington Court probably occurred, at most, once a decade.

Carrying his port, Robert strolled out onto the terrace. Miss Lindquist was not seated in the corner, so he lit a cheroot, propped one booted foot on the bench, and puffed contentedly as he contemplated. Lady Padbury would have to revoke her edict when they arrived in London. She could not puff off one daughter and ignore the other. Not if she wanted to receive invitations to the more select events. Karolina's mother had been the daughter of an earl; Lydia's mother was a minor baronet's daughter.

Frowning slightly, he wondered if Karolina had made her bows to Society. She was three-and-twenty, so she would have been presented in '07 or '08. Although he'd been in the Peninsula during the latter Season, he had been in Town for the former and he did not recall meeting her there. Nor was he likely to have forgotten the event. Straightening abruptly, he considered the possibility that she had not made her come-out and that her stepmother had no intention of presenting her this Season. If that was the viscountess's plan, it was doomed to failure. Robert had a few plans of his own.

Chapter Three

Robert had almost given up on Miss Lindquist when he heard the quiet closing of a door followed by the soft yet rapid footfalls of a person who feared herself late for an appointment. Although gratified by her eagerness, he disliked that she believed herself tardy. After all, they had not set a time to meet, nor specifically planned to do so. Neither of which explained his lightened heart at the sound of her approach. Nor the fact that he had been out on the terrace for nearly an hour.

He greeted her as she came around the corner of the house. "Good evening, Miss Lindquist. I hoped this lovely, star-filled sky would draw you outside."

"Good evening, Lord Elston." As she turned her face heavenward, the hood of her cloak slipped back a bit. He had a glimpse of delicate features limned in the moonlight like a cameo, perfectly suited to her petite frame, and a swath of pale hair before she turned toward him. "It *is* a lovely evening, isn't it?"

"Indeed it is."

She stared up at him for a moment, as if studying his features, then retreated to the same shadowy corner she had occupied last night and sat on the bench.

"How were your charges today, ma'am?"

"Quarrelsome." Her words were accompanied by a weary sigh.

"I hope that is not a frequent state."

"Rather more frequent than I would like, but not unexpected with children."

"How many are in your charge?"

"Four."

An only child, Robert found it difficult to imagine a family of six children. Seven with Karolina, who was several years older. "With all the time Padbury spent out of the country, I daresay he must have enjoyed being reunited with his wife and family." Belatedly realizing the double entendre inherent in his remark, he flushed. "I beg your pardon—"

"There is no need to apologize, Lord Elston. Padbury did enjoy the time he spent with his family." She shifted on the bench, then raised her chin defiantly. "Although it is common knowledge hereabouts, you may not be aware that Padbury did not . . . He could not have fathered two of the children. He had not seen his wife for more than a year prior to their births."

Lady Padbury cuckolded her husband? Robert's opinion of the viscountess, never high to begin with, plummeted further. "Yet Padbury apparently accepted them."

Miss Lindquist nodded. "Yes. He said they were innocents and should not suffer for their mother's actions."

Curiosity overruled Robert's excellent manners. "And he did not denounce her?" Padbury had not divorced her, although he'd certainly had grounds for bringing such an action before the Ecclesiastical Court and, eventually, Parliament.

The governess shook her head. "No. He believed his long absences were at least partially to blame for her behavior."

Something in her voice told Robert she didn't agree. He thought as she did—after all, the wives of soldiers and sailors were parted from their husbands for as long or longer and few considered it an excuse for infidelity—but he did not pursue the matter. They had already crossed the line in taking the conversation this far. "He confided in you, ma'am?"

"About some matters. Most, probably. I oversaw the estate during his absences."

"Did you? I hope Padbury realized what a treasure he had in you, Miss Lindquist. Had you any training in estate management?"

"Only what he taught me. And yes"—he saw the gleam of her teeth in the moonlight as she smiled—"I believe he valued me as he ought."

"Good."

Silence reigned for several minutes, but Karla did not find it uncomfortable. It was like that between two friends who do not feel the need to entertain each other. Then they both spoke simultaneously. "Lord Elston—"

"Miss Lindquist—"

The marquess deferred to her. "Please continue, ma'am."

"I was merely going to invite you to smoke a cheroot, if you wish."

"You do not find the smell objectionable?"

"Not at all. My father smoked them."

"Mine did too occasionally, but my great-aunt declares them 'nasty, stinking weeds.'" His tone was wry.

"Did your mother object?"

"I don't remember. She died when I was ten."

Karla winced at her thoughtless words. She knew that, although "Miss Lindquist" would not. "My condolences, sir. It is not easy to lose one's parents, is it?"

"It is damnably—er, deucedly hard."

She held up a hand to forestall his apology for swearing in her presence. "Are you going to smoke?"

"No, ma'am. It isn't done, you know."

"What isn't done, my lord?"

"Gentlemen do not smoke in front of ladies. Not even if invited to do so."

Karla shook her head. "Society has rules for everything, doesn't it?"

"So it seems." A wry smile accompanied the words.

Oh, how she regretted deceiving him! Karla wanted to speak to him, but she still feared he would scorn her—and pity her—if she confessed her lie and the reasons for it. She watched as he leaned back against the stone baluster of the terrace and crossed one booted ankle over the other. He was at ease while her stomach was in knots. Before she lost her nerve altogether, "Miss Lindquist" needed to pass on a message from Karolina.

"I gave Karolina your message, Lord Elston. She remembers you well, but—"

"But she was unable to grant my request because the viscountess ordered her to remain abovestairs and take her meals in the schoolroom."

Karla gaped at him. "How did you know?"

"Charles told me."

"H-he did?"

The marquess nodded. "He thinks it very unfair of Lady Padbury to treat Karolina so. And the boy is right. It *is* unfair."

Karla was heartened by the knowledge that both her half-brother and Elston felt as she did. Not that it would change anything.

"Tell me, ma'am, how similar is Karolina's situation to yours? Given what Charles said today, and what you told me last night, there seems to be little difference."

"There is very little difference, my lord." *None at all, in fact.* "The viscountess deems us a threat to Lydia's chances of snabbling an eligible *parti.*"

The marquess's left eyebrow arced upward, but all he said, in a bland, almost drawling tone, was, "Lady Padbury ought to rethink her strategy."

"Oh? Why?"

"Most mothers would consider me an eligible *parti,* yet Lady Padbury has not granted my quite unexceptional request to speak with Karolina. Such behavior is not likely to endear the viscountess or her daughter to me."

"I daresay she hasn't considered that aspect of it."

"Likely not." After a few moments of silence, he inquired, "Has Karolina made her bows to Society?"

"No, my lord, she has not."

"Does Lady Padbury intend to present both Karolina and Lydia this year?"

"I do not believe so. The viscountess has spoken only of Lydia."

"Would Karolina like to have a Season?"

Karla could not help but wonder at the reasons behind Lord Elston's questions. At first she'd thought he hoped for an opportunity to see her in London, but there seemed to be more to it than that. "Yes, my lord, she would. There is little opportunity here for her to meet eligible men and . . ."

"Go on, Miss Lindquist."

"And she would thrive in a home of her own, with a husband and children to love."

"We all thrive when loved."

Silence reigned again until Karla could no longer contain her curiosity. "Do you think the viscountess will give Karolina a Season?"

"I don't know, Miss Lindquist, but I will do my best to persuade her." He smiled, an almost boyish look of mischief on his handsome face. "And should my persuasions not be sufficient, I shan't hesitate to enlist the aid of some formidable allies."

"Oh? And who might those be?"

"Lady Blackburn. My great-aunt Lavinia." He named a number of ladies whom she did not know, then ended with, "Lady Julia Castleton. She will be presenting her great-niece this year, and Beth is Karolina's age."

Karla voiced a concern. "Will they be considered on the shelf?"

"No, ma'am, they will not, although they will be older than most young ladies making their bows."

Her head whirling at the possibility that she might have a Season, Karla stood. "Lord Elston, I wish you success with your plan." She looked up at him, a strong, powerful silhouette against the moonlight. "If tomorrow evening is pleasant, perhaps I will see you out here and you will tell me how you go on."

"I will be leaving in the morning, Miss Lindquist. There is no point in remaining if I cannot speak with Karolina." With one long stride, he stood in front of her. "Surely she will tell you if my plan succeeds."

Karla nodded. "Yes, she will."

"Will you be in London, too, Miss Lindquist?"

"No, my lord." Karla could not play two roles in so public a venue. Nor did she want to continue her misbegotten masquerade. "I will stay here with the children."

"Fortunate for the children, unfortunate for me. I have enjoyed your conversation, ma'am, and greatly appreciate your counsel."

She dipped a curtsy. "Thank you, Lord Elston. I, too, have enjoyed our conversations." After a quick look up at him, she turned to leave. "Good night, my lord. I wish you a pleasant journey."

"Good night, Miss Lindquist. And thank you."

She had taken only a few steps when he spoke again. "I

know a gentleman should not ask, but how old are you, ma'am?"

Taken aback, she could only stammer, "I-I am . . . not yet thirty, my lord."

"Have you no dreams of a home and family of your own?"

"Of course I do. I daresay every young woman does. But a governess's dreams are not likely to become reality."

"Who can say what the future holds?" he murmured. "Good night, Miss Lindquist."

"Good night, my lord."

After smoking another cheroot, Robert went inside to find his hostess. She and Miss Lydia were in the parlor, sitting in glum silence. The viscountess's embroidery rested on the sofa beside her; her daughter paged desultorily through an issue of *Ackermann's Repository*. When he entered the room, both women straightened in their seats and smiled.

"You sat a long time over your port, my lord." Miss Lydia's tone was rather accusatory, as well as sulky.

"Gentlemen sometimes do, my dear." The viscountess sent her daughter an admonitory glare. "Although I am surprised, Elston, that you and Charles found so much to discuss. He is only a boy, after all."

"Charles may be young, ma'am, but he has a good head on his shoulders."

"How kind of you to say so. I am sure he was quite gratified by your condescension in speaking to him at such length."

Robert disliked toadying in any form, but Lady Padbury's blatant attempt to curry favor was, for some reason, particularly distasteful. He gritted his teeth to resist the nearly overpowering urge to give her a setdown. "Charles has been back at his books for some time. I have been out on the terrace smoking a cheroot."

The viscountess's smile dimmed slightly, but Robert continued before she could say anything. "I will be leaving early in the morning. Thank you for your hospitality these past two days."

"Leaving? But you have—"

"If you remember, ma'am, I arrived intending only to pay a call."

A calculating gleam entered Lady Padbury's eyes. "But I thought you wanted to see Caroline."

"I did. And I still do. My call on Miss Lane will have to wait until you are in London for the Season."

"But Caroline won't—" Lydia interrupted, only to be overridden by her mother.

"Hush, Lydia. Do not interrupt his lordship."

Robert looked over at the girl. "Pray continue, Miss Lydia."

"I was only going to say that Caroline won't be going to London."

Wearing what he hoped was a suitably astonished expression, Robert turned to the viscountess. "Surely that isn't true, ma'am. To give one daughter a Season and ignore the other would invite the opprobrium of the *ton*. Especially if you ignore the elder in favor of the younger. The high sticklers won't countenance such behavior."

Lady Padbury looked thoughtful, so he pressed his advantage. "Padbury was well liked, as was the first viscountess. If you fail to do your duty to their daughter, many doors will be closed to Miss Lydia." If the viscountess shunned her stepdaughter, Robert vowed to use his influence to see her—and, by extension, her daughter—censured.

"Now, since I have a long journey tomorrow, I will bid you good evening. I look forward to seeing you and your daughters in Town, ma'am." Robert gave them a rather curt bow, then turned on his heel and left the room, quite pleased with his success in launching his plan.

Robert left Paddington Court the next morning after an early breakfast with Charles. The boy professed his sorrow at the marquess's departure and his enjoyment of his lordship's company and conversation. Informed of Robert's campaign to ensure Karolina would have a Season, the young viscount declared himself an ally and vowed to do all that he could to convince his mother of the benefits of presenting both Karla and Lydia this spring.

As they walked outside, Charles rather diffidently said, "Lord Elston, if you like, I could write and tell you how things go on here. So you would know if the plan is succeeding."

"That is an excellent idea and would be very helpful. But . . ."

"But what, sir?"

"Well, I am rather fond of receiving letters. If I gain a new correspondent, then he suddenly stops writing, I would be very disappointed."

"Oh." His expression crestfallen, the boy kicked a pebble on the drive. As he watched its flight, he suggested, "I could continue to write you after I go back to school, but I daresay you won't find the letters very interesting."

Robert was pleased by his protégé's perspicacity. "I am certain I will find them very interesting indeed." With a wink, he added, "You can tell me things you can't tell your mother and sisters. Ask me things, too."

Charles's smile brightened the overcast morning. "Capital, sir!"

After giving the boy his card and instructing him to send his letters to Elston Abbey for the next fortnight, then to Symington House in London, Robert climbed into his traveling coach. As the horses turned onto the carriage drive, he glanced back at the house. A curtain twitched at one of the third-story windows and a shadowy figure appeared briefly, until the first curve of the drive removed her from his sight. Robert could not help but wonder if it had been Karolina or Miss Lindquist.

Jane, the Countess of Blackburn, was still at the breakfast table when her butler entered carrying a silver salver. "A caller at this hour? It cannot be much past ten o'clock."

"It has just gone ten, my lady," Hughes replied, offering the little tray so she could take the card it held. "The gentleman apologized for the early hour and said he would be pleased to await your convenience."

She picked up the card. "Oh, do show Lord Elston in. He brings news of Karolina Lane." Jane looked down at her yellow muslin round gown and wished she'd dressed more fashionably this morning. "The marquess will have to take me as he finds me."

"If I may say so, my lady, you look lovely. Like a beam of sunshine."

Jane smiled at the retainer who had known her since she had come to Blackburn Park as a bride thirty-five years ago. "Thank you."

"I will show Lord Elston in. Do you think he will want breakfast?"

"Probably not, but I will ask. If he does, please give Cook my apologies for the disruption in routine."

Tapping the calling card against the table, Jane waited for the butler to return with her guest.

"The Marquess of Elston, my lady," Hughes intoned from the doorway.

Elston entered the room and bowed. "Thank you for receiving me, Lady Blackburn."

"I am delighted that you called, Lord Elston. Will you join me?" She smiled and motioned him to the seat at her right. "What can Hughes bring you?"

"I had breakfast with Charles, but I will have a cup of coffee with you, my lady."

Jane nodded to her butler, then turned her attention to the marquess. "I am all agog to hear what you learned of Karla, but I shall contain my curiosity until Hughes returns with your coffee."

Elston smiled, then crossed one elegantly clad leg over the other. "No need for that, ma'am. I am happy to pass on what I learned, with or without coffee.

"First off, I should say that I never spoke with, or even saw, Karolina. All of my information comes from Charles and Miss Lindquist."

"Miss Lindquist?"

"The governess."

Jane frowned in puzzlement. "Lady Padbury dismissed the governess, a Miss Meadows, several months ago. I was not aware a new one had been engaged."

"She isn't new to Paddington Court, ma'am, merely new to that role."

Jane felt her frown deepen but made no effort to banish it. "I don't understand, Lord Elston."

"Elston, please, my lady. I am a few years younger than your son, although I do not know him well. He was three forms ahead of me at Eton."

"Elston it shall be, then."

Hughes entered with the coffee. Jane waited until he had

served the marquess and left. "Tell me of Miss Lindquist. You said she has been at Paddington Court for a time but only recently taken on the role of governess?"

"Yes. She has lived there more than twenty years."

"What? I cannot believe that. I would have met her— or at least heard of her—long before now. What is her given name?"

It was Elston's turn to frown as he sought to remember. "I think it is Catherine."

"Hmm. And she is a relative of the first Lady Padbury?"

"Yes. Miss Lindquist told me she was considered a member of the family until Padbury died and . . . tolerated was the word she used, I believe, by the current viscountess after his death. It was not until Miss Lydia left the schoolroom and began appearing in local society that Miss Lindquist was forced to become useful."

"Forced?"

Elston took a sip of coffee, an expression of intense concentration on his lean, austerely handsome face. "It is difficult to separate what she told me from my impressions, but I am almost certain she said she is allowed to stay because she is useful and because Lady Padbury fears being censured should she cast Miss Lindquist out."

"And so she would be." Jane still could not believe that she had not met a member of the family, even a distant one, who had been at Paddington Court for so long. "We have strayed from our original topic. My fault, I fear, but allow me one last question about Miss Lindquist before you tell me what you learned of Karla."

"You may ask as many as you like, my lady."

"How old is Miss Lindquist?"

"I encountered her on the terrace after dinner whilst smoking a cheroot, so I never saw her clearly. But"—he smiled—"when my curiosity overruled my manners last night and I asked, she said that she was not yet thirty."

"Hmm." Jane had a strong suspicion that the lady he'd encountered was Karolina, although she could think of no reason why her young friend would conceal her identity from the marquess.

"Now, Elston, what did Miss Lindquist and Charles tell you about Karla?"

"Miss Lindquist said Karolina's situation is not much different from her own. I took that to mean that Karolina, too, was banished from receiving callers and such. Charles confirmed that later. He told me Lady Padbury fears gentlemen won't pay attention to Miss Lydia if Karolina is in the room and, therefore, has ordered her stepdaughter to remain abovestairs when there are guests. During my visit, Karolina was told to take her meals in the schoolroom with the younger children."

Jane meant to hold her tongue until Elston finished, but she could not. "Hortense must be mad! How can she think banishing Karla will increase Lydia's popularity?"

"Perhaps because the gentlemen will have no choice but to talk with Lydia."

"Or choose not to call at all."

The marquess nodded. "As you say, my lady."

"What else did you learn?"

"Karolina has not been presented, nor had a Season."

"That I knew. When Hortense did not present Karla the year she was seventeen, I offered to do so the following year and was told that she did not want a Season."

"Miss Lindquist says otherwise."

"Given what you have told me so far, I cannot doubt it." Jane looked down at her hands, clasped tightly together in her lap. "Oh, if only I had asked Karla herself!"

"Do not torture yourself with 'if onlys,' my lady."

She tried but failed to summon a smile. "I almost fear to ask what else you learned."

"I thought perhaps Lady Padbury intended to present Karolina and Lydia this year, but Miss Lindquist said the viscountess has spoken only of Lydia. I decided to do what I could to ensure that Karolina has a Season, too. When I took my leave of Lady Padbury and Miss Lydia last night, I said I looked forward to seeing Karolina in London. Miss Lydia was quick to tell me 'Caroline' wouldn't be in Town."

He interrupted his discourse to ask a question. "Why do Lady Padbury and Miss Lydia call Karolina 'Caroline'? Charles is the only family member I met who pronounced her name properly, although he generally calls her Karla, as does Miss Lindquist."

"I asked Hortense once, years ago. She said Karolina was a heathen name and she would not use it. She always pronounced it correctly when Padbury was present, however, so I suspect it is just a way—one of many, apparently—to demean Karla."

"After Miss Lydia said 'Caroline' would not be in Town," the marquess continued, "I pretended astonishment and told Lady Padbury that the high sticklers would condemn her for presenting her daughter and ignoring her stepdaughter, thus closing many doors to Lydia."

"Well done, Elston!"

He grinned like a young boy. "I was rather pleased."

"As you should be. I assume Hortense changed her mind?"

"I don't know. She looked thoughtful, as if considering what I'd said, so I left her to her musings."

"What can I do to help?"

He thought for several moments before replying. "I don't know what to tell you, my lady. Charles—who, by the way, is quite outraged at his mother's treatment of Karolina—offered to write me, to let me know how things go on. I accepted, after obtaining his promise to continue the correspondence after he returns to school."

"May I ask why?"

The marquess looked a bit uncomfortable at the question. "It must be difficult for a boy that age to be fatherless. There are some questions a mother cannot answer."

"Ah." Jane nodded, biting the inside of her cheek to keep from smiling. "You will be an excellent mentor for him."

"I will do my best, my lady."

"I know you will. And I will do my best to make Hortense see the advantages of presenting both Karla and Lydia."

"Thank you, Lady Blackburn. I was hoping for your support." Elston stood, then bowed over her hand. With a cheery "I will see you in London, my lady," he departed.

Jane smiled at his retreating figure—and wondered if she might effect a match between the so very eligible Marquess of Elston and Miss Karolina Lane.

Chapter Four

*T*wo days of hard travel over abominably muddy roads brought Robert and the faithful Higgins to Newark, a town straddling the border between Lincolnshire and Nottinghamshire. It was late afternoon when they arrived, so Robert took rooms at one of the larger posting inns, hoping the accommodations would prove superior to those of the previous night. Fortunately, they did. The rooms were free of dust, the furniture polished to a glossy shine, the sheets clean and dry. After enjoying a hot bath, Robert spent the evening in front of the fire in a private parlor, studying the ever-growing pile of estate papers he carried with him. The next morning, after a bracing but extremely muddy cross-country ride, another bath, and a leisurely breakfast, they set off once again. Their destination was Woodhurst Castle, seat of the Marquess of Kesteven. Although acquainted with the marquess, a fellow member of White's as well as a friend of his father's, Robert was more interested in encountering Kesteven's twin daughters, Ladies Deborah and Diana Woodhurst.

As Higgins tooled the coach up the carriage drive a few minutes before two o'clock, Robert could only hope his luck held. He knew that sooner or later on one of these calls he'd find the family had already left for London to prepare for the Season, but he would prefer that it happen later. Meeting the ladies informally, before they were primped and primed and plunged into the rather shallow world of the *ton,* gave him a better opportunity to judge their characters and personalities.

Fortune still smiled upon him. Not only was the family in residence, but the marchioness and her daughters were receiving callers. At least, they agreed to see him. After surrendering his hat, gloves, and greatcoat to a footman, Robert was escorted by the butler—whose name, if he remembered correctly, was Stephens—to the drawing room.

"The Marquess of Elston," the manservant proclaimed.

Robert bowed to the company, which included Kesteven, his marchioness, an aspiring dandy in his early twenties, and two blond misses, as alike at first glance as two peas in a pod. The marquess, who was seated on a sofa next to his wife, reading aloud as the ladies embroidered, rose and strode across the room to greet him.

"Wrexton! This is an unexpected pleasure."

After a look over Robert's shoulder, the marquess's delighted expression faded to a somber one. "I forgot for a moment that your father is gone. You are Elston now." Kesteven gripped Robert's shoulder. "My condolences. You must miss him sorely. I do."

Robert nodded. "Some days it is impossible to believe he won't be waiting at the Abbey when I return."

"You haven't been in Gloucestershire, then?"

"No, sir. I left a few days after Christmas for Scotland. I needed time alone—" Robert stopped speaking when the marquess squeezed his shoulder.

"The first holiday is always hard."

The marchioness came to stand beside her husband. "Good afternoon, Elston."

Robert bowed. "Good afternoon, my lady. Thank you for receiving me."

"It is always a pleasure to see you. Please"—she took his arm and escorted him toward a group of chairs and couches near the fireplace—"join us. I was just about to ring for tea."

"Thank you, my lady."

"I will ring, m'dear," Kesteven told his wife.

The marchioness paused beside the sofa on which her daughters sat, dressed in identical white muslin gowns sprigged in blue. "Elston, I don't believe you have met our younger children. May I introduce our daughters, Lady Deborah and Lady Diana, and our younger son, Lord Henry.

"My dears," she continued as the young people rose, "this is the Marquess of Elston."

Robert bowed to the young ladies, then to the dandy. "It is a pleasure to meet you, Lady Deborah, Lady Diana, Lord Henry."

The trio curtsied or bowed and expressed their pleasure in making his acquaintance.

Robert escorted Lady Kesteven to her seat on the sofa facing the one occupied by the twins, then took the chair she indicated, which was close enough to hers for comfortable conversation.

The marquess, returned from his errand, sat next to his wife. "What brings you to this area, Elston?"

"As I was telling you earlier, my lord, I left Gloucestershire after Christmas and spent two months in Scotland. Now I am returning to Elston Abbey and, on the way, visiting my estates and calling on people my father spoke of before he died."

Kesteven smiled. "Reminiscing about our days at Eton and Oxford, was he?"

Robert squirmed inwardly, disliking the direction the conversation had taken due to his stretching of the truth. "A bit, yes."

The arrival of the butler with the tea tray temporarily halted their discourse. Robert glanced around the room, which, despite its vast proportions and elegant furnishings in shades of green and gold, felt comfortable and cozy. After the marchioness poured tea for everyone, he changed the topic to spare himself further lies. "Lady Kesteven, will you be in London this Season?"

"Indeed we will. Deborah and Diana will be making their bows this year."

"We would have done so two years ago had Grandmama not died," the twin on the right said. If they had returned to the same places after helping their mother distribute the refreshments, it was Lady Diana who spoke. "And last year I had influenza."

Robert took a sip of tea. "I imagine you are looking forward to the Season. Most young ladies enjoy it."

"Indeed we are," they chorused.

They would undoubtedly achieve great success. For many men, blue-eyed blondes with creamy complexions were the epitome of English womanhood. This lovely pair—and they were very pretty girls—would have the added attraction of their remarkable similarity. As he looked from one to the other, Robert marveled that anyone could tell them apart.

"I daresay people tell you this all the time, but you are incredibly alike. I imagine the gentlemen of the *ton* will compete to be the first to be able to identify you."

The twins smiled, revealing identical dimples. "Very few people can," the girl on the left said.

"Even Papa confuses us sometimes," her sister added mischievously.

"Now, Di," Kesteven chided with mock gravity, "don't be telling tales on your old papa. Elston will think me an unnatural father."

"Not at all, sir." Robert smiled at the marquess, grateful for his unwitting confirmation of the girls' identities. They sat in the same positions as when Lady Kesteven had introduced them—Deborah on the left, Diana on the right. "I marvel that anyone can tell them apart."

"Lord Elston, do you think it would be better if we dressed differently in London? To make it easier for people to tell us apart," Lady Deborah clarified.

Lady Diana glared at her sister. "Why should we make it easy for them?"

"Why shouldn't you?" The marchioness's query was also a gentle reproach. "You often do not dress identically."

"But, Mama . . ."

Robert ignored the discussion between the girls and their mother, pleased with himself for having found the means— or a means—to distinguish the twins. Lady Deborah's voice was the A above middle C, rising and falling slightly as she spoke but always returning to that note; Lady Diana's was nearly a quarter-step lower. Few people would notice the difference, but as a violist he was attuned to nuances in pitch.

"Mama ought to dress you in pinafores and send you back to the schoolroom!" It was the first time Lord Henry had spoken since he'd been introduced.

Robert did not know if it was the young man's words or the suddenness of his pronouncement that halted his sisters' quiet bickering. Lady Deborah said nothing, but a hurt expression clouded her pretty blue eyes.

Lady Diana glared at her brother. "A leader of the *ton* and an arbiter of fashion, are you?"

Henry snorted. "Of course not, but I know better than to argle-bargle in front of a guest." Lady Diana flushed at the pointed reproof, and her brother's tone gentled. "If you want a fashionable opinion, ask Elston."

Now the cynosure of all eyes, Robert flicked an imaginary piece of lint off the sleeve of his bottle green coat, then crossed one pantalooned leg over the other. When he raised his gaze, one of the twins stood before him.

"May I pour you another cup of tea, Lord Elston?"

Grateful for her intervention, he handed Lady Deborah his cup and saucer. "Thank you, my lady. No cream or sugar, please."

As she walked to the tea tray, Lord Henry crossed to sit on the sofa next to Lady Diana, then took her hand and began speaking softly, his expression earnest.

When Lady Deborah returned, she took the chair next to Robert's, which her brother had occupied earlier. After a sip of her tea, she faced him, a rueful half smile adorning her countenance. "Lord Elston, I apologize for my—our—rudeness. I hope our brangling did not . . ." She hesitated a moment as if not sure how to finish the sentence. "I hope you were not too appalled by our bickering."

Robert smiled, hoping to put her at ease. "In truth, my lady, I found it rather fascinating." Her eyes widened, and it was clear she doubted his sincerity. "I have neither brothers nor sisters, so the interactions between siblings are a mystery to me. Rather like uncharted territory would be for an explorer. I, however, need not risk life and limb to make discoveries, merely observe friends and acquaintances with their siblings."

As the disbelief faded from her countenance, he continued. "Although you and your sister disagreed, it was obvious that you respect each other's opinions. You listened to what Lady Diana—and your mother—said, as they did when you spoke."

"You are very observant, my lord." It was not clear from her tone whether she thought it a virtue or a fault.

"I was a soldier for four years, Lady Deborah. My skills at observation were well honed on the Peninsula."

She tilted her head slightly to one side. "How do you know I am Deborah?"

Doubt surfaced for a moment. He replayed her question

in his mind before he answered. "I noticed earlier that your speaking voice is just a tiny bit higher than your sister's."

"Really?" She seemed pleased by the observation. "No one has ever noticed—at least, no one commented if they did." Her dimples flashed as she smiled at him. "I did not realize it myself."

"The difference is very slight."

"Observant, indeed!" A frown creased her brow. "But Diana is not here for you to compare . . ."

"I am a musician, so perhaps I have a more highly developed sense of pitch than some people."

"I, too, am a musician, my lord, so I don't believe that accounts for it. What instrument do you play?"

Music was a private pleasure for Robert, not a public one, so he answered rather obliquely. "I would guess that, like many young ladies, you play the pianoforte."

She nodded. "I do, although I prefer the harpsichord."

"With either instrument, when you press a key, it produces the note you require."

"Usually." She grinned. "Unless I press the wrong key."

Robert felt a matching smile quirk the corners of his mouth. "True. With string instruments, however, the player must create the correct pitch."

"So they must." She considered the idea for several moments, then inquired, "Do all string players have such a highly developed sense of pitch?"

"The good ones do. Those who don't are not often asked to perform."

Her eyes danced with amusement. "I imagine not."

"Are you a violinist or a cellist, Elston?" Robert had not realized Lady Kesteven was listening to their conversation, but he was neither surprised nor offended by the knowledge.

"Neither, my lady. I am a violist."

"I have never seen a viola," Lady Deborah said. "What do they look like?"

"A viola looks like a violin, only larger. They share three strings—the G below middle C, D, and A—but the viola has a lower one, making it a tenor to the violin's soprano."

"How much larger than a violin is a viola?"

"About half again as long as a violin"—Robert held up his hands to indicate the viola's length—"and a bit wider."

Lady Deborah's eyes narrowed as she tried to envision the instrument. A few seconds later, she shook her head. "I cannot quite imagine it."

"If you like—and if your lady mother does not object to me prolonging my call—I will send my man to the village to retrieve my viola so you can see it. Or I can call again tomorrow to show it to you."

"Of course you may extend your call, Elston," Lady Kesteven declared.

"You chose the inn's hospitality over ours?" The marquess's voice was gruff, and hinted at hurt feelings.

Robert maintained a neutral tone as he attempted to explain his actions without giving further offense. "I arrived too late yesterday to call, my lord. And I did not know—nor did the innkeeper—if you had already departed for Town."

"You could have sent a note," Kesteven muttered *sotto voce.*

"If you are planning to stay at the inn tonight, Elston, I shall be sorely vexed," averred the marchioness. "Do, please, stay with us."

"But—"

Lady Kesteven overrode his protest before he even voiced it. "I will send a servant into the village to collect your things." Her gaze implored him to accept.

Robert gave in gracefully. "Thank you, my lady. I would be honored to enjoy your hospitality." Unlike the last such invitation, he had no qualms about accepting this one. "But you needn't send anyone; my man can easily accomplish the errand."

"My man will accompany yours," Kesteven offered. "Two can pack more quickly than one."

"If you wish to send someone, sir, a groom or coachman would be better. Higgins—my man—has been doing double duty this trip."

"Your valet can drive a coach?" This from Lady Deborah, in tones of astonishment. "Papa's valet would never agree to do so, even if he possessed the skill."

Robert smiled. Higgins was as far from the high-in-the-instep fellow she described as chalk from cheese. "Higgins may not be a typical valet, but he serves me well. He was my batman in the army."

"Ah" was her only reply. Kesteven, however, seemed to understand. "I will ask Stephens to bring your man up so you can give him your orders. And I will have my coachman accompany him."

"Thank you, sir."

As he dressed for dinner in the spacious, pleasantly appointed chamber to which his host and hostess had shown him, Robert considered his unusual journey. At the rate he was traveling—with rain turning the roads into muddy quagmires and afternoon calls extending into visits of a day or two—it would be nearly a week before he reached Elston Abbey. Tomorrow was Sunday, so they would not travel then, Higgins firmly believing that to do so was to invite an accident.

There was one call to make between here and home— near Leicester, about forty miles away. From there, it was another eighty miles or so to the Abbey. With good roads and strong, well-matched teams, it was possible to travel forty miles in a day, but they would not be on one of the mail routes, so their progress would be slower. As eager as he was to return home, Robert did not begrudge the delay. He was pleased with the success of his campaign, and deemed the time well spent.

Dinner was a lively affair, far different from those Robert had shared with his father and his great-aunt Lavinia. He was seated on Lady Kesteven's right, with Lady Deborah on his right. Lord Henry was opposite Robert, with Lady Diana across from her twin. There was a great deal of good-natured teasing and bantering among the younger members of the family. Kesteven also received a share, and gave as good as he got.

Much of the conversation centered on the coming Season and the twins' entrance into Society. That led back to the discussion of whether or not the girls should dress alike, which Lady Diana attempted to resolve by asking Robert's opinion.

"I cannot give you a good answer. I am not a twin, so I have little notion of the bonds between you and your sister. I would think the decision rests, at least in part, upon how much of your sense of identity is due to being a twin."

Lady Diana appeared much struck by his words, so Robert ended his faltering explanation. Quitting while ahead, so to speak.

Lady Deborah's murmured "very perceptive" had him turning toward her, one eyebrow raised in question.

"Part of the difficulty, my lord, is that Diana and I approach this decision from different perspectives. For her, it is a question of what would be most fashionable, and garner the most attention. For me, a matter of individuality. I don't want to be perceived merely as one of the Woodhurst twins, but as myself."

"Ah." Now he understood the question—and the problems. "If fashion were the sole basis of decision, then I would recommend dressing identically. Although I cannot recall any twins who have come out recently, I would imagine that is the accepted style. Certainly two identically lovely girls will receive more attention than one.

"However, since there are other considerations, I suggest similar, but not identical, gowns. Dresses of the same style and color, but with sashes of different colors," he clarified. "Or different trims. That will allow you to benefit from the advantage of being twins, but also help you to be perceived as individuals."

"That is a perfect solution!" Lady Diana enthused.

"Indeed it is." Lady Deborah smiled at him. "Thank you, Lord Elston."

Over the port, Lord Kesteven talked at length about a bill he and Elston's father had planned to introduce during this Parliamentary session. By the time Robert slipped outside to smoke a cheroot, he had somehow—and he had no idea how it had happened—agreed to sponsor the bill with Kesteven. The cause was a worthy one, but the newly elevated peer had not intended to be so active his first year in Lords. He'd imagined sitting quietly through most of the sessions and, perhaps, if he felt very strongly on a topic, giving his maiden speech. Now, thanks to his host, Robert had both a subject and a tentative date for his initial oration. Not to mention a huge sheaf of papers to study.

He stomped, unseeing, through the flower gardens, reaching the far end with fists clenched and teeth gritted against the storm of emotion that racked his body. *What the devil was my father doing riding neck or nothing in the local hunt when he promised to sponsor a bill this session?*

Robert kicked the trunk of a tree that blocked his path, yelped as pain jolted through his foot, then hopped to a nearby bench and dropped onto it.

His anger spent, he sighed and buried his face in his hands. *What kind of man am I that I rail at my father for dying?* Robert felt woefully unprepared to take over the duties of the marquessate, but that was no excuse for such uncontrolled—and uncharacteristic—rage.

He had thought putting his theoretical knowledge of estate management into practice would be the biggest challenge he faced this year. Well, that and choosing a bride. Now he had committed himself to a serious, and time-consuming, study about the problems of children forced to work in mines, mills, and factories. With all his other responsibilities, time was an increasingly precious—and ever fleeting—commodity.

If only . . .

No. He would not torment himself with "if onlys." He had more than enough to occupy his mind; he need not seek more.

With a weary sigh, Robert rose and walked toward the house, hoping his absence had gone unnoticed. He had no wish to offend his hostess, and he had not yet honored his promise to show Lady Deborah his viola.

As he approached the house, he saw one of the ladies coming toward him, but the light shining through the windows was not sufficient for him to identify her.

"Elston?"

Recognizing the marchioness's voice, Robert lengthened his stride and quickly covered the ground between them, chagrined that his hostess had been required to search for him. "I beg your pardon for my rag manners, Lady Kesteven. I came outside to smoke a cheroot. I hope I have not overset your plans for the evening?"

"I did not come out here to berate you, Elston, but to talk with you. Shall we walk in the gardens?"

He offered his arm. Lady Kesteven tucked her hand into the crook of his elbow. "I had not planned anything for this evening except a quiet night at home, so you have overset nothing. Although—"

"I have not forgotten my promise to Lady Deborah."

The marchioness smiled. "I was sure you had not. You

are a man of your word." She indicated a path on their left. "It was not my intent to hint about your promise to my daughter, either, but to apologize if my invitation created havoc with your plans."

Robert halted and turned to her, an eyebrow raised in question.

"I know you are traveling home, that you intended only to call this afternoon." In her haste to explain, Lady Kesteven's words nearly tumbled over one another. "But William misses your father sorely, and I don't like to see my husband grieving. I was thinking only of him, not of your plans, when I invited you to stay with us."

After a quick breath she continued, less rapidly than before. "I will understand if you must leave in the morning, and so will my husband, but it would mean a great deal to him if you could stay for a day or two."

"You have not overset my travel plans, my lady. I was honored by your invitation, and I shall enjoy deepening my acquaintance with you and your husband."

Resuming their stroll, he attempted to lighten her mood. "Just think, ma'am. Not only have I had the pleasure of meeting your younger children, but I have the jump on all the other bachelors in the realm in claiming acquaintance with your daughters."

The marchioness laughed. "So you have."

"I will gladly avail myself of your gracious hospitality for another day, but I must leave Monday morning."

She stopped, peering solemnly up at him. "Thank you, Elston. Your visit, short though it must be, will mean a great deal to William. And to me."

Uncomfortable, Robert motioned toward the house. "Shall we return inside, my lady? I have a promise to keep to your daughter."

After he escorted Lady Kesteven to the door of the drawing room, Robert continued upstairs to get his viola. Returning a few minutes later, he found Lord Henry and one of the twins playing backgammon, the other girl playing a Mozart sonata on the pianoforte, and Lord and Lady Kesteven conversing quietly on a sofa. The marchioness smiled at him when he entered, then motioned him to a nearby chair. Robert put his instrument case on the floor and sat down to listen.

The twin performing was a very talented musician, playing with both accuracy and feeling. He wondered if the girls' musical skill was as identical as their appearance. If so, when called upon to perform after dinner or at musicales, they would outshine the other young ladies in Society. In all the years he'd been on the town, Robert had heard only a handful of performances of this caliber. The musical members of the *ton* who grimaced through such entertainments would be pleased to know their ears would be spared occasionally this Season.

His applause at the end of the piece was heartfelt—and was rewarded with a smile.

"That was lovely, Deb," commended the marchioness.

"Indeed it was, Lady Deborah." Robert crossed the room to escort her to a seat.

"I am glad you enjoyed it, my lord." He received another smile, more dazzling than the first, when she spotted the case beside his chair. "You brought your viola! Will you show it to me, please?"

"Yes, of course. After your sister performs." To judge by the gamesters' exclamations, Lady Diana had been trounced by her brother, but she made no move toward the pianoforte. "If she is going to."

"I don't imagine she will. Diana disdains to practice"—Lady Deborah clearly found this incomprehensible—"and tangles her fingers in knots when called upon to play."

"Ah." So their musical abilities were not equal. Their talent might well be, but not their appreciation and application of it. "In that case . . ." Robert smiled at his companion, then lifted the viola case onto his lap. Removing the instrument, he handed it to her, and waited to see what she would do.

She surprised him. Again. Most people plucked at the strings and twisted the pegs, but after laying the instrument carefully in her lap, Lady Deborah ran her hands—elegant hands with long, slender fingers—over the wood, as if committing the size and shape to memory. She pushed a string against the fingerboard near the pegs, then another, closer to the bridge. When her tactile examination was complete, she picked the viola up by the neck, her other hand supporting the bottom. "You hold it on your shoulder when you play?"

"Support it against the front of your shoulder"—he placed his hand at the proper position on his left shoulder—"beside your neck, and tuck your chin to hold it in place."

Her eyes narrowed in concentration, she followed his instructions. Since she was seated to his left, he could not see if she held it properly, so he grabbed the bow and rose to stand in front of her.

"Just so, my lady." With an elaborate flourish worthy of an Elizabethan courtier, he presented her with the bow. "You are ready to play."

Laughing, she demurred. "I don't know how. Besides, I would much rather hear *you* play." She stood and, with a shy smile, handed him the instrument. "Thank you for showing me your viola, Lord Elston."

"It was my pleasure, Lady Deborah." And it had been a pleasure. So much so that he would play without his usual protestations. "There is very little solo music for the viola, but I know a sonata for viola and harpsichord. With your assistance and"—he turned to Kesteven and his wife—"your parents' consent, I will play it."

The marchioness nodded approval. "That would be lovely, Elston. Run along to the music room and practice your part, Deb. We will come down in half an hour or so."

A smile of pure delight graced Lady Deborah's countenance when he handed her the sheet music.

By the time Lord Elston entered the music room half an hour later, Deborah had translated the figured bass of the harpsichord part into an accompaniment in the baroque style that would have pleased the composer. Whether it would meet the standards to which the marquess was accustomed remained to be seen. She had done her best in the time provided and could only hope he found it acceptable.

As he removed his viola and bow from their case, Lord Elston gave her one of his rare smiles. "I hope we can play through this at least once before our audience arrives. I fear I am sadly out of practice."

"Oh dear. I was counting on your proficiency to cover my shortcomings, my lord."

"Given your marvelous performance earlier, Lady Deborah, I am certain you will do quite well. Would you play an A for me, please, so I can tune the viola to the harpsichord?"

She gave him the A above middle C and watched, fascinated, as he adjusted one of the pegs with his left hand while bowing with the right.

"An octave lower, please."

She complied. He nodded, apparently satisfied, and moved to the next string, playing both together and adjusting the lower one. A frown creased his brow as he continued tuning. When all four strings were adjusted to his satisfaction, he turned to her, his expression rueful.

"Would you be offended if I removed my coat? It is not cut fully enough to allow me to play comfortably."

"I shan't be offended at all, my lord. Shall I ring for your valet?"

Lord Elston laid his instrument and bow on a nearby table. "That will not be necessary. It is not *that* tight."

He turned away, and Deborah averted her gaze until she heard his footsteps. After draping the dark corbeau coat across a chair against the wall, he picked up his viola and bow, then crossed the room toward her. *Oh, but he was a fine figure of a man! The cut of his waistcoat emphasized the breadth of his shoulders as well as his lean waist and hips.* As the fingers of his left hand danced soundlessly across the viola's strings, the muscles in his shoulder and upper arm rippled the linen of his shirt.

Taking a position slightly behind and to the left of her, he inquired, "Are you ready to try the two parts together?"

"Yes." She took a deep—and hopefully calming—breath, then began to play.

"Well done, my lady!" he proclaimed when they reached the end.

Delighted by his enthusiastic compliment, she glanced over her shoulder at him and smiled. "That was lovely, my lord. You are very talented."

"I think—"

The entrance of her family prevented her from learning the marquess's thought. After her parents, Henry, and Diana were seated, Lord Elston stepped forward to introduce the piece, explaining that Handel had written it for harpsichord and viola da gamba and later transcribed it for the viola. Then, resuming his position behind her left shoulder, he leaned over and whispered, "I am ready whenever you are, my lady."

Deborah played the opening measures and was soon caught up in the music's magic. At the end, as her family's applause broke over them, Lord Elston offered his hand, led her out from behind the harpsichord, and, still holding her hand in his, bowed first to their audience, then to her, a delighted smile wreathing his countenance.

Much later that evening, Deborah crossed the sitting room that separated her bedchamber from Diana's and, after a cursory knock, entered her twin's room. Di sat at the dressing table, brushing her hair, so Deborah perched on the end of her sister's bed.

Meeting her eyes in the mirror, Diana smiled. "Today was not quite as boring as we expected, was it?"

Stifling the giggle her sister's drawled understatement provoked, Deborah returned the smile. "No, it certainly wasn't." Then, unable to contain her admiration any longer, "Isn't Elston the most wonderful man!"

Diana shrugged. "Judging from Mama's comments before we joined you in the music room, he is a most eligible *parti*."

"Of course he is. He is intelligent, handsome, talented—"

"Handsome? I thought him rather somber and austere."

"He is in mourning—"

"I was not referring to his clothes, Deb. His face is rather austere, don't you think? Like a monk. Or a scholar."

Deborah looked askance at her sister. "I don't agree. And there is nothing monkish or scholarly about those shoulders!"

Diana smiled mischievously. "Quite the Corinthian, judging from his figure." A few moments passed in silent contemplation of the marquess's physique. "Still, I cannot help but wonder if he ever laughs. He seldom smiles."

"He smiled several times today," Deborah countered. "And he has an almost boyish grin. It quite transforms his face."

"Really?"

"Oh, yes." She nodded vigorously. "And a dimple in his left cheek."

Simultaneously they sighed their appreciation, having

long ago agreed that a single dimple was a very admirable trait in a gentleman.

After plaiting her hair, Diana crossed to the bed, then scrambled beneath the covers. "I take it you would not be averse to seeing him in Town? And that you would not refuse an invitation to dance or drive with him?"

"Of course I would not refuse!" Scowling at her ninny of a sister, Deborah slid off the bed and headed for the door. "I daresay you wouldn't either."

"Probably not" was the mirthful rejoinder.

Quitting her provoking sister's chamber, Deborah closed the door rather forcefully. As she drifted off to sleep, she replayed their performance in her mind. And dreamt of waltzing with Elston.

Chapter Five

*S*unday passed quietly but pleasantly. Robert spent most of the day with Kesteven, who reminisced about his half-century friendship with the late Lord Elston. After dinner, Robert and Lady Deborah repeated their performance of the harpsichord and viola sonata, to the delight and enjoyment of both audience and musicians.

Monday morning after a convivial breakfast, Robert took his leave of the Woodhurst family, promising to call when he arrived in Town. It was a bright, sunny morning, albeit a bit chilly, with a few puffy clouds gracing the blue sky. As the coach bowled along toward Leicester, Robert considered Kesteven's twin daughters. Lady Deborah was lovely, intelligent, well-mannered, sweet-tempered, and a wonderful musician. Lady Diana was equally lovely, but did not measure up to her sister in other respects. Deborah was demure and dignified; Diana, bold and brash. Both had the gift of laughter, but Diana seemed to laugh at people, Deborah with them. Robert was astonished that two people who looked so incredibly alike possessed such different personalities.

Lady Deborah was a worthy candidate for his marchioness, but he was much less certain about Lady Diana's suitability. It was damned disconcerting to think of having a wife he could not distinguish from another man's until she spoke, but, even so, he would pursue the connection in London. Afternoon calls, dances, and drives in the park would either deepen their acquaintance into friendship—and, perhaps, something more—or it would not. By the end of the Season, he hoped to have pared the list of ladies from seven down to one. Or, at most, two.

After meeting three of them, Robert was hopeful that

one of his parent's choices would be a lady he could respect, and for whom he'd feel affection. It was unrealistic to hope for a love match, but, in time, affection might mature into that tender emotion. At the moment, Lady Deborah was at the top of his mental list of prospective brides; Miss Clarissa Merrick at the bottom. 'Twas a pity he had not been able to meet Karolina Lane during his visit to Paddington Court. Robert could not help but wonder what kind of woman the lovely little girl he had befriended so many years ago had become.

Unaware that she was the subject of Lord Elston's musings, Karla stared across the luncheon table at her stepmother, wondering if she misheard the viscountess's last statement.

"Isn't it exciting, Karla?" Charles exclaimed. "You are going to London for the Season!"

She had not misunderstood: her stepmother was going to present her—and Lydia, of course—to Society. "Exciting, indeed, Charles." Despite her racing heart, Karla's tone was even. "I hope that, until Easter term begins, you will be my escort around Town. There will be so many sights to see."

"Your first priority must be the modiste, which Charles is not likely to find very interesting." Lady Blackburn smiled at the boy, as if apologizing for introducing such practicalities. "But once Karolina and Lydia have new clothes, I know they will enjoy exploring museums and such with you. And"—the countess's voice lowered to a conspiratorial whisper—"be sure to take them to Astley's Amphitheatre. The performers there, both human and equine, are quite spectacular."

Karla turned to their guest. "Will you be in London for the Season, my lady?"

"Oh, yes. I am looking forward to it. I shall enjoy introducing you and your sister to my friends. And to their sons."

Karla would not have thought such a dignified lady could grin, but there was no other way to describe Lady Blackburn's beaming, and slightly amused, smile.

"I hope you will tell us how to go on before you begin those introductions."

The countess reached over and gave Karla's hand a gentle, reassuring squeeze. "Of course I will, my dear. I will help you order new wardrobes, too, if you like."

"I would like that very much, my lady." Karla much preferred the simple elegance of Lady Blackburn's gowns to the flounces and ruffles her stepmother favored.

"I am quite capable of guiding Lydia's and Caroline's choices." The viscountess's expression bordered on a frown, as if she was not quite certain whether her sense of fashion was being questioned.

"Of course you are, Hortense," the countess agreed. "But think how much quicker and simpler it will be with my assistance."

"Hmm."

"The sooner the girls are properly turned out, the sooner you can make calls." Lady Blackburn presented this compelling argument as if it were the veriest commonplace.

After a moment's consideration, the viscountess conceded with a graciousness that surprised Karla. "In that case, we would be pleased to have your assistance."

"Excellent!" Lady Blackburn smiled. "How soon can you be ready to leave?"

As Karla climbed the staircase to the schoolroom after the countess's departure, her knees suddenly buckled. She sat on a stair, one hand clutching her stomach. *Oh, Lud!* If Elston was in Town for the Season, she was doomed. Once he realized she had deceived him, he would denounce her. And she would deserve his scorn. *Why had she allowed her pride to overrule common sense? Why hadn't she confessed her masquerade before he left?* The answer to both questions was the same: she had not wanted him to know of her humiliating situation. After all, the hero of a lady's dreams is supposed to respect and admire her. Elston had starred in that role for seventeen years; Karla could not have borne it if he'd pitied her.

If only . . .

No. She would not torture herself with "if onlys." Squaring her shoulders, she rose and continued upstairs. What was done was done. Now she must deal with the consequences of her folly.

Late in the morning on their second day of travel, Robert and Higgins reached their destination, a village near the

Earl of Foxton's estate about ten miles south of Leicester. Robert did not know the earl, nor would he be particularly interested in making the gentleman's acquaintance if not for the fact that Foxton's daughters were listed in the codicil as prospective brides. Since it was too early to pay calls and he was not yet ready for luncheon, Robert hired a horse. A brisk ride would allow him to stretch muscles cramped from sitting in the carriage all morning, as well as to explore the countryside.

As he turned his mount onto the path a groom had recommended, Robert's thoughts turned to the earl's daughters. Of the three, only the middle one, Lady Mary, remained unwed. It was unusual for a younger sister to marry before an elder one, and Robert could not help but wonder why Lady Mary, five-and-twenty and the oldest of the unknown ladies, remained a spinster. Perhaps she was not as pretty as her siblings. Maybe she'd been engaged and her fiancé had died. Or her single status might result from some flaw in her character. All three possibilities were equally likely Robert thought, guiding his horse toward a small copse.

At the sound of angry voices, he turned away, intending to ride around it. When the words penetrated his consciousness, he changed direction again, this time moving toward the speakers.

Dismounting at the edge of the copse, Robert looped the horse's reins over the branch of a leafy shrub. Then, with the stealth that had made him one of Wellington's best scouts, he moved silently through the trees.

"You are a fool, Mary Foster!" a woman proclaimed. "I know you enjoyed that little scene you just enacted. I only hope you find the loss of Lizzie's friendship equally amusing."

Robert neared the clearing in time to see the shorter of the two women cross her arms over her chest and sneer at her companion. It was not an expression that flattered her plain, rather heavyset countenance. Standing in the shadow of a large, gnarled oak, he watched and eavesdropped shamelessly. "You are the fool, Charlotte, if you think Lizzie will reject my friendship."

"I did not say she would reject your friendship. I said you would lose hers."

"It is the same thing—"

"No, it is not." Robert agreed with the taller woman—Charlotte—even as he wondered what Foxton's daughter had done.

Lady Mary shrugged. "The same or different, it doesn't matter for it will not happen. Not for this. Indeed, Lizzie will probably thank me."

"Thank you for seducing the man she loves? Don't be daft."

"I did not seduce him—"

"Maybe not, but I doubt Lizzie will see it that way. I am surprised you let Harry kiss you. You don't even like him!"

Lady Mary's laugh was mocking. "I didn't let him do anything. I kissed him."

"Why?" Robert waited as eagerly as Charlotte to hear the response.

Lady Mary shrugged again. Her companion apparently did not deem that a suitable reply. "Don't think you can put me off. I want an answer." It sounded as if she spoke through clenched teeth.

"We do not get everything we want in this life, Charlotte."

"Is that it? You stole Lizzie's beau because your sister's husband chose her over you?"

Robert thought the muttered phrase that followed the query was "Not that I blame him." He quite agreed. Having heard more than enough to convince him Lady Mary would not be a suitable bride—for all three of the reasons he'd considered—he retraced his steps, then mounted and returned to the village.

After returning the horse to the stable, Robert informed Higgins they would continue their journey after luncheon. Although obviously surprised by the abrupt change of plan, the valet merely said, "Very good, my lord," and placed the stack of shirts he was holding back into the trunk from which he had just taken them. The innkeeper was not as amiable, but a haughtily raised eyebrow followed by a frigid stare put him in his place.

Three days later, on the nineteenth of March, an hour after dusk, Robert spied the towering bulk of Elston Abbey against the horizon. There were more stately homes in the realm, and many newer ones, but Robert loved every quirk of the old monstrosity. Built in the late fifteenth century as a Benedictine monastery, the old stone building had seen—and survived—much. It had been renovated several times over the years by various ancestors, but all of the changes blended harmoniously with the original design.

Lights shone in most of the ground-floor windows, so Robert surmised his great-aunt had received the message that he hoped to arrive tonight. Either that or she was entertaining. The latter possibility was unlikely, but not impossible. Given his fatigue and his travel-stained appearance, Robert hoped she had not invited half the county to greet his return.

"Welcome home, my lord!" the gatekeeper exclaimed.

"Thank you, Hobson. It is good to be home."

"Lady Lavinia has been anxiously awaitin' yer arrival. Sent a footman down here twice already." The old man snorted. "As if ye'd get lost betwixt here and the door."

Robert smiled slightly. "We haven't been lost yet, so I have every confidence that Higgins can get us to the house without difficulty."

"O' course I can." With that, the valet-cum-coachman started the team up the carriage drive.

Before they rounded the last curve, the huge double door opened and the butler and two footmen emerged. The latter men ran down the steps; the former's pace was more stately, in keeping with his age, dignity, and higher station. By the time Higgins halted the coach, two grooms had joined the group waiting to welcome the marquess.

The butler opened the carriage door and let down the steps. "Welcome home, Lord Elston."

Robert stepped down onto the drive. "Thank you, Wilcox. I am glad to be home."

"As we are to have you here, my lord."

He walked toward the house. "I trust everyone has been well, and that no problems have arisen."

After a quick look to make certain the footmen were unloading the luggage, Wilcox followed. "Lady Lavinia has missed you sorely—"

"As I have her."

"But Mr. Markham has been able to deal with all estate matters, I believe."

Robert resisted the urge to take the front steps two at a time. "Please send a message to Markham to meet me in the estate office in the morning. At half past ten."

"Yes, my lord."

After entering the great hall, Robert paused for a moment, looking around and reveling in the joy of being home again after nearly three months away.

"Robert!" Lady Lavinia Symington erupted from the winter parlor, which had originally been the abbot's study, at a speed which belied her nearly seventy years.

Catching his beloved great-aunt in a hug that lifted her off her feet, Robert kissed her on both cheeks before setting her down. Then, keeping one arm around her shoulders, he tucked her against his side and grinned down at her. "Good evening, Aunt Livvy. What a lovely welcome home."

Color blossomed on her cheeks. "You rascal. Is that a proper greeting for your aged aunt?"

"It is a proper greeting for you, darling Livvy. When you are aged, I will greet you more sedately."

"And just when do you think I will attain that venerable status?"

"Hmm." Robert pretended to consider the question. "In a dozen years or so."

"Did you hear that, Wilcox?" Lady Lavinia inquired of the butler, who was a decade younger. "When we are eighty, we will be old and properly revered."

Wilcox bowed. "You will be, my lady. Lord Elston may well consider me ancient now."

The butler's tone revealed that the matter was of some concern to him. "Nonsense, Wilcox," Robert reassured.

The servant smiled slightly, then reverted to his usual, formal mien. "When would you like to have dinner, my lord?"

They usually dined at six o'clock and it was well past that now. "Aunt Livvy, you should not have waited for me," Robert chided.

"I would much rather wait and eat with you than dine alone."

Remorseful at all the meals she had eaten alone in the past few months, Robert leaned down and bussed her cheek. "Give me half an hour to bathe and change. Then

I shall attempt to atone for my absence by entertaining you with tales of my travels."

As he strode toward the stairway, Robert heard her mutter, "Foolish boy."

During dinner, Lady Lavinia apprised Robert of the noteworthy events in the area during his absence: the vicar's wife had presented him with a lovely daughter on Valentine's Day; Gibbs of the home farm and his wife were the proud parents of yet another son, their fifth; the squire's daughter—the girl whose attempt to compromise Robert into marriage had sent him fleeing to Scotland—had eloped with a half-pay officer; Viscount Lorring's eldest son was reportedly smitten with a general's daughter he'd met during the Christmas holidays at his cousin's home in Derbyshire. Robert wanted to tell his great-aunt of the decision he had reached in Scotland, and of meeting three of the young ladies listed in the codicil, but found he could not bare his soul in front of the servants.

After his aunt rose from the table, leaving him to enjoy his port in solitary state, he poured a glass and carried it outside to smoke a cheroot. There was no terrace at Elston Abbey, but despite that lack, Robert's thoughts turned to Paddington Court and the ladies he had met—or not met— there. He wondered if Karla would get her Season, if Miss Lindquist's charges had been quarrelsome today. That thought led to Charles, and Robert hoped the young viscount had honored his promise to correspond. Reminding himself to check the accumulated mail after Aunt Livvy retired, Robert took one last puff of his cigar, drained his glass, and went inside to join his great-aunt.

When he reached the door of the parlor, Robert stood for a moment looking at the woman who had raised him after his mother died. Aunt Livvy was taller than average— a Symington trait more pronounced in the men than in the ladies—and, over the past few years, she'd become more rounded. Not plump exactly, just not as slender as she used to be. She had the same chocolate brown eyes he himself had—another family feature—but her hair, which in his boyhood had been as black as his own, was now snowy white. The spectacles perched on her nose as she frowned down at her embroidery were a recent addition, but did not detract from her beauty. As always, he was amazed no man had ever perceived what a treasure Lady Lavinia Symington was.

"Such a frown, Aunt Livvy. You will get wrinkles."

She smiled at his teasing and patted the sofa cushion beside her. "More wrinkles you mean. I doubt anyone would notice another."

He peered at her face, his eyes narrowed in mock concentration. "Well, darling aunt, it does appear that you have one or two, but any discerning gentleman would be so entranced by your beauty that he would overlook them."

"There is no point in dumping the butter boat over me, Rob. I have a mirror. I even look in it occasionally."

"Why did you never marry, Aunt Livvy?" he asked, his tone serious. "It can't be because you did not receive proposals. You must have had dozens of them."

"Not dozens, dear, but more than one or two." She turned to face him. "I accepted one, too, from a man I liked and admired and believed I would come to love. Unfortunately, he died a few weeks before our wedding."

"Have you been mourning him ever since?"

"No. I grieved for several years, for I fell deeply in love with him during our betrothal, but I have not been mourning for half a century."

"Did you never again receive an offer from a man you liked and admired?"

She shifted, as if uncomfortable with the topic. "Many years later I did, but I was happy with my life and I had a hard time imagining him as a part of it."

Robert tensed. Then he willed his muscles to relax and, with a slight effort, kept his tone conversational. "How old was I when you received that offer?"

She lifted a hand to stroke his cheek. "You must not think I refused solely because of you, dear. As I said, I had a hard time imagining him in my life, or myself as part of his."

After a moment's pause, she tilted her head to one side, her expression bemused. "Why are we discussing such ancient history?"

He captured her hand in his and squeezed it gently. "Because, darling Livvy, I cannot fathom why the gentlemen of Gloucestershire haven't leapt to claim you as wife."

"Spoken like a fond nephew."

"Well, I am a fond nephew." His teasing smile felt as if it fell short of the mark.

"You are, and I am a doting aunt. Great-aunt." She waved a hand, dismissing the distinction. "But you know that already."

He squeezed her hand again, then raised it to his lips. "Indeed I do."

"Have you been considering marriage, Rob?"

"You know that I must. You were present when the codicil was read and you heard the solicitor's monologue on my duty, as the last male Symington, to secure the succession."

"I don't dispute that you need an heir. I would, however, disagree if you tell me you must choose a wife from your father's list of ladies. *You* are the one who is marrying. You must please yourself, not your father."

Robert shifted position, leaning back into the curved corner of the sofa so he could watch his aunt's reactions to what he was about to say. "Can I not try to do both? I did a great deal of thinking about this in Scotland. Although at first I thought the codicil had been written in anger, I now believe it was written in love."

Aunt Livvy reached for the green embroidery silk. She nodded but said nothing.

"I resolved to try to honor my father's last request, but not at the sacrifice of my happiness. After I have met all the unmarried ladies on the list, if I do not believe I could be happy with any of them, I will look elsewhere. But I will consider them first."

"That is a sensible, as well as an honorable, decision."

"Fourteen are unmarried, but three are still in the schoolroom."

"Only three?" She peered at him over the top of her spectacles. "I thought four."

Robert was momentarily stunned by the knowledge that his great-aunt had given his plight such consideration. He should not have been surprised—Livvy loved him with all her heart and always had—but he was. Surprised and deeply moved. He leaned over and kissed the top of her bent head. "I love you, Aunt Livvy."

She smiled up at him. "I love you, too, Rob." After a rather searching glance, she resumed their conversation.

"Aren't Manvers's youngest, Donnebrook's youngest, the Baddington chit, and Greenwich's daughter all too young?"

"Lady Christina was presented at the Queen's Birthday Drawing Room in January, so I assume she will make her bows this Season."

A slight frown creased his aunt's brow. "I fear my memory is not as good as it once was. Is Lady Christina Greenwich's daughter or Donnebrook's?"

"Greenwich's."

Livvy stitched in silence for several seconds. "Are you acquainted with any of the eligible girls?"

"Had you asked me that question in December, I would have answered four. Now, however, I can say I know—or know of—eight of them. Nine, really, but I have not seen one since I was a stripling, so I count her as an unknown."

His aunt's eyebrows soared toward her hair. "Indeed? Do you plan to tell me how you met four of the ladies while secluded in Scotland?"

"Perhaps," he drawled. Disappointment flashed across her features before she bent over her work. "I was only teasing, Aunt Livvy. Of course I will tell you."

He stretched his legs out, crossing them at the ankle. "I planned the journey back from Stranraer so I could visit two of the estates and call on several ladies' families."

"Clever boy. On whom did you call?"

"First on Lord and Lady Merrick. I met their daughter, Clarissa, but I cannot imagine myself married to her." Involuntarily, he shuddered. "Next I visited Paddington Court. If you recall, the codicil specified 'Miss Karolina Lane, the eldest daughter of Viscount Padbury.' "

Livvy nodded. "I remember. I thought it an unusual stipulation and didn't understand why your father excluded the viscount's younger daughters."

"Father didn't like the second Lady Padbury. Presumably he found that reason enough not to include her daughters. She has one, Miss Lydia, who will be making her come-out this Season."

Robert thought for a moment, seeking the words to convey his impressions of the viscountess and the situation at Paddington Court. "It was a very strange visit. Karla—Miss Lane—is the girl I knew years ago. I was looking forward to renewing our acquaintance, but the viscountess did everything she could to prevent a meeting between us."

"How so, dear?"

"She lied about her stepdaughter's whereabouts. At tea, Lady Padbury said Karla—whom she and Miss Lydia persist in calling 'Caroline'—was visiting a tenant; then she purportedly dined at the vicarage."

"If they did not expect you to call, Rob, that might well have been the case."

"It might," he agreed, his tone rather grim. "Except that Lady Blackburn, who was visiting when I arrived, told me that Karla hasn't been seen in the village for months. Not even in church."

"I remember Jane Blackburn." Livvy smiled in reminiscence. "She was a delightful girl, and the belle of her Season."

"She is a very nice lady, and still quite lovely. She is also very concerned about Karla. Lady Blackburn and I have launched a campaign to convince the viscountess to present Karla to Society."

"Lady Padbury cannot present her daughter if her stepdaughter has not made her bows!"

Robert nodded. "Exactly so. I made quite a point of telling the viscountess that the *ton* would close their doors to Miss Lydia if Karla was not also presented."

The arrival of the tea tray halted their conversation. Declining tea, Robert crossed the room to pour himself a snifter of brandy. Then, leaning one shoulder against the mantel, he resumed his tale.

"I have strayed a bit from my intended story. Suffice it to say, I spent two days at Paddington Court and never saw Karla. Her half-brother, the current viscount, told me Lady Padbury expressly forbade Karla to come downstairs during my visit. And there is another young woman, Miss Lindquist, a relative of the first Lady Padbury, who is in a similar situation."

"Infamous!" Livvy's cheeks flushed with outrage. "Who is this Lady Padbury?"

"I don't know her maiden name, but I remember Father telling me that her father was a minor baronet."

"Were you and Jane Blackburn successful in convincing

Lady Padbury to give her stepdaughter a Season? If so, you will meet Karolina in London."

"I don't know if my words were sufficient persuasion, but Lady Blackburn may have better luck. Charles—the young viscount—also intended to try." After a pause, he added, "Charles volunteered to write and let me know if our campaign succeeds."

"I hope it does." His aunt's determined tone reminded Robert of his boyhood. Unspoken but nonetheless clear was "if not, I shall have a great deal more to say."

He wondered if he could persuade her to accompany him to London. When he was a boy, she had regularly accompanied his father, claiming the Abbey was too large and too quiet when Robert was at school, but sometime during his years on the Peninsula, she had stopped going to Town for the Season. Before he could formulate his request, his aunt asked another question.

"What other young ladies did you meet?"

"I met Kesteven's daughters, Ladies Deborah and Diana Woodhurst. They are twins, as alike in appearance as two peas in a pod, but with quite different personalities."

"Can you imagine either girl as your wife?"

"I do not yet know them well enough for that," he hedged, reluctant to say more even to his beloved aunt.

Livvy looked over at him, as if sensing there was something he wasn't saying. "Will you pursue the acquaintance in Town?"

With a nod, he granted her a partial victory. "Yes, I will."

"Good."

As he sipped his brandy, Robert wondered how much work awaited him here. He wanted to arrive in London before the Season was too far advanced. Otherwise he might be too late to court some of the young ladies.

"Did you meet anyone else, dear? And which girls do you already know?"

"I am acquainted with Greenwich's, Winton's, Montrose's, and Chesterfield's daughters, but I cannot imagine being married—happily married—to any of them."

He took another drink of brandy. "The same is true for Foxton's middle daughter, Lady Mary. Although I didn't meet her, I learned enough about her to know that she and I would not suit."

"Gossip may contain a hint of truth, but sometimes it is pure fabrication."

He turned away to place his snifter on the mantel, as well as to avoid his aunt's too perceptive gaze. "My knowledge did not come from gossip. I inadvertently overheard an argument between Lady Mary and a friend that convinced me her character is flawed."

Aunt Livvy's eyebrows soared again, but she said only, "When will you leave for London?"

"In a week or two, after I attend to the matters here that require my attention."

"Good." She placed her embroidery in her lap and secured the needle in the corner of the fabric. After several moments of unnecessary smoothing, she glanced up at him and spoke with uncharacteristic hesitancy. "Would you dislike it excessively if I accompanied you to Town?"

Robert contained his shout of joy with an effort. Enveloping his aunt in a hug, he pulled her to her feet. "Darling Livvy, I would like it above all things."

"Truly?"

"Yes indeed."

"Then I had best scrutinize my wardrobe and make plans."

As he escorted his aunt upstairs, Robert made another resolution. Since he had to enter the Marriage Mart, he would look about and see if he could find a worthy gentleman for his aunt. Bellingham, perhaps; George's father had been a widower for two decades, but he might well want to share the rest of his life with a companionable, loving woman like Livvy.

Stopping outside the door to his aunt's bedchamber, Robert kissed her cheek, then turned toward his own rooms. *Another campaign successfully launched.*

Chapter Six

*S*ome days Karla could not quite believe that her step-mother was going to give her a Season. On others, mostly when Lady Blackburn was present, Karla delighted in the prospect of making her bows to Society. She was a bit old to be having a come-out, but Elston had assured her—or, more precisely, Miss Lindquist—that another young lady her age was being presented this year. Better late than never, as the old proverb said.

The thought of Elston stopped her in her tracks, amid open trunks and a pile of gowns waiting to be packed. She looked forward to seeing him again, to meeting him as herself and, hopefully, continuing their childhood friendship. Although she knew the latter was unlikely, especially after he realized she had deceived him, that did not stop her from wishing it might be so. *If only she hadn't . . .*

A knock halted her circling thoughts. "Is it safe to enter?" The visitor peeked around the open door, her face downcast, but the mahogany hair with its off-center silver streak was instantly recognizable.

Karla skirted the obstacles to the doorway and drew Lady Blackburn inside. "Quite safe, my lady," she answered on a giggle. "And you need not study the carpet. There are no fearful sights, although the room is far less tidy than usual."

The countess lifted her gaze, her hazel eyes with their distinctive gray rim widening as she surveyed the chamber. "What are you doing up here, child, other than driving your maid to distraction?"

"Packing. At least, I am trying to—"

"Where is your maid?"

Karla stifled a sigh and escorted her visitor to a chair. "I don't have one."

Lady Blackburn's eyes widened farther. "You don't have a maid." Each word was distinctly articulated, as if doing so would make the meaning clearer.

"No, my lady."

"She quit because she wishes to stay in the country?"

"No, my lady." Karla walked the few steps to the window and looked outside. "I have never had a maid."

The countess muttered something, then ordered, "Ring the bell and have Smithers brought up here."

Karla cringed. Things were going from bad to worse. "If I ring, no one will answer."

There was a moment of silence; then gentle hands grasped her shoulders and turned her around. "Why is that, my dear?"

Karla blinked back the tears that flooded her eyes at the countess's compassionate tone. "Because I am treated little better than a servant."

Enveloped in Lady Blackburn's loving embrace, Karla laid her head on the countess's shoulder and allowed her emotions free reign. After several minutes, she swiped at her eyes with the back of her hand, then stepped back and groped for her handkerchief.

"Here." Lady Blackburn handed her a snowy-white, lace-trimmed scrap of linen. Then, her steps militant, the countess walked to the bellpull and gave four strong tugs.

Having found her own handkerchief, Karla wiped her eyes and blew her nose. "That should throw the servants into a pother."

"Good." The words were calmly spoken, but the gleam in Lady Blackburn's eyes was anything but. "I was hoping you used the same system of rings I do."

"One for the butler, two for a footman, and three for one's maid or valet?"

"Exactly so."

A moment later, they heard footsteps pounding up the stairs, then running down the hallway. A red-faced footman burst into the room, followed by a chambermaid. "What's amiss?" the manservant huffed.

"What is amiss," the countess stated in a crisp yet calm voice, "is that you have not broadcast to the entire county the viscountess's orders for you to ignore your late master's daughter. Nor have you let it be known that Miss Lane's stepmother treats her quite shabbily."

The footman opened his mouth to protest, but Lady Blackburn's carefully worded complaint allowed him no excuse. Now it was embarrassment, not exertion, that colored his face. "No, my lady. I mean, yes, my lady."

"If something similar happens again, you will immediately notify one of the Blackburn Park servants."

Squaring his shoulders, the footman bowed. "Yes, my lady. I will."

The chambermaid bobbed an awkward curtsy. "I will, your ladyship."

"Good." The countess studied the pair for a moment. "Now you"—she pointed to the maid—"will escort Smithers up here. And you"—she indicated the footman—"will tell the rest of the staff what I just told you."

"Yes, your ladyship." The maid curtsied again and left the room.

"All of them?" the manservant asked, alarmed. "Even the butler and the viscountess's maid?"

"All except the butler, Lady Padbury's maid, and Miss Lydia's," the countess amended.

The footman's expression eased. "Very good, my lady."

After the man left, Lady Blackburn resumed her seat. Karla braced herself for the coming inquisition.

"Why didn't you tell me what was happening?" The countess's tone was stern, but her eyes were full of compassion.

"I was too ashamed."

"The shame is not yours, child; it belongs fully to your stepmother."

Perhaps it had been pride, and fear of being pitied, but Karla wasn't about to confess that.

"Why did you lie to Elston?"

Karla sank onto the window seat and covered her face with her hands. *How in the world did Lady Blackburn know about that?*

Some moments later, the countess sat beside her. The silence seemed to grow and swell, mocking Karla for her cowardice. As she nerved herself to meet her neighbor's gaze, a knock at the door heralded the entrance of the chambermaid and Lady Blackburn's dresser.

"Smithers, it seems that the viscountess has neglected to provide Miss Lane with a maid. Would you see to the packing of her gowns?"

The chambermaid stepped forward and curtsied. "My lady, I would like to help Mrs. Smithers." She twisted her hands in her apron, then blurted, "I ain't never packed no fancy gowns, but—"

The maid's desire to help brought Karla to her feet. "Thank you, Molly. If Smithers needs assistance, she can show you how it is done."

The countess's dresser studied the younger servant for a moment, then nodded decisively. "I would be pleased to have your help." After a quick survey of the room, Smithers inquired, "Are all the gowns to be packed on the bed, Miss Lane, or are there others in the wardrobe?"

"They are either on the bed or already in the trunk by the dressing table. But"—Karla gestured helplessly—"I have never packed gowns before, so . . ."

"Molly and I will take care of everything, Miss Lane, while you and my lady enjoy a cup of tea."

"Thank you, Smithers. And you, too, Molly." Karla smiled at the helpful pair before leading Lady Blackburn out of the room.

In the morning room over tea and sandwiches, Karla confessed her deception to the countess. Lady Blackburn, in turn, revealed that Elston had provided the information that allowed her to deduce the ruse. Karla's confession to the marquess still loomed on the horizon, but she was too drained to worry about it now. She still trembled from the force of the emotions that had racked her as she'd unburdened herself: fear, then mortification, quickly followed by relief. Confession might be good for the soul, but it was exhausting.

"Karla?"

Chagrined at being caught wool-gathering, she closed her eyes for a moment before facing the countess. "I apologize, my lady. I—"

"No, my dear. It is I who must beg your pardon for not

realizing how done in you are. Please forgive my foolish prattling."

Karla mustered a smile. "You never prattle, Lady B. Nor are you foolish."

The countess rose. "Come, child. After a few hours' sleep you will feel much more the thing."

"But—"

"No buts. After I see you settled, I will talk with your stepmother. Whatever she expected you to do today, she will have to do herself."

The countess led her upstairs. As they approached Karla's room, Smithers and Molly emerged, the packing completed. After thanking both women, Karla stood, drooping with fatigue, while Lady Blackburn undressed her like a child, then tucked her into bed and kissed her brow. "Sleep well, my dear. I expect to see the roses back in your cheeks when I call tomorrow."

Her eyes once again swimming in tears, Karla closed them and obeyed her benefactor's command.

Robert's days at Elston Abbey fell into a pattern. After breakfast with Aunt Livvy, he met with Markham, his bailiff. The meetings were often quite long, and frequently necessitated a great deal of riding about the estate. Although he missed luncheon with his aunt more days than not, Robert was always well fed by whichever tenant family he and Markham were visiting at the time. Some days Robert returned to the house in time to pay calls or receive callers with his aunt. He made an effort—generally successful—to be home, bathed, and changed in time for tea. And he and Aunt Livvy always had dinner together, either at the Abbey or at the home of whichever neighbor was providing the evening's entertainment.

There were many such entertainments. Too many, as far as he was concerned. Many a night he sat in his study long after midnight, reading about the plight of children working in mines and factories or catching up on his correspondence. To his great delight, Charles had honored his promise to write. In typical schoolboy fashion, his letters were either short and concise or long and rambling. Robert preferred the latter, although the former had predominated for the past week as the Lanes prepared to move to Town.

Karla was going to get her Season, and Charles was to be her escort to museums, churches, and other marvels of the metropolis for a few days, until Easter term started.

Robert had been hoping to see the boy in London, but would not arrive until after Charles returned to school. Their correspondence was flourishing, however, and Robert felt certain it would continue after the viscount returned to Harrow, even if the letters were less frequent.

Realizing that he'd read the same paragraph twice and still had no idea what it said, Robert closed his book. Hopefully tomorrow he would have more time for his studies. Feeling weary to his bones, he closed his eyes for a moment. Trying to envision a six-year-old blond, blue-eyed sprite transformed into a young lady of three-and-twenty, he fell asleep.

London! Karla found it hard to believe she was really here. The journey of nearly two hundred miles had taken eight days, due to Lydia's delicate stomach. Karla was thankful she had ridden most of the way in Lady Blackburn's coach, even more grateful for all the countess's lessons about the *ton* and its ways. So many rules governed the behavior of young ladies! Karla hoped she would remember them all and not disgrace her mentor.

Lady Blackburn had asked if Karla could stay at Blackburn House, but the viscountess had flatly refused the request. Although Karla agreed with her stepmother that people would ask questions if she did not reside with her family, she thought the countess's answer—that she wanted, just once, to sponsor a young lady in Society and had chosen her neighbor as protégée—would be readily accepted by anyone rag-mannered enough to inquire.

The countess's kindness and concern were vastly different from the viscountess's coldness, and wonderfully welcome to Karla. With all her heart she wished her stepmother had granted Lady Blackburn's request. It was possible the viscountess would change her mind, but given that she had granted her stepdaughter a Season only to avoid the *ton*'s opprobrium, Karla knew a reversal was highly improbable.

The coach halted—finally!—outside a narrow townhouse. Four stories tall, it was constructed of stone, its wooden trim painted black. There was a large fanlight above the door and the windows shone in the afternoon sunlight. Compared to Paddington Court the townhouse seemed small, but it was obviously well maintained. Unfortunately, Karla had no idea if it was Padbury House or Blackburn House. The former was in Curzon Street, the latter on Upper Brook Street. Both were fashionable addresses, but Upper Brook Street was near the entrance to Hyde Park and, she presumed, must have more cachet.

"Curzon Street at last, my dear. I daresay you will be as glad to get out of this carriage as I am." A wry smile accompanied the countess's words.

So this is Padbury House. Karla returned her companion's smile. "I will be delighted to sit on something that does not bounce, but I will miss your company."

Lady Blackburn brushed the back of two gloved fingers against Karla's cheek. "You will see me nearly every day. And you are welcome to visit Blackburn House whenever you wish—morning, afternoon, or evening."

"Thank you, Lady B." Impulsively, Karla hugged the countess. For a second, she feared she had overstepped, but Lady Blackburn returned the embrace.

A footman swung open the door, ending the affectionate moment. Karla followed the countess out of the carriage, then looked around to see if the other vehicles in their little cavalcade had arrived. Her stepmother's traveling chaise was parked in front of the countess's, but neither the servants' coach nor the baggage wagon was present. Perhaps there was a back entrance for the servants through which they would carry in the trunks.

Charles erupted from the viscountess's carriage as if his coattails were on fire. Racing toward Karla and the countess, he said, in a near shout, "Finally, we are here!" Belatedly remembering his manners, he halted a few feet in front of them and bowed. "Ladies, may I escort you inside?"

Karla could see that Lady Blackburn was fighting a smile, as she was. But the countess took Charles's arm and, with the graciousness that was an integral part of her character, asked his impression of various sights on the road into Town. As she followed them up the walk, Karla wondered what was keeping her stepmother and Lydia. Stifling a sigh, she turned and began to retrace her steps, but the footman standing at the coach's open door shook his head, so she reversed direction again. Whatever the problem, her help was not required.

The front door opened just as Charles and the countess reached the steps. Harris, who had traveled to London last week to set the townhouse in order, ushered the young viscount and Lady Blackburn into the house. Although she would have liked to stay outdoors enjoying the lovely spring afternoon, Karla hastened inside.

"Good afternoon, Harris." As the butler assisted her out of her pelisse, she whispered a question. "Everything is in order here?" His nod indicated there were no immediate problems. "Please bring a tea tray to . . ."

"Tea in the drawing room right away, Miss Lane." Lowering his voice to a whisper, he added, "Top of the stairs on the left, miss."

As Charles and the countess ascended the stairs, Karla glanced around the entry hall before following them. It seemed vaguely familiar, but she couldn't say she remembered it. Not that she'd really expected to—she had not been here for almost twenty years—but she'd hoped some of the rooms would hold memories of her parents.

The tea tray arrived; the viscountess and Lydia did not. Karla and Charles made an effort to entertain Lady Blackburn, but all three of them were tired and disinclined toward conversation. After drinking a cup of tea, the countess made her *adieux*.

"Rest well tonight, Karla. You will need all your energy in the morning when we visit the modiste and order new wardrobes for you and Lydia."

"What is so fatiguing about choosing a few gowns?" Charles offered his arm to escort Lady Blackburn downstairs.

"Choosing a few new gowns is not terribly tiring, but your sisters will be ordering dozens. Morning dresses, carriage gowns, riding habits, evening attire, and ball gowns. And they must pick the pattern, fabric, and trim, for each one."

"Oh my!" Karla had not had a new dress since before Lydia's entrance into Yorkshire society and had been looking forward to ordering a few new gowns, but the prospect of such a marathon of shopping was quite daunting.

"If we complete our business at the modiste's tomorrow, then Tuesday we will turn our attention to shoes, hats, and accessories," the countess cheerfully informed them.

Charles helped Lady Blackburn don her pelisse. "I'm glad I'm not a girl!"

Smiling, she stepped in front of the mirror to put on her bonnet. "Is a visit to the tailor so different?"

"Not so very different, perhaps, but men's clothing—my clothing—doesn't require a different pattern for each coat and waistcoat. And my shirts are all of the same pattern and fabric."

"That may be true now, Charles, but not when you are older."

Noting her half-brother's skeptical expression, Karla rejoined the conversation. "Papa's coats were of a variety of patterns. His waistcoats, too. I imagine the same is true for most men."

Charles nodded, conceding the point, then offered his arm to escort Lady Blackburn to her carriage.

Karla thought she was prepared for the shopping expedition. Before they'd left Yorkshire, she had spent several hours one afternoon studying the latest fashions in *Le Belle Assemblée* and *Ackermann's Repository,* and she and her half-sister had debated the merits of various styles last night after dinner and this morning at breakfast. When Lady Blackburn arrived, she joined Karla and Lydia at the table and, over a cup of coffee, pointed out styles and colors she thought would flatter each girl. Karla was delighted that the countess's suggestions—gowns in pastel colors with simple lines and few embellishments—matched her own ideas. As soon as the viscountess appeared, the quartet set off for Madame Celeste's.

When they crossed the threshold of the elegant shop in Bond Street, the proprietress herself came forward to greet Lady Blackburn. "Madame la Comtesse, eet is a pleasure to see you in Town again. You come for ze Season, yes?" Her English, although heavily accented, was easily understandable.

"Yes, Madame, I am here for the Season, and in need of some new gowns. But first we must choose wardrobes for these two young ladies."

Introductions were performed as the modiste studied all three Lane ladies with a critical eye. After seating her customers on two sofas set opposite each other, with a table of pattern books in between, Madame clapped her hands and ordered an assistant to bring a tea tray. "Now, mesdames, I shall measure you while ze mademoiselles look at ze patterns."

Karla chose styles for morning gowns, carriage dresses, evening gowns, and ball gowns, all of which received Lady Blackburn's approval. After Karla was measured, she and her mentor turned their attention to fabrics and colors.

"What do you think of this silk for the ball gown with the tucked bodice?" Karla asked, running her fingers over the delicate pale pink fabric.

"It is the perfect choice." Lady Blackburn pointed to a bolt of fabric. "Do you like this pale blue muslin? It would make a lovely morning gown."

"Indeed it would. Would it be better for the one with the ruffled lace at the neckline or the one with the petal-like sleeves?"

"The gown with the tulip sleeves was the one I had in mind, but it would be lovely for either dress. What do *you* think? Your opinion is the one that matters, since you will be wearing the gowns."

After a moment's thought, Karla made her decision. "The tulip sleeves, I think."

Exclaiming over the colors and textures, they matched fabric and trim to the patterns they had chosen. As they strolled back toward Lydia, the viscountess, and Madame, Karla placed a hand on Lady Blackburn's arm, halting her. "Thank you very much for your help, my lady."

"You are quite welcome, but you didn't need help. Your own taste is excellent."

Karla blushed with pleasure at the compliment. "Thank you, Lady B. I only hope my stepmother won't think I have been too extravagant in my choices."

"Extravagant? My dear, you have been anything but."

"Caroline!" The viscountess's voice cut through the quiet shop like a hot knife through butter. "Madame is waiting to hear your selections."

Karla hastened to the alcove where they sat. The modiste appeared far from impatient, chatting desultorily with

Lydia and her mother. Karla seated herself on the sofa
opposite her stepmother and half-sister, then smoothed the
crumpled edges of the list she had compiled as she made
her choices.

Madame smiled, clearly pleased at such organization.
"Meess Lane, you will show me ze patterns you have chosen, please, and describe ze fabrics. Then, when Madame
le Vicomtesse approves, I write eet in my order book."

"It will take me a few minutes to find all the patterns,
Madame." Karla picked up the book from which she had
selected the most designs and leafed through the pages.
Beside her, Lady Blackburn began searching another
volume.

"Just find one, Meess Lane. Then we go on to ze next.
Ordering a new wardrobe ees not ze work of a moment."
The Frenchwoman chuckled.

Karla smiled. "No, it is not." She shifted the book so the
modiste could see the first design. "This morning gown, in
the white muslin sprigged with blue flowers."

The viscountess bustled over to stand behind Karla, so
she, too, could see the pattern. Lydia trailed behind her
mother.

"A very good choice, Meess—"

"No. That is not acceptable."

Karla glanced at her stepmother in surprise, as did Madame Celeste and Lady Blackburn.

"You dislike ze design, Vicomtesse, or ze fabric?"

"The gown is too plain. There are no flounces, no
ruffles."

"Meess Lane has not ze height for ruffles; they are for
taller girls like Meess Lydia."

The viscountess glared at the modiste. "I believe I know
what is best for my stepdaughter, Madame." She turned to
her daughter, motioning toward the pattern books. "Lydia,
find the ruffled morning gown you chose."

The modiste mumbled something in her native tongue,
but she spoke so quickly Karla did not understand the
comment.

"What is ze next design, Meess Lane?"

Karla turned to the gown with the tulip sleeves. "This
one, in the pale blue muslin."

Madame nodded. "It will look lovely—"

"The pattern is acceptable," the viscountess decreed, "but in the darker blue muslin."

"Isn't that too dark? We are supposed to wear pastels." Karla dared not protest too much, but neither did she want a gown she disliked.

Lady Padbury crossed her arms over her ample bosom. "Dark colors wear better."

The modiste resorted to French again. Lady Blackburn, after a glance at the viscountess's face, commented, "Muslin is muslin, Hortense. Regardless of color, it wears the same."

The viscountess did not yield. "Make it in the dark blue, Madame."

The modiste picked up her pencil, but it was obvious she did not agree with the choice.

Lydia dropped a pattern card in Karla's lap. "Here is the ruffled morning gown."

Lady Padbury smiled at her daughter. "That is much more the thing. And it would make up very well in that sprigged muslin, don't you think, Caroline?"

For someone else, perhaps, Karla thought rebelliously, but not for her. "I am not overly fond of ruffled dresses."

"What a strange girl you are." The viscountess turned to her daughter. "What fabric did you choose for this gown, Lydia?"

"The light green muslin."

"Madame, make it in the buttercup yellow for Miss Lane."

The color was, if possible, even more unflattering than the design. Karla's hands clenched in her lap. "I would prefer the pale pink."

Seeing the glint of battle in her stepmother's eye, she attempted a compromise. "Or the yellow for this pattern." Karla pointed to her next choice.

After a moment's thought, the viscountess conceded. "We'd best take both. You will need a number of morning gowns."

Karla stifled a groan, wishing she'd remained silent. Now, instead of one dress disastrous in both style and color, she had a lovely pattern in a color that would render her well nigh invisible and an unflattering design in a becoming hue. Her luck was definitely out with morning gowns; hoping for a change of fortune, she switched to evening attire.

"A word with you, Hortense." Lady Blackburn rose and walked out of the alcove.

"Not now."

"Indeed now." The countess stood in front of a display of satin, one foot tapping impatiently.

"What is so important—"

"Now, Hortense."

Lady Padbury huffed out a breath and rose. "If you insist."

"I do."

Karla looked from one woman to the other, then at Lydia, who shrugged her incomprehension.

When the viscountess was out of earshot, Madame picked up her pencil. "Your next choice, Meess Lane?"

Grabbing the opportunity the countess had provided, Karla found the pattern for her favorite of the ball gowns. "This one with the tucked bodice, in the pale pink silk."

The modiste wrote swiftly. "Excellent choice."

"You don't think it too plain?" Lydia queried, her tone hesitant.

"Next, Meess Lane?" To Lydia, Madame explained, "Gowns with simple lines are more flattering to petite ladies. You will see. When she wears zees gown, your sister will look *très élégant*."

Karla found the next design, an evening gown. "This one, in the peach lutestring." She turned several pages. "And this, in the ivory silk."

The modiste nodded and added both to her order book. "Ze ivory is more flattering for you than white."

"Those will be pretty, Caroline. I chose this pattern"— Lydia pointed—"but in pale blue."

"You will look lovely in it." Karla smiled at her half-sister. "This spencer in rose sarsenet. And that one in the fine Clarence blue merino."

Madame and Lydia both nodded approval, the former's pencil flying across the page of her book.

"This evening gown in the rose pink crepe with blond lace trim. And—"

The return of her stepmother and Lady Blackburn distracted Karla. Judging by the viscountess's expression, she had not enjoyed the conversation.

As if nothing untoward had occurred, Karla showed her next selection to the modiste. "This ball gown in the cream cambric with the sky blue ribband trim."

"It will do, I suppose." The viscountess sounded like a woman sorely tried. "But in white. White is, after all, *de rigueur* for young ladies."

"I have white, Vicomtesse." Despite her words, the modiste wrote "cream."

"This walking dress in . . ." Karla peered at her list, unable to decipher what she had written. "Do you remember what color we chose, Lady Blackburn?"

The countess leaned over to see the pattern. "The bishop's blue sarcenet—"

"Nile green." The viscountess's tone was adamant. Karla knew that protest, no matter how delicately worded, was futile.

And so it went. Karla's frustration increased each time her stepmother vetoed the color or style of a gown. Not a single one of her choices survived unscathed. The final straw was a carriage dress for which Karla and Lady Blackburn had selected a rose pink merino with black braided trim.

"The mustard bombazine," the viscountess declared.

"No," Karla protested. "It is too dark and too heavy."

Her stepmother ignored her. "The mustard bombazine," she repeated.

"No." Karla stood, anger warring with humiliation. "I am sorry, Madame, but I do not want it. I will make do without a carriage dress." Then, seeking only to escape, she hurried toward the door.

She had not been prepared for this shopping expedition at all.

Chapter Seven

*B*linded by tears, Karla did not see the two ladies on the sidewalk outside the shop until she nearly bowled over the younger one.

"I beg your pardon." Despite her determination not to cry, a sob escaped. She groped in her reticule for her handkerchief. "I am sorry. I—"

"Oh dear." The younger lady offered a small, lace-trimmed linen square. "Is there something we can do to help you?"

Karla mopped her streaming eyes. "It is kind of you to offer, but I fear there is no solution to my problem."

The older lady placed a comforting hand on Karla's shoulder. "Is there somewhere we can take you? Someone who might be able to assist you?"

As Karla sought to formulate a reply, the door opened behind her. The young lady turned slightly and curtsied. "Good morning, Lady Blackburn."

"Good morning, Lady Julia, Miss Castleton." The countess curtsied to the older lady and inclined her head to the younger one before enfolding Karla in a hug. "May I introduce you to my friend and neighbor? She has had a very trying morning."

"Of course you may introduce us. But first"—the elder lady motioned to a crested carriage standing at the curb—"may we convey you somewhere?"

"Thank you. If you would be so kind as to take us to my home."

"It would be our pleasure." Then, to the hovering footman, "Blackburn House, James."

Before Karla and the countess could follow the other

ladies into the elegant town chaise, the footman who accompanied them that morning approached Lady Blackburn and bowed. "My lady, would you like me to deliver a message to the viscountess?"

"Yes, please. Tell her that Miss Lane has gone home with me. We will return to Padbury House in time for tea."

"Very good, my lady." The footman bowed again, then stepped back and watched as Karla and the countess were handed into the carriage.

As the chaise moved smoothly into the traffic on Bond Street, Karla attempted to gather her scattered wits—and her composure. "I feel remarkably foolish."

"There is no reason for that, surely." The tall, slender brunette seated beside her had an unusual accent. "After all, you did not upset yourself."

Karla could not help but be cheered when the unknown young lady again came to her rescue. "Thank you very much for your kindness." Glancing over at the older woman, whom Lady Blackburn had addressed as "Lady Julia," she added, "And thank you, ma'am."

The countess appeared distracted. As Karla pondered whether it was ruder to introduce herself or to converse with ladies with whom she was not acquainted, Lady Julia cleared her throat. "Jane, I believe you were about to introduce us."

"I beg your pardon." Lady Blackburn's smile was a bit rueful. "Lady Julia, Miss Castleton, may I present Miss Karolina Lane, a neighbor of mine in Yorkshire. Karla, this is Lady Julia Castleton and her great-niece, Miss Beth Castleton."

"I am pleased to make your acquaintance, Lady Julia, Miss Castleton." Karla mustered a wobbly smile.

Lady Julia, a slender, silver-haired, elegantly dressed woman in her sixties, studied Karla for a moment. "You are the daughter of Viscount Lane and his first wife, are you not?"

"Yes, my lady."

"You look very like your mother."

The thought cheered Karla immensely. "Thank you, my lady. I don't remember Mama well—not her features, that is. To me, she is more of a memory of love and comfort and the scent of roses."

Miss Castleton touched Karla's hand fleetingly. "That is a wonderful memory to have. But how unfortunate that you don't have a portrait or miniature of her."

The words stirred a recollection. "Her portrait used to hang in the drawing room when I was little, but I have not seen it in years. I daresay my stepmother had it removed to the attics."

"She would," Lady Blackburn muttered.

"I do not believe I am acquainted with your stepmother, Miss Lane." Lady Julia's tone seemed to indicate that this was a shocking omission on the part of the second Lady Padbury.

"My half-sister and I are making our come-outs this Season, my lady, so you will have the opportunity to meet my stepmother."

"If you wish." The countess's mumbled remark garnered an Inquiring Look from Lady Julia.

Miss Castleton turned to Karla with an eager smile. "I, too, will be making my come-out. A shocking thing at my age, I know, but—"

Karla studied her companion. "You cannot be much more than twenty, not so much older than other girls making their bows. I, however, am three-and-twenty. Practically on the shelf."

"On the shelf? Pah!" Lady Julia clearly thought her foolish beyond permission. "*I* am on the shelf, Miss Lane. You are far from securing a place there."

Miss Castleton scrutinized Karla from head to toe. "I guessed you were nineteen, Miss Lane. Will you feel better knowing that I, too, am three-and-twenty? I must confess, I am delighted to know another girl my age is being presented this Season."

Karla nodded. "It is enormously comforting, Miss Castleton. I feared all the other girls would be seventeen, like Lydia." Suddenly shy, she ducked her head and added, "I do hope we can be friends."

"I think we already are." Miss Castleton's smile lit her blue eyes and curved her mouth. "As friends, I hope you will call me Beth."

"I would be honored, Beth. I am Karolina. Or Karla."

"Karolina." In her new friend's lilting voice, it sounded musical, almost magical. "What a lovely name! Mine is actually Julia Elizabeth, but I have been called Beth since I was a babe."

"It suits you, I think. More lively than Julia." Color flaming in her cheeks, Karla turned to Beth's great-aunt. "I beg your pardon, my lady. It was not my intent to disparage your name."

With a smile, Lady Julia accepted the apology. "As a girl, I thought myself misnamed because 'Julia' conjured visions of languid ladies reclining on chaise longues."

"Exactly so, ma'am," Karla grinned, charmed to discover this fanciful aspect of the elegant spinster's character.

Their arrival at Blackburn House halted the conversation, but only temporarily. The Castletons accepted the countess's invitation to share a pot of tea, so they might acquaint the newcomers with recent happenings in Town. Seated in the stylishly appointed but comfortable drawing room, which was furnished in cream and blue with a bit of crimson for contrast, Karla felt the tension easing from her muscles. She would have to deal with the repercussions of her defiance, as well as her stepmother's sartorial edicts, but not for several hours. Until then, she would enjoy her time with Lady Blackburn, and the company of her new acquaintances.

After the butler brought in the tea tray and the countess served her guests, the conversation was general for a time. Since she didn't know any of the people being discussed, Karla allowed her thoughts to drift. And, as they so often did, they quickly gravitated to the Marquess of Elston. The mention of his name immediately returned her attention to her companions.

". . . and I met several of the gentlemen at house parties before the Season started. Viscount Dunnley and his brother, Captain Middleford; their cousin, the Earl of Weymouth; and his friend, the Marquess of Elston," Beth was saying.

"I do not know Captain Middleford well, but the other three are surely the most eligible—and charming—bachelors in the *ton*." Lady Blackburn smiled. "Knowing them before the Season begins gives you quite an advantage, Miss Castleton."

Beth's answering smile was wry. "As an American, I daresay I will need every advantage."

"Nonsense! You are a lovely, charming, well-mannered young lady." Lady Julia's words brought a flush to her niece's cheeks.

"You, my dear aunt, are prejudiced." Beth reached over and squeezed Lady Julia's hand. "And I love you for it."

"But I am not," the countess said, "and I quite agree with Lady Julia."

Karla came to the rescue of her blushing friend. "Beth, have you made the acquaintance of any of the other young ladies making their bows this Season?"

"Quite a few. Lady Christina Fairchild, the Duke of Greenwich's daughter, and Lady Sarah Mallory, the Earl of Tregaron's daughter, were presented at Court when I was. As was Miss Harriett Broughton. I have met Miss Spencer and Miss Cathcart, too, but I know Lady Christina, Lady Sarah, and Miss Broughton best. We share a love of music and will be performing at Mrs. Broughton's musicale next week."

"You are much braver than I. Were I to attempt such a thing"—Karla shuddered at the thought—"I would be so nervous, I'd make a mull of it. If I didn't faint first."

"What instrument do you play?"

"I play the pianoforte, although not as well as I would like. I am a better singer, but my voice is not strong. Nor high."

Beth rose and moved to the chair next to Karla's.

"You are in for it now, Miss Lane." Lady Julia's warning was accompanied by a gurgle of laughter. "Once Beth gets on the subject of music, she can talk for hours."

Karla smiled at the older lady, who moved to join the countess on the sofa so they, too, could enjoy a comfortable coze. When she turned back to Beth, Karla could almost see the wheels spinning in her new friend's mind.

"Would you be nervous if you were singing as part of a group, Karla?"

She pondered the question for several moments. "I am sure I would be, but perhaps not as much. I cannot say for certain, never having done so."

"Are you willing to try?"

"I would be willing to try singing in a group, if that is what you are asking. But not publicly. At least, not yet."

Despite her qualms, Karla's interest was piqued. "What do you have in mind, Beth?"

"Nothing specific. I was just thinking it would be nice if some of the young ladies known as instrumentalists had an opportunity to show another aspect of their talent."

"How many are instrumentalists?" There would be a measure of anonymity in a large group. Or so she hoped. "And what instruments do they play?"

"I play the violin, but I also love to sing. Tina—Lady Christina Fairchild," Beth clarified, "plays the pianoforte and Lady Sarah is a harpist, but I imagine they sing as well as they play. And that is extremely well indeed."

"Oh." Karla wondered if her talent was too meager to join such a group.

"Harriett, like you, prefers singing to playing the pianoforte. I don't know if Miss Spencer and Miss Cathcart sing, but I will find out."

Beth counted the musical ladies on her fingers as she named them. "Tina, Sarah, Harriett, you, and me, for certain. Possibly Miss Spencer and Miss Cathcart. Harriett is a soprano, as am I. You are an alto. I suspect Tina is, too, although I could be mistaken—her speaking voice is about the same pitch as mine. Sarah is undoubtedly a soprano. If we had another alto, that would be three for each part."

"What about Miss Cathcart and Miss Spencer?"

"Both sopranos I suspect." Beth tapped a finger against her lower lip. "Does your sister sing?"

"Lydia is my half-sister, and you should ask her to sing only if you want to clear the room. Quickly."

Beth grinned. "Is she truly that bad?"

"I am afraid so. But she is a tolerable pianist."

"I will find out what parts Miss Cathcart and Miss Spencer sing. Surely there must be altos other than you and Tina coming out this Season."

Karla took a sip of her now-tepid tea and nerved herself to ask Beth a question. "You mentioned earlier that you are acquainted with Lord Elston. I knew him years ago, when I was a little girl. He was Viscount Wrexton then, a very grand young man of twelve to my six-year-old eyes, but he was kind enough to befriend me during a difficult time. What is he like now?"

Beth's beaming smile caught Karla off guard, causing her to wonder if her friend hoped for more than friendship from the marquess. "I would guess he is much the same, for he was very kind to me recently when I was similarly circumstanced. In truth, I was a little surprised. When we were introduced, he seemed reserved and . . . aloof."

"My first impression was much the same, but that may have been due to the difference in our ages."

"Last I heard, he planned to come to Town for the Season, although I don't know when he will arrive. But Weymouth would. Shall I ask him?"

Karla wanted to know but was not about to reveal her interest. "There is no need to do so on my account. I merely wondered if I might see him here, since he is the only gentleman of the *ton* with whom I am acquainted."

"Are there no Town beaus in . . . Yorkshire, was it?"

"Yes, Yorkshire. The only peer near Selby is Lady Blackburn's son, and he spends nearly all his time in London."

Beth glanced over at the countess. "Despite that, they must be close. She came to London for several weeks last November to serve as his hostess."

Karla nodded. She had missed the countess sorely then, for that was when the viscountess had issued the ultimatum that so drastically altered her stepdaughter's life.

"Speaking of hostesses . . . I shall host an afternoon of singing on Thursday, if you do not already have an engagement. I don't believe there are any social events scheduled then, so the other girls should be free to join us."

"I have no idea what my stepmother's plans are. We only arrived yesterday." Just mentioning the viscountess was enough to sink Karla into gloom. She knew, with the same certainty she knew the sun would rise in the east tomorrow, that her stepmother would exact punishment for her behavior at the mantua-maker's this morning. Running out had been rude, but . . .

"Karla? Is something wrong?"

The concern in Beth's blue eyes—the same kindness and compassion Karla had seen in Lady Blackburn's when she'd discovered the truth about her young friend's situation—was almost Karla's undoing. She ducked her head, blinking rapidly.

Beth's hand gently grasped hers and pulled her out of the chair. "Let's sit in the window seat, shall we?"

Unable to trust her voice, Karla nodded and followed her friend's lead. When they were seated, still holding hands, Beth repeated her question.

"You must think me the veriest goosecap—"

"I don't think any such thing." Beth's staunch avowal was heartening.

"I did a very foolish thing this morning. But I don't regret it, for if I hadn't done it, I might not have met you."

"When you ran out of Madame Celeste's shop?"

"That was part of it."

"I must own I have been wondering about your mad dash. But," Beth teased, "if you'd waited another minute, Aunt Julia and I would have been inside and we would have been introduced in the usual way."

"I daresay we would have, but I think my 'mad dash' was better."

"Really?" One golden brown eyebrow rose inquiringly. "And why is that?"

"Because if we'd met in a perfectly unexceptional manner, it might have taken me days, or even weeks, to discover what a wonderful person you are."

Beth's one-armed hug was strong. And vastly comforting. "That is quite a compliment. I am sure I do not deserve it, but I shall treasure it all the same."

Several moments passed in silence. Karla contemplated the whimsies of Fate—and thanked heaven that she had not run out sooner.

"Would you like to tell me what happened? Talking about a problem often makes its burden lighter."

"That isn't likely in this case. But I would like to tell you, if you don't mind."

"Of course I don't mind! I asked, didn't I?"

Karla told everything from the anticipation with which she had entered the shop to the despair she'd felt leaving it, as well as the cause of the latter emotion.

"Mustard bombazine for a carriage dress?" Beth shuddered. "Did your stepmother purposely choose unflattering styles and colors or does she just have appalling taste?"

Karla giggled—and Beth blushed. "I ought to have phrased that more politely, but we shall blame such frankness on my American upbringing, if you please, not on a shocking lack of decorum."

"American frankness. Of course." Karla's grin faded as she reviewed the events in the modiste's shop. "I don't know if the viscountess's pattern choices were deliberate or not—she favors ruffles and other such embellishments on her gowns—but despite Lady Blackburn's intervention, the colors were intentionally chosen."

A movement across the room drew both girls' eyes. Lady Julia stood, smoothing her gloves as she rose. "Beth, darling, we need to leave. We promised Castleton we would be back in time for luncheon."

"May I call upon you tomorrow, Karla?" her new friend inquired.

"Please do, but if my stepmother is still angry, she may not allow me callers."

"Highly unlikely. Aunt Julia is a force to be reckoned with in Society." Beth's grin was wicked. "You must call on us Wednesday. It is our At Home day and it seems half the *ton* congregates in our drawing room."

"Where—"

Beth turned and pointed out the window. "Castleton House is just down the street and around the corner to the right, on Grosvenor Square."

"Padbury House is on Curzon Street."

When Lady Julia bent to pick up her niece's reticule, both girls stood and strolled to join the older women. A few feet from their destination, Karla received another hug.

"Have I your permission to tell Aunt Julia about your visit to the modiste?" Beth asked in a whisper. "She might have some helpful ideas."

Karla hesitated only a moment; foolish pride had gained her naught. "You may tell her if you wish."

"I will call tomorrow," Beth promised. Then she and her aunt thanked the countess for her hospitality and departed.

After they left, the room felt empty, despite Lady Blackburn's presence.

Robert and his bailiff had spent the day in a field, helping his tenants shore up the sides of a ditch weakened by recent rains. And he'd enjoyed every minute of it. Well, perhaps not the slide down the ditch's muddy bank—although that event, and his laughing acknowledgment of his mud-covered appearance afterward, had dissolved the last bit of the laborers' reserve at having their lord and master working beside them—but he'd enjoyed the rest of the day. As he guided his horse toward home, Robert felt at peace with himself and his life. With a glance heavenward, he thanked a benevolent deity for showering his life with blessings.

The muscles in his back and legs protested when he rose in the stirrups to jump a low stone fence, but his exuberance was undiminished. Sore muscles, muddy clothing, and scraped knuckles were his reward for a hard day's work. His cronies in Town would not recognize him at the moment, but his people did, and that was far more important.

His ebullience spilled forth in a laugh of pure happiness. Robert relaxed the reins and raced homeward, a smile on his face and joy in his heart.

His arrival in the stableyard caused unexpected consternation. After a sweeping glance, O'Malley, the head groom, crossed his arms over his chest and demanded, "What happened, m'lord? I know ye weren't tossed."

Dismounting, Robert grinned at the Irishman. "What makes you think I wasn't?"

Peebles, the oldest groom, snorted. "Give over, do. Ye ain't been unhorsed since ye was a tyke."

"Nor was I today. A misstep near the edge of the drainage ditch in Paxton's field is the cause of the mud I am wearing."

"What'd ye do? Ye ain't wet enough to have tripped and fallen in."

"I . . . ah, measured my length in the mud as I was sliding down the bank."

As the grooms convulsed in paroxysms of laughter, Robert bowed. "Delighted as I am to provide you with such amusement, my horse needs attention. As do I, before my aunt catches sight of me." A wry smile accompanied the words.

He pointed to the youngest of the stable lads. "Run up to the house and tell them to have Higgins meet me in my study with my dressing gown."

The boy nodded and trotted off, only to stop after a few paces. "Want I should tell 'em ye'll be wantin' a bath, m'lord?"

"No need, lad. Higgins will have already taken care of that."

As he strolled toward the house, Robert wondered what the ladies listed in the codicil would do if they saw him now. Smiling at their probable reactions, he decided it was just as well they could not. He did not look at all like one of the fashion leaders of the *ton*. But next week that would change. Aunt Livvy had told him at breakfast she would be ready to leave in the morning. Next week his marriage campaign would move to its second phase as he began waging the battle to find a bride.

On Thursday morning Karla ventured into the polite world for the first time without her stepmother. The occasion was Beth Castleton's singing party. Lydia was in a huff because she had not been invited; the viscountess was angry because Karla wouldn't take her half-sister along, invited or not. But Karla, with propriety on her side, had stood firm against their demands. Her reward for such uncharacteristic staunchness was Lady Blackburn as her chaperone. Karla could not have been more delighted.

Castleton House was one of the largest homes on Grosvenor Square. After they were greeted by a tall, rather stern-faced butler, Karla was escorted down the hall to the music room by a footman while the butler accompanied Lady Blackburn upstairs to the drawing room where Lady Julia and the mothers or chaperons of the other young ladies were conversing.

Upon entering the music room, Karla was greeted with a hug from Beth. "I am so glad you are here. Come and meet the other girls."

Beth led her to the side of the room where four young ladies were seated in a circle, chatting among themselves. All four, as well as Beth and Karla, were clad in white muslin with sprigging of varying designs and colors. After seating her last guest, Beth stood in the middle of the group and waited until she had everyone's attention.

"I am going to ask all of you to introduce yourselves to the group, instead of introducing each of you to one another."

With a curtsy, she began. "I am Beth Castleton, the only

surviving daughter of the earl's younger brother and his wife. I was born and raised in America, hence my accent, and I have lived in England with my uncle and great-aunt for a little over a year. At the shockingly advanced age of three-and-twenty, I will be making my bows this Season. I play the violin and pianoforte, the former better than the latter, but I love to sing. I also have a passion for mathematics." Groans and looks of disbelief greeted the statement, but Beth's smile was undiminished. "Other favorite pastimes are riding and dancing."

After another curtsy, she sat down. "Lady Christina, your turn."

The young lady who rose and walked to the center of the circle of chairs was petite, raven-haired, and dark-eyed. Although not beautiful in the classical sense, she was a very pretty girl. "I am Tina Fairchild, daughter of the Duke and Duchess of Greenwich. I am seventeen and will be making my come-out this Season. I play the pianoforte and sing, but I much prefer the former."

"Are you a soprano or an alto?" someone asked.

"An alto. My favorite pastimes . . .Well, the answer depends on whom you ask. My mother would say it is getting into mischief." Laughter greeted this sally. "I, however, would say it is music and riding and dancing. I have lived all my life in London or Greenwich, but I would love to travel and explore other countries."

After a glance at their hostess, who nodded her approval, Tina curtsied to the group and resumed her seat.

"Before the next girl introduces herself, may I ask a question?" This from a dark-haired girl directly across from Karla.

"Of course you may," their hostess replied.

"You didn't say what part you sing, Beth. Are you an alto?"

"No, a soprano." After smiling at the young lady who asked, Beth turned to the girl on her right. "Lady Deborah, will you go next?"

Beth had not mentioned Lady Deborah on Monday, so Karla knew nothing about the tall, slender Beauty with curly blond hair and blue eyes who walked to the center of the circle.

"I am Deborah Woodhurst. I am twenty and, by twelve minutes, the eldest daughter of the Marquess and Marchioness of Kesteven, but I have two older brothers."

"You are a twin?" Tina's voice and expression conveyed disbelief.

"I am." Deborah smiled. "My sister is identical in looks, but her personality and interests are rather different."

Tina groaned. "I am doomed if there are two of you." At Deborah's puzzled expression, the duke's daughter added, "How can a squab of a girl with dark hair and eyes possibly gain the gentlemen's attention if there are two tall, blond, blue-eyed Beauties in the room?"

"By being your charming, vivacious self," Deborah answered.

Tina shook her head, apparently unconvinced that being herself would do the trick, but she perked up when the dark-haired young lady across from Karla said, "Some gentlemen will not ask a tall girl to dance. At least, my brother won't. He is only a few inches taller than I am and he never asks a lady to dance unless he knows she is at least three inches shorter than he is."

Tina's outrageous "I do hope you will introduce me to your brother" drew smiles or laughter from all the girls.

After a moment's hesitation, Lady Deborah continued. "I play the harpsichord and the pianoforte, but prefer the former, and I enjoy singing. In this group, I will be singing alto, although I have the range for either part. I enjoy riding, and I am hoping to do a great deal of dancing this Season. As, I imagine, we all are." Smiling, she curtsied, then sat down.

Beth nodded to the girl seated opposite Karla. "Lady Sarah."

Lady Sarah was another tall, slender Beauty, but with a more curvaceous figure than any of the others. Her hair was the blue-black of a raven's wing and she had the most vividly blue eyes Karla had ever seen, framed by incredibly long, curly eyelashes. "I am Sarah Mallory, daughter of the Earl and Countess of Tregaron." The lilting voice sounded almost like singing. "I am twenty-one. I play the harp, both the concert harp and the small harp, and like most Welsh, I love to sing. I am a soprano. Other favorite pastimes are riding and sailing, dancing and embroidery. Oh, and shopping. I *adore* shopping." She joined in the laughter her last comment provoked, then curtsied and resumed her seat.

When Beth turned to Karla, she hoped her knees would not disgrace her. Standing in the center of the group, she was almost overcome by shyness, but encouraging smiles from Beth and Sarah helped her find her tongue. "I am Karolina Lane, or Karla if you prefer, daughter of the late Viscount Padbury and his first wife. My father was a member of the Diplomatic Corps, so when I was a little girl I lived in a number of European countries."

"Which ones?" Not surprisingly, the question came from Tina.

"I remember Spain, Russia, and several German kingdoms."

"And when you were older?"

"When I was six, my father married again and because my stepmother does not like traveling, we did not accompany my father. I have six half-brothers and -sisters, one of whom, Lydia, is being presented this year."

"Are you also making your bows, Karla?" Deborah asked.

"Yes. I am three-and-twenty but I have never had a Season."

"How old is Lydia?" This from the girl who had not yet been introduced.

"Seventeen."

"I daresay your stepmother's dislike of travel accounts for her decision to present you together."

Karla shrugged, but silently blessed Deborah for the suggestion, which was far more palatable than the truth. "Since I was six, I have lived in Yorkshire, so I know very few members of Society. It is wonderful to know that, after today, there will be friendly faces among all the strangers." Everyone nodded in agreement, some more vigorously than others.

"I play the pianoforte and sing—I am an alto—but I much prefer singing to playing. I like riding and dancing, and I am an avid reader."

"Novels?" several voices queried.

"I *adore* novels." Karla's imitation of Sarah's inflection was not perfect, but it was close enough to provoke another round of laughter. Karla curtsied and resumed her seat, happy that she had managed a creditable introduction despite her rubbery knees.

The last girl stood without prompting from their hostess. Her looks were not as striking as the others', but even so, she was pretty. An inch or so taller than Karla, her brown hair was the color of rosewood and she had lovely hazel eyes. "I am Harriett Broughton. I am nineteen years old and will be making my come-out this year. I am a soprano and pianist, but, like Miss Lane, I prefer singing.

"I like dancing, but I have a terrible fear that I will forget all the steps when I reach the dance floor, and I love to read. And, again like Miss Lane, I am delighted to meet all of you and to know there will be friendly faces at social events because I find it difficult to converse with strangers."

As Deborah, Beth, and Karla nodded their agreement, Tina frowned. "I never have any problem talking with people I have just met."

"That is because you are a chatterbox," Beth teased.

"And you probably haven't a shy bone in your body," Harriett opined.

Tina grinned. "No, I don't."

With the ease of an experienced hostess, Beth soon had them all gathered around the pianoforte—Sarah, Harriett, and Beth on one side, Karla and Tina on the other, while Deborah played. Fortunately for Beth's plan, their voices blended well. Two hours later, they had a repertoire of five songs, and their hostess rewarded them by ringing for a tea tray.

In the midst of the polite conversation that always accompanies tea, Tina suddenly waved an arm, nearly knocking Harriett's cup from her hand. "Look at us. Two girls with inky locks, two brunettes, and two blondes. All we need is a pair of redheads to please all gentlemen's tastes, both with our looks and our talent."

Giggling like schoolgirls, they all set down their tea to avoid further mishaps.

"One of each pair is even tall," Karla added.

"I think our appeal, aside from out talent, is that we have three Beauties"—Beth pointed to Sarah, Deborah, and Karla—"and three very pretty girls. Some gentlemen prefer the former, but others will not want a wife more beautiful than themselves."

The latter comment sent them all into the whoops, although Karla felt certain it was more accurate than not.

"Despite the many aspects of our appeal to the gentlemen of the *ton,* there is one glaring discrepancy," Harriett noted. "We have the daughter of a duke, a marquess, an earl, and a viscount, as well as an earl's niece. You need only replace me with a baron's daughter to cover all the ranks of the peerage."

Everyone protested vehemently. In the three hours they'd spent together, they had become such firm friends that ousting Harriett—or anyone else—was unthinkable.

Chapter Eight

After one final look in the cheval glass, Karla picked up her shawl, reticule, and gloves and left the haven of her room. Three intensive mornings of shopping on Bond and Oxford Streets (after a rather nasty argument with her stepmother regarding the first) had ensured that the Lanes would be fashionably dressed. Rather, Lydia would be. Karla was doomed to wearing unflattering styles and colors chosen by her stepmother. She might be in fashion, but she would not be well dressed. Without Lady Blackburn to back her arguments, assuming that the viscountess would even listen to them—an impossibility since the countess was not invited to accompany them—Karla was unable to overrule her stepmother. Not without impossibly straining relations between them.

Three rather nerve-racking afternoons of paying calls had resulted in a gratifying number of invitations. Tonight, only four days after their arrival in Town, Karla and Lydia would make their first appearance in Society, at a soiree at Castleton House. According to Lady Blackburn, Lady Julia Castleton was one of the premier hostesses of the *ton*—and rather selective in her guest list.

Karla was a bit surprised they had received one of the coveted invitations. Although she had, somehow, favorably impressed Lady Julia at their first meeting (and subsequent ones), Karla did not believe her stepmother had fared as well. Perhaps the invitation was a result of her friendship with Beth Castleton; perhaps not. Regardless of the reason behind it, Karla was happy to know there would be familiar faces at her first social event, including all of the friends she had made this morning.

She had been introduced to dozens of people in the course of their afternoon calls. Although she'd made an effort to pair names and faces, Karla knew she would not remember them all. She could but do her best tonight, and hope that Society would forgive any lapses in her memory.

As she approached the drawing room, she heard Lydia's excited chatter and the murmured responses of another woman. Karla could not determine if it was her stepmother or Lady Blackburn who spoke, but suspected it was the latter. At tea, the viscountess had been nearly as excited as her daughter about their first foray into the *beau monde*. Karla only hoped all of the Lanes would make a favorable impression this evening. Charles, who would be leaving for school the next morning, had also been invited, but Karla's concern was not on his behalf. His manners were excellent and his awe at being included would ensure he did not overstep the bounds of propriety.

She paused for a moment outside the door, glancing down at her gown. She had received two evening gowns from Madame Celeste, one yesterday and one today, as well as two morning dresses and a spencer. This gown, of peach lutestring, was her favorite for evening. The other was completely unfamiliar, as if someone else had ordered it. Karla had paid attention to her stepmother's choices, or thought she had, but she had no recollection of the stark white satin gown with its triple row of ruffles at the neckline and flounced hem. Although the gown fit her perfectly, she felt overwhelmed by the heavy fabric and vastly uncomfortable with its embellishments, which seemed to swallow her whole. Shaking off the memory, Karla mustered a smile and walked into the room.

Before she could utter a greeting, the viscountess jumped from her seat, staring. "You are to wear the white satin tonight, Caroline."

"I prefer to wear this gown."

"White satin?" A frown wrinkled Lady Blackburn's brow. "I do not recall a gown of that fabric."

Karla turned to the countess. "I did not recall it myself."

"Of course you didn't, silly." Lydia rose and linked her

arm with Karla's. "Mama ordered it for you after you left Madame Celeste's that first day."

Karla glanced from her half-sister to her stepmother, then back. "Is that the only one she ordered for me?"

"Oh, no. She chose at least half a dozen."

With a muttered oath, Lady Blackburn rose from her chair and stalked—there was no other word to describe it— toward the viscountess, who was too busy glaring at her daughter to notice. Charles, apparently recognizing the countess's ire, retreated to the far end of the room. Karla ignored Lydia's artless prattle and strained to hear the low-voiced conversation between her stepmother and the countess.

Lady Blackburn seated herself on the sofa beside the viscountess. "The gowns you ordered for Karla, were they her choices or yours?" Karla, furious at her stepmother's underhanded trick, marveled at her friend's neutral tone.

"Mine, of course, since I had no idea what Caroline had chosen."

"She had a list, Hortense. Did it occur to you to consult it?" It sounded as if the countess spoke through gritted teeth.

"A list?" The viscountess frowned. "I don't recall a list."

The countess's jaw clenched momentarily. "The gowns you chose, were they styles and colors you would wear yourself?"

"The designs were similar to those Lydia chose," the viscountess said. "The colors, whites and pastels." Karla stifled a sigh. If she was fortunate, the colors might be flattering, but the gowns were probably awash in ruffles.

"Do you not think it would have been wiser to allow Karla to make her own choices? She is the one who will wear the gowns."

The viscountess shrugged. "Perhaps, but I thought it better to order them then, so they would be ready when Lydia's are."

"Another day would not have mattered."

The viscountess lifted her hands in a "how was I to know?" gesture.

Lady Blackburn slumped back against the sofa cushions. "Tell us about the gowns, so Karla will know what to expect."

Lydia and Karla gave up their pretense of conversation and listened openly. After her stepmother described two gowns so heavily embellished as to be almost caricatures of the latest styles, Karla sank into a chair, shaking her head in disbelief. Lydia detailed four more before Lady Blackburn jumped up and glared at the viscountess.

"The girl is making her come-out, not going into service!"

"But the patterns are all the crack and pastels are *de rigueur*—"

"Dark blue is not a pastel, Hortense," the countess snapped. "Neither is purple."

"But—"

"Tell me this: did you choose gowns for Lydia in those colors?"

A flush stained the viscountess's cheeks. "No, but—"

"I have told you before that you must treat both girls equally."

"They have the same number of new gowns!"

Lady Blackburn rubbed her temples and sighed wearily. "Number is not the only factor, Hortense. Are the gowns of the same quality? Were they chosen to flatter the wearer?"

"That haughty Frenchwoman would not permit shoddily made gowns. As for whether or not they are flattering, we won't know that until the girls wear them."

The countess snorted. Delicately, to be sure, but it was a snort all the same. "You may lie to yourself, Hortense, but you will not lie to me. Nor to your stepdaughter. We"—she indicated herself, Karla, and Lydia—"know the gowns you chose for Karla will not become her. And"—the countess's voice hardened—"you did it deliberately."

"I did no—"

"You believe that if Karla's gowns are unflattering, she will not attract attention, leaving Lydia in the limelight. But you are wrong, Hortense. Dead wrong."

"No—"

"Which do you think draws more attention: a quiz or a girl who is unexceptionally attired?"

Karla watched the color drain from her stepmother's face.

Lady Blackburn nodded. "Finally, you comprehend the point I have been making for weeks. If you treat Karla differently than Lydia *in any way,* it is not your stepdaughter who will suffer the *ton*'s opprobrium, it is you. And, perhaps, Lydia."

"Me?" Lydia jerked to her feet. "But I—"

The countess's gaze skewered the younger girl. "Do not dare to tell me you didn't know what your mother was doing. You are not that stupid."

Lydia dropped back into her chair, clearly chagrined.

"What should we do?" the viscountess inquired, gaze and voice beseeching.

Shooting a look of disgust at his mother, Charles rose. "Right now, we should go to the Castletons' soiree."

Judging from her stepmother's stunned expression, she had completely forgotten the engagement. "But what about Caroline's gowns?" she wailed.

Charles stopped walking and looked at his mother in disbelief. "Tomorrow, perhaps Lady Blackburn will go with you to the modiste and help you resolve the problem of Karla's clothing." As he resumed walking, he muttered, "Although why she would, I don't know, since it is your fault." Fortunately, only Karla and the countess heard the boy's last remark.

Reaching them, the young viscount bowed gracefully to Lady Blackburn, then offered his arm to escort her to the carriage.

Robert and his great-aunt arrived at Symington House on Upper Brook Street the evening of April fourth. Higgins had not been happy about traveling on Sunday, but had grumbled only once, predicting disaster. Fortunately, they arrived safely, and without the slightest problem. Under normal circumstances, Robert would have heeded his valet's scruples, but this Season would be different than any other, and he was ready to launch his search for a bride. He was even, in some ways, looking forward to it.

The day before they left Gloucestershire, he had received a letter from George informing him that all seven prospective brides, as well as the four Robert knew and had immediately eliminated from consideration, were in Town. Beth had become quite friendly with the three young ladies she'd already met, and had made the acquaintance of three others: Miss Lane and Ladies Deborah and Diana Woodhurst.

Robert blessed, again, the impulse that had led him to confide in his friends.

His great-aunt was exhausted from the journey, not having slept well while they were on the road, and retired early. After she did, he went to his study, dispatched a note to George, and began sorting through the small mountain of mail and invitations awaiting his attention. By the time he went up to bed, Robert had made a list of all the events to which he had been invited and written acceptances to several in the coming week. He would consult with his friends before deciding which of the others to attend.

Monday was cool and rainy, but despite the weather, Aunt Livvy was determined to visit a mantua-maker and refurbish her wardrobe. Notes to Lady Julia Castleton and Lady Blackburn, requesting the name of their modiste, yielded not only Madame Celeste's name and direction, but also offers to accompany Lady Lavinia. Robert, who had been prepared to sacrifice himself on the altar of familial duty, breathed a sigh of relief. Aunt Livvy had known Lady Julia since they'd made their come-outs together half a century ago, so she sent a note of thanks to the countess, then accepted her old friend's offer and set off for Castleton House a short time later.

By noon, Robert had received neither a note nor a visit from George. Since the message he'd dispatched the previous evening had warned of possible danger, Robert's first call that afternoon was at Bellingham House on Portman Square.

"Good afternoon, Hargrave. Is Weymouth at home?"

The butler bowed. "Good afternoon, Lord Elston. Lord Weymouth has been in Dorsetshire for the past week, but we expect him back this afternoon."

"Please see that he receives the note I sent last night as soon as he arrives."

"Yes, my lord."

With a smile of thanks, Robert departed. His second call was at Castleton House on Grosvenor Square.

"Good afternoon, North." Robert handed the butler his hat and a calling card. "Are Lady Julia and Miss Castleton at home?" Monday was not one of Lady Julia's At Home days, but he hoped the inclement weather had kept the ladies indoors.

"They are, my lord. If you will follow me, please."

Since the butler had not inquired if the ladies would see him, Robert assumed Beth had given orders that he was to be admitted whenever he called. He followed North to the morning room, where Beth was reading to Lady Julia as she embroidered.

Beth greeted him with a beaming smile when he was announced. "Elston, how lovely to see you again!"

"I am equally delighted to see you, Miss Castleton." He bowed to her great-aunt. "Good afternoon, Lady Julia. You both look wonderfully well."

Lady Julia waved him to a chair. "We are in fine fettle. I am enjoying watching my darling girl cut a dash in Society."

Beth blushed. "Aunt Julia!"

"Well, child, I am and you are."

Robert was delighted to hear it. "I was very sorry to miss your come-out ball, Miss Castleton. Especially after having reserved a dance."

"I know that you have other obligations right now, my lord. As for your dance, you may claim it any time."

"Do you attend Lady Throckmorton's ball this evening?" She nodded. "Then I request the first minuet and the third waltz, if you have not already promised them."

"Both are free, unless the third waltz is the supper dance." She hesitated, then said rather timidly, "If Weymouth doesn't return from Dorsetshire, you may have the third waltz even if it is the supper dance, if you'd like."

Robert accepted with a smile. "I would be honored, Miss Castleton. If George makes a timely arrival, and I daresay he will, you may put me down for anything but a reel after supper."

She returned his smile with a shy one of her own. "Thank you."

"Is George expected back today?"

"He hoped to be."

"Is my errant friend your escort? I would be pleased to stand in for him."

"Dunnley is doing the honors tonight." Lady Julia's wry tone evidenced her enjoyment of her great-niece's success.

After half an hour Robert took his leave. Beth stood, too, telling her great-aunt that she would walk him to the door. As soon as they were out of earshot, she turned to him. "There are two things I need to tell you. Six of the ladies on your list will be at the ball tonight. I will introduce them to you, if you like."

He smiled down at her. "I would like that very much." After several seconds, he prompted, "And the second thing?"

"We—you and I, that is—met at a house party in Scotland." She glanced down, then again met his gaze. "When I first arrived in Town, I did not expect the *ton* to question my absence, so I was unprepared for the inquiries. A house party was the best, and most accurate, story I could contrive."

"Truthful, too, if we ignore the abductions, rescue, and all that preceded your arrival in Stranraer."

They reached the entry hall, where the butler stood ready to hand Robert his hat, gloves, and cane. After donning them, he bowed over Beth's hand. "Until tonight, Miss Castleton."

"I am looking forward to the evening, my lord." A gleam of devilment danced in her eyes. Although he hated to douse it, Robert had little choice. He bent his head to hers and, in a whisper, passed on the warning he'd written to George, asking her to give the news to him if she saw him before Robert arrived at the ball.

Although obviously distressed by the message, Beth nodded and summoned a shaky smile. *"Au revoir,* Elston."

He tipped his hat to her, then turned and walked out into the rain.

Karla stared at the image in the cheval glass, fighting back tears. The ball gowns that had arrived thus far were ones her stepmother had chosen, not the two choices she had made during the distraction provided by Lady Blackburn that first day at Madame Celeste's. While it would be charitable to say the gown did not suit her, Karla was not feeling at all charitable at the moment. She thought it looked hideous. And so did she.

The Throckmorton ball was her first. But instead of Cinderella or a princess from a fairy tale, she resembled the wicked witch. Her dream of dancing with handsome gentlemen was just that—an impossible illusion. No man in his right mind would want to be seen even talking to her.

Feeling tears well, she blinked rapidly. She would *not* cry; she refused to give her stepmother that victory.

Karla started when a knock sounded on her bedchamber door. Dabbing at her eyes with a handkerchief, she turned toward the portal. Mary, the chambermaid who had been assigned to assist her, opened the door and peeked inside.

"This message just came for you, Miss Karla. From Castleton House."

"Thank you, Mary."

After delivering the missive, the maid took another look at her mistress, then shook her head and left the room, mumbling under her breath, "It's a crime, it is. The spiteful old besom ought to be shot fer makin' Miss Karla wear that ugly gown."

The real crime was . . . the other ball gowns were even uglier.

Chapter Nine

After inching his way up the stairs, Robert greeted Lord and Lady Throckmorton and, after being announced by the butler, entered the ballroom. He stood for a moment in the doorway searching for Beth Castleton, to whom he was promised for the first minuet, or her great-aunt. In a group of dowagers, he spotted Lady Julia's silvery-gray hair adorned with a dainty lace cap, then saw her great-niece standing a few feet away amid of a group of young ladies and gentlemen, chattering gaily. He recognized Dunnley's tawny head and Howe's dark curls, but Robert was not acquainted with the other gentlemen in the group, nor with the young ladies. He circled the room toward them, stopping occasionally to speak to acquaintances.

He paid his respects to Lady Julia and the women seated nearby, then joined the group around Beth, greeting her and the two gentlemen he knew. When she glanced down at the card dangling from her wrist, which Lady Throckmorton had said was a list of the dances, he studied it, too, smiling wryly when he saw the minuet was next.

"Yes, Miss Castleton, I left it a bit late. I did not expect such a tangle of carriages outside, nor such a crowd on the stairs. I have been too long in the country, I expect." Nodding at her card, he added, "A clever idea. Lady Throckmorton could start a new fashion."

When the gentlemen dispersed to find their partners for the next set, Robert offered his arm to lead his friend onto the dance floor. "You look lovely tonight, Beth." She was pretty as a picture in her apricot silk gown, a smile curving her mouth and brightening her blue eyes.

"Thank you, sir. You are very handsome as well."

They moved through the patterns of the minuet chatting amiably. At the conclusion of the dance, he tucked Beth's hand in the crook of his arm to escort her back to Lady Julia. As they promenaded, Robert realized he needed to ascertain whether or not he would be dancing the third waltz with Beth.

"I don't know if George has returned. I left a note for him at Bellingham House but have not received a reply. Since the third waltz is the supper dance, I shall hope to partner you then. If George cuts me out, have you found a dance for me later in the evening?"

"Have you promised the second country dance after supper?"

"I have requested no dances except with you."

"Elston, such talk could turn a lady's head!"

"That of a simpering miss, perhaps, but not yours."

She sighed theatrically. "I don't even know how to simper."

A smile tugged the corner of his mouth. "You needn't learn. Simpering is vastly overrated."

When they reached her aunt, Robert bowed over Beth's hand and thanked her for the dance. Then, lowering his voice, he inquired, "Has George's absence left you without a partner for another set?"

"Yes, for the first cotillion, but I am not concerned about that, only worried about Weymouth." She bit her lip, opened her mouth, then closed it again without speaking.

"What were you going to ask?"

She darted a glance at her aunt before replying. "You said you had not yet promised any dances. Would you think me terribly forward if I asked you to dance with some of the other young ladies whose cards aren't likely to be full?"

"I would think you quite wonderful for looking out for your friends. Whom do you recommend for my next partner?"

Beth looked around the room. "Miss Broughton. Do you know her?"

Robert had to grit his teeth to keep from laughing at his ally's oh-so-innocent tone. "No, but I assume she is the brunette in white standing next to Mrs. Broughton." Beth nodded. "Then I shall take myself off to request an introduction and ask your friend to dance."

He turned to go, but stopped when she said, "Thank you,

Elston. Harriett is rather shy, but a delightful girl. She likes music and reading."

Thanking Beth with a smile, he strolled around the perimeter of the ballroom to meet the fifth of his prospective brides.

Karla's heart had leapt when Elston was announced. He was so very handsome in his charcoal gray coat, white silk knee breeches, and silver-gray waistcoat. His cravat was elegant yet simple, his collar points of a fashionable but moderate height. She watched him as he stood in the doorway, scanning the room as if searching for someone. Watched, too, as he walked to join the group around Beth Castleton and Viscount Dunnley. *Lucky Beth!*

Karla would have liked to join them, but she did not want to be seen near such fashionable people when she looked so hideously ugly. It wasn't just her ball gown, although it was certainly horrid enough to give her pause, but also her red-rimmed eyes. The note she'd received from Beth had been more than Karla's fragile composure could withstand. Knowing that Elston would be at the ball, that he might see her looking worse than a quiz, had turned her into a watering pot. But she had not cried because of the gown. Or not solely because of it.

Also, she was reluctant to inflict her stepmother, who was in a far from pleasant mood, on Lady Julia. The viscountess's current bout of grumbling—and it seemed she had done nothing but complain since they'd left Curzon Street—concerned the blindness of the gentlemen present, none of whom had asked Lydia or Karla to dance the first two sets.

So despite the fact that she very much wanted to join the group around Beth, to tell her or another member of The Six (the name Karla had given the group of musical young ladies who had met last week at Castleton House) about the horrible gowns she would be forced to wear this Season, she stayed where she was, in the shadow of a fat column on the opposite side of the room, and watched from afar. Thus, she saw Elston offer his arm to lead Beth onto the dance floor for the minuet, witnessed the smiles they exchanged before and after the dance. *Oh, lucky, lucky Beth!*

                        *   *   *

Robert stopped in front of Mrs. Broughton and bowed. "Good evening, Mrs. Broughton."

"Good evening, Lord Elston."

He looked at her daughter, one eyebrow rising slightly. Mrs. Broughton did not disappoint him. "I don't believe you are acquainted with my daughter, Harriett, my lord. Harriett, this is the Marquess of Elston."

As he bowed, Miss Broughton curtsied gracefully. She was a pretty girl, perhaps a bit shorter than most, with striking hazel eyes. There was a hint of red in her brown curls, which gleamed like the rosewood table in the drawing room at Symington House after a polishing. Not a very romantic image, Robert thought, and one he'd best keep to himself.

"Are you enjoying the ball, Miss Broughton?"

"Yes, I am. Lady Throckmorton must be pleased it is such a crush."

The orchestra played the introductory bars of a country dance. Robert glanced around but saw no gentleman hastening toward them. "If you have not promised this dance, might I have the honor of your company for this set?"

She looked at her mother for permission, as was proper. When it was granted, Miss Broughton turned back to him, smiling. "I would be pleased to dance with you, my lord."

He offered his arm, then led her to join the nearest set. The movements of the dance necessitated some conversational pauses, but he learned, among other things, that she was nervous about singing at her mother's musicale the following evening and that she had become friends with a number of the other girls making their come-outs this Season, including Beth, Lady Christina Fairchild, Lady Deborah Woodhurst, Lady Sarah Mallory, and Miss Karolina Lane, most of whom would also be performing. Fortunately, the mail he'd sorted through last night had included an invitation to the musicale, which he'd already accepted.

At the conclusion of the dance, he escorted his partner back to her mother. "I enjoyed our dance, Miss Broughton. I look forward to hearing you perform tomorrow."

She blushed rosily, then blurted, "There are many others far more talented than I. Miss Castleton, Lord Bellingham, Lady Christina, Lady Deborah, Lady Sarah, Lord Howe—"

"Howe?" he questioned, eyebrows soaring. The man was a Corinthian whose sporting abilities were widely admired, but Robert, who knew him well, could not recall ever hearing the baron's name mentioned in connection with music.

Miss Broughton nodded emphatically. "Yes. He has a very fine bass voice."

Selwyn, a young dandy, was approaching, so Robert bowed over Miss Broughton's hand and requested another dance after supper, then nodded to her mother, who was deep in conversation with Lady Moreton, and resumed his stroll around the room.

Karla felt a pang of envy when Elston led Harriett onto the dance floor. *How many of The Six will he dance with tonight?* Much as she wished to be included in that select group, Karla was not at all certain she wanted the elegant marquess to see her this evening. The same pride that had launched her deception at Paddington Court troubled her now, for she would much rather renew her acquaintance with him when she was becomingly dressed. But she had learned from her folly and would not make the same mistake again. If Fate decreed she must meet Elston tonight, so be it.

She was pleased when one of the dowagers seated nearby persuaded a young relative to dance with Lydia, but not nearly as happy when Lady Blackburn's son came over to speak with her, then requested that Karla honor him with a set. Although she was flattered that he asked, she knew she looked a fright and she did not want to expose herself to any more stares and snickers than she had already received. But that was hardly grounds for refusing, so she lifted her chin, squared her shoulders, and allowed Blackburn to lead her onto the floor.

Much to Karla's dismay, it was a country dance in which the ladies lined up opposite the gentlemen. The ladies could not see her horrid gown without craning their necks, but the gentlemen had an unobstructed view as they waited for the music to commence. Fortunately, the movements of the dance did not permit much conversation as they moved toward the top of the set. Unfortunately, the time would come when they would dance from the top of the line to the bottom and everyone would see her ghastly gown then.

It was small consolation to know that there was another set in the room whose members could not see her in the wretched thing.

The whispering among the ladies began the moment she and Blackburn started down the line. Encouraged by the gentle squeeze he gave her hand, Karla pinned a smile on her face and did her best to ignore the stares. It was surely the longest set she'd ever danced down, seeming to stretch for miles, and the whispers rustled along it at the same speed she and the earl did. Finally, they reached the bottom and Karla had a few seconds to relax.

She used the time to study her partner. Although she had known Geoffrey, Lord Blackburn, all her life, she had seen little of him in recent years because he was quite active in government and spent most of his time in London. The earl was three-and-thirty and slightly above average height, with his mother's gray-rimmed hazel eyes and mahogany hair, as well as the beginnings of the off-center silver streak that distinguished his parent's locks. He was a good-looking man, not as handsome as Elston, of course, but definitely a gentleman who drew a lady's eye. When next they came together in the patterns of the dance, Karla's smile was genuine, for she appreciated Blackburn's kindness in asking her to dance. Even if that dance was a bit of an ordeal.

The second time down the line was easier. Far from pleasant, but easier. Being the cynosure of all eyes was difficult enough when looking one's best, nearly unbearable in her present circumstances. But dancing was dancing, an activity she enjoyed. She was even able to forget, for a few minutes at a time, the ugly gown she wore.

She sighed with relief when the dance ended, eager to retreat. His lordship, however, had other ideas.

"Would you care for some lemonade, Miss Lane?"

Karla's mouth had already formed a refusal when she realized that he intended to promenade around the room whether she wanted refreshments or not. Since there would be fewer people in the supper room and since walking there would not allow time for a perambulation around the ballroom before the next set began, she amended her answer. "Thank you, my lord. A glass of lemonade would be welcome."

"Good girl." Then, softly so only she would hear, "Don't allow your stepmother the victory. Imagine you are wearing your favorite gown and hold your head high."

It was good advice, and well intended, but even so, her face blazed as a blush of absolute mortification climbed from her collarbone to her hairline.

"I am sorry, Karolina. It was not my intention to distress you." The whispered apology conveyed the earl's anguish.

She glanced up at him and nodded, not trusting her voice. All her effort was concentrated on not bolting back to the shadowy recesses beside her column. Elston was standing about ten feet in front of her, talking with a man in scarlet regimentals whose left arm was in a sling.

Chapter Ten

$\mathcal{R}$obert nodded to Blackburn as he walked past with a quiz on his arm. Not at all what one would expect of the fastidious earl, but perhaps he was trying to curry favor by singling out a politician's wallflower daughter. A second glance at the pair caused Robert to revise his assessment: the girl was a Beauty; 'twas only her gown that was ugly, overwhelming her petite frame. Idly, he wondered who she was. If he had the dressing of her, he would garb her in delicate fabrics and frocks with flowing lines. With an inward chuckle at his foolishness in planning a wardrobe for a stranger, he returned his attention to Captain Ashton and the news from the Peninsula.

Robert introduced the captain to Beth Castleton as a partner with whom she could sit out the first cotillion and, in turn, was presented to Lady Sarah Mallory and her parents, the Earl and Countess of Tregaron. The Welsh girl was a Beauty, tall, slender, and curvaceous, with midnight-black hair and vivid blue eyes framed by long, curly lashes. After social pleasantries were exchanged, Robert turned to Lady Sarah.

"I understand from Miss Castleton that you are an accomplished musician. Both a harpist and a singer."

"How kind of Beth to praise my talent." Lady Sarah's voice had the musical lilt distinctive of the Welsh. "I enjoy playing and singing, but Beth's skills exceed mine."

Robert could not decide if Lady Sarah's praise of the American girl was sincere or merely an attempt at maidenly modesty. Nothing in her tone or facial expression hinted at the latter; rather, it was the absence of either that caused him to wonder. "Will you be performing at Mrs. Broughton's musicale tomorrow evening?"

"Yes, I will. Are you planning to attend, my lord?"

He inclined his head. "I am looking forward to it." Although it was the socially acceptable response, Robert's words were sincere. He *was* looking forward to the event, which would allow him to determine the musical talent of several of the ladies on the list, as well as hear Beth perform.

"I would be honored if you would grant me a dance this evening, Lady Sarah. If you have any that are not yet promised."

Smiling slightly, she handed him her card. "I would be pleased to dance with you, my lord."

Despite the absence of a court of admirers, her card was nearly full. Only a country dance and two reels remained. "The last country dance?" When she nodded her acquiescence, Robert scrawled his initials beside the penultimate set.

He returned the card and bowed over her hand. "I shall look forward to dancing with you later."

Dunnley joined them just as the musicians played the opening bars of the cotillion. Lady Sarah smiled impartially at the two men, then accepted the viscount's escort onto the dance floor. Robert took his leave of her parents and continued his stroll around the ballroom.

Karla regained a measure of composure as she drank a glass of lemonade. Blackburn introduced her to two gentlemen, Lord Durwood and Sir Kenneth Peyton, both of whom requested a dance. She hoped that when they came to claim their sets and were introduced to her stepmother and Lydia, they would also ask her half-sister to tread a measure. If not, Karla feared she would never hear the end of it.

Returning to the ballroom on the earl's arm, Karla looked around, hoping to see Beth. Instead, she saw Elston return Sarah's card and bow over her hand. *Lucky Sarah!* Viscount Dunnley joined them and led Sarah onto the floor for the cotillion, so the marquess's dance must be later in the evening. Blackburn quickened their pace slightly and Karla glanced up at him, then realized he must have a partner for this set. He was too much of a gentleman to allow her to make her own way back to her stepmother's side, so she did not suggest it.

When they reached Lady Blackburn, who was a few feet closer than the viscountess, Karla slipped her hand from the earl's arm and curtsied. "I enjoyed our dance, my lord. Please give my apologies to your next partner for delaying you."

His lips quirking, the earl bowed. "I was hurrying because I feared I had delayed you, Karolina."

Amazed that he thought her so popular, Karla could only shake her head. He plucked her card from her wrist and claimed another set, then took his leave. As the countess gazed fondly at her son's departing back, Karla peeked to see which dance Blackburn had chosen.

"Lady B! He picked the supper dance!"

"Who did, my dear?"

"Your son!"

Lady Blackburn smiled. "Geoffrey has excellent taste. Of course he chose you for his supper partner."

Karla rolled her eyes; there was no "of course" about it. "You are prejudiced, but I love you for it."

"My dear—"

"Oh no!" It was an anguished moan.

"What is it, Karla?"

"He didn't ask Lydia for a dance."

"And you fear she and your stepmother will cut up stiff about it?" A militant look entered the countess's eyes. "Leave them to me."

Although she doubted Lady Blackburn could say anything to deflect the viscountess's wrath, Karla nodded. "If you wish." Then she returned her gaze to the room and its occupants, searching for Beth or another member of The Six. And, of course, for Elston.

A few minutes later, she saw Beth promenading with an army captain whose left arm was in a sling. Karla thought he was the man Elston had been talking with earlier, but since her attention had been riveted on the marquess, not his companion, she was not certain. Although she did not know the military gentleman, Karla prayed the pair would continue their stroll to her corner.

Fortune smiled upon her. A few moments later Beth

spotted Karla, and the American girl's eyes widened in dismay—or horror. After greeting Karla and Lady Blackburn, Beth presented her escort, Captain Ashton. As the gentleman exchanged pleasantries with the countess, Beth took Karla's arm and drew her a few feet away.

"If that gown reflects your stepmother's preferences, then I can only conclude she has no sense of fashion." Beth's frankness, as well as her outrage, was oddly comforting.

"It does. And it is the most flattering of all her choices." Karla fought to keep her voice even. "The rest—and there are at least half a dozen of them—are worse. Either in color, style, or both."

Beth gave Karla's hand a sympathetic squeeze. "That is difficult to imagine."

"The ball gowns and evening gowns are the worst. The morning and afternoon gowns are not quite as bad."

"A small blessing, perhaps, but a blessing all the same." Beth glanced around to be sure they could not be overheard. "Is there nothing you can do?"

"A few days ago, after a rather heated discussion with Lady Blackburn, my stepmother finally saw the error of her ways, but by then most of the ball gowns and evening gowns had already been pieced and cut. Madame Celeste will remove the ruffles and flounces from the ensembles that aren't finished, and will attempt to do so for this gown and a morning gown, but I am stuck with the fabrics and colors."

"I will visit tomorrow and bring Moira, my maid. She may have some ideas." Beth smiled and lowered her voice. "Did you get my note? Elston is here tonight."

"I received your message but there wasn't time to send a reply. I . . . I saw Lord Elston earlier."

"Did you speak with him? I know you were looking forward to renewing your acquaintance with him."

Beth did not know the half of it—and thank the Lord for that! Karla hoped for a chance to resume her childhood friendship with the marquess, but she dreaded confessing her masquerade as Miss Lindquist. "No, I have not spoken with him."

"I am sure you will have the opportunity to do so later this evening."

Beth's certainty was a bit daunting, especially since Karla

knew she looked like a quiz—or worse—in the horrid gown, but she managed to nod. "Perhaps."

A Look from the countess caused both girls to remember their manners—and Beth's partner. Captain Ashton waved off their apologies, bespoke a dance with Karla later in the evening, then was presented to Lydia and the viscountess. He requested a set with her half-sister, for which Karla was grateful although Lydia was not: She lied and claimed her card was full. And was castigated for it by her mother and Lady Blackburn as soon as Beth and the captain were out of earshot.

Robert continued his perambulation around the perimeter of the ballroom, hoping to see either Lady Blackburn or Lady Padbury. Beth had told him this afternoon that Karla would attend the ball and he was eager to renew his acquaintance—and his friendship—with her. Glimpsing a lady in the far corner whose mahogany hair was accented by a silvery swath, he quickened his steps, but stopped when he saw the Marchioness of Kesteven.

"Good evening, Lady Kesteven." Robert bowed.

"Wrex—Elston! How nice to see you this evening." The marchioness's smile indicated that her words were more than a social pleasantry.

"Would you honor me with this dance, my lady?"

"It is difficult to refuse such an excellent partner, but I am chaperoning my daughters this evening."

Robert arced a brow. "Is there a rule that chaperones may not dance?"

"I think there must be." She nodded toward a corner where a group of matrons sat. "They always sit or stand at the edge of the floor, watching their charges."

"One would think they could observe better on the dance floor."

"There, they might forget their charges in the pursuit of their own pleasure."

Surveying the group of women, he drawled, "I cannot imagine the lady in the striped turban lost in frivolity."

The marchioness laughed. "Nor can I."

"If I cannot entice you to dance, my lady, tell me how your daughters are enjoying the Season."

"You may ask them yourself after this set. Your prediction was correct, you know, and they have followed your excellent advice."

Robert thought back to his visit at Woodhurst Castle. "My prediction that the gentlemen of the *ton* would compete to be the first to be able to tell the girls apart?"

"Yes. No one outside the family can as yet, except you and one of the other girls making her bows this Season."

"Who is this discerning young lady?"

"Miss Castleton."

He smiled slightly. "I am not surprised. She is extremely intelligent, and very perceptive."

"So it would seem."

The cotillion ended and the twins returned to their mother's side. After taking leave of her partner, Lady Deborah greeted Robert with a smile and a curtsy. "Lord Elston, how very nice to see you again."

He bowed. "The pleasure is mine, Lady Deborah."

"I had not heard you were in Town." Lady Diana's impolite salutation earned her a look of reproach from her mother.

"I arrived last night." Robert's response was deliberately rather curt.

"Well, if you are hoping to dance with us, you are much too late. Our—"

"Diana!" Lady Kesteven and Lady Deborah reproved in unison, clearly shocked. The marchioness grabbed her youngest daughter's arm and, after murmuring their excuses, dragged her a few steps away.

Lady Deborah studied the toes of her dancing slippers for several moments before meeting his gaze. "I apologize for my sister's rudeness, Lord Elston. I cannot imagine why she said such a thing."

That was obvious from her bemused expression. Her embarrassment was equally apparent. Robert smiled, hoping to put her at ease.

"Your sister is quite capable of making her own apologies," he said, his tone gentle but firm. "There is no reason for you to do so." Then, after a moment's pause, "I am, however, disappointed to hear that all your dances are promised."

That earned him a smile. One that conveyed both regret and her own disappointment.

"May I—"

Mr. Radnor's arrival interrupted Robert's query. After greeting the gentleman, whom he had known for years, Robert took his leave. He kept his pace to a stroll, but his steps led inexorably toward the corner of the room where Lady Blackburn stood. Lady Padbury and Miss Lydia were seated nearby, the latter talking to the Beauty in the atrocious ball gown.

With mingled elation and dread, Karla watched Elston approach. Her attention was distracted for several moments when a young dandy, Lord Selwyn, stopped to speak with Lady Blackburn, then was presented to the Lanes. The baron won the viscountess's favor by asking Lydia to partner him in the next dance, a Scottish reel. As the young lordling escorted her half-sister onto the dance floor, Karla realized Elston was only a few steps away. Her heart racing, she watched him bow over Lady Blackburn's hand, then turn and greet the viscountess with little more than a nod of his head. Karla did not know the rules governing gentlemen's bows, but she could not help but wonder if his shallow obeisance was due to the fact that he held her stepmother in considerably less esteem than the countess.

Karla's heart was thumping hard enough to pound its way out of her chest when the marquess turned to her.

"I know you met years ago as children, but . . ." Lady Blackburn smiled at them both. "Karla, may I present the Marquess of Elston? Elston, this is Miss Lane."

As Karla curtsied and Elston bowed, he seemed to scrutinize her features—and her gown. "I daresay you don't remember me, Miss Lane. When last we met—seventeen years ago, I believe—I was Viscount Wrexton."

The idea that she might have forgotten him made Karla smile. "I remember you very well, my lord, and your kindness to a bewildered little girl."

"Are you enjoying all the Season's activities?"

"For the most part, I am, although the *beau monde* is rather intimidating compared to Yorkshire society."

The marquess smiled slightly. "For Gloucestershire, too."

"Probably for every county in the country," Lady Blackburn added.

"I hadn't considered that, but it is comforting to know

every young lady making her bows is feeling the same." Thinking of the irrepressible Tina Fairchild, Karla grinned. "Well, perhaps not *every* young lady."

One of Elston's brows rose and his smile broadened. "I cannot help but wonder which young lady prompted that remark, but I shall refrain from asking."

"Thank you for sparing my blushes, my lord."

The viscountess joined them, stepping between Karla and the marquess. "When did you arrive in Town, Elston?"

He moved a pace to the side and turned slightly so he again faced Karla and Lady Blackburn. The subtle slight might have gone unnoticed by the viscountess, but his rather curt tone did not. "My great-aunt and I arrived last night."

"I was delighted to learn that Lady Lavinia accompanied you." With a mischievous smile the countess inquired, "Has she visited the modiste yet?"

He nodded. "She went this morning. Apparently the visit was a success."

"You should have called on us this afternoon, Elston. Lydia has been looking forward to your arrival." Her stepmother's arch tone and presumption of familiarity made Karla cringe inside.

"I had a number of calls to make this afternoon and was not able to visit everyone I wished." The marquess's words were polite, but Karla thought there was a slight edge to his voice.

"I had the same problem when I arrived in Town," Lady Blackburn said. "It took me several days to make them all."

"I imagine the same will hold true for me."

The viscountess took a deep breath, which Karla knew presaged an argument of some sort. Fortunately, Elston spoke before her stepmother found her voice. "Would you care for a glass of lemonade, Miss Lane?"

"Yes, I would. Thank you, my lord."

Karla expected him to decamp—and never return—but he was made of sterner stuff and offered his arm to escort her to the refreshment room. After a quick glance at Lady Blackburn for permission, Karla tucked her hand in the crook of his arm and made her escape, ignoring her stepmother's obvious displeasure.

"Do you make a practice of rescuing damsels in distress, Lord Elston?" Karla tilted her head back to smile up at the tall, handsome marquess.

He met it with one of his own—not a polite quirking up of the corners of his mouth, but a genuine smile that spread from his mobile lips to his chocolate brown eyes. "As a gentleman, I try to. But surely, as old friends, we need not be so formal. Just Elston, please. Or Wrexton, if you prefer."

"Thank you, Elston. I . . . I was not certain you would wish to pursue our childhood friendship."

"Not wish it? Miss Lane, I have been looking forward to renewing our friendship since my visit to Paddington Court."

His obvious sincerity gladdened Karla's heart. "Thank you. I have been hoping it would be possible." Then, more hesitantly, fearing her request might overstep the bounds of propriety, "I hope you will call me Karla, as you used to."

"I cannot do so in such a public venue. At least, not until it is common knowledge that I have known you from the cradle."

"Have you indeed? I only remember your visit when Papa married my stepmother, and another a year or so before that."

"I *rocked* your cradle, Karla. After your christening and on several other occasions."

She could not think of a suitable response to such a statement. After all, she couldn't thank Elston for being her champion almost from birth; he had no idea she imagined him in that role. Fortunately, they reached the refreshment room and she was spared the necessity of replying. Accepting a glass of lemonade from a footman, she sought the courage to confess her deception.

Elston guided her to a small table set in a bay window and seated her, then sat across from her, toying with a glass of wine. "Is your stepmother treating you well here in London?"

Although she could not imagine what prompted such a question, Karla answered truthfully, if not in any detail. "As well or better than at home in most respects."

"Does she allow you the same freedoms she allows Lydia?"

"I am allowed to visit friends, if that is what you are asking."

"That wasn't what I meant." His fingers tightened on his glass and he looked down for a moment.

"What did you mean?" She brushed a finger against one whitened knuckle, then quickly returned her hand to her lap.

"I hope you won't find my question too offensive." He caught her gaze and asked, baldly, "Does your stepmother choose your gowns, or do you?"

Dismayed, both by the question and the color she felt burning her cheeks, Karla looked away. "She chose most of them." Suddenly, and quite unexpectedly, the whole story of that first humiliating trip to Madame Celeste's came pouring out.

Embarrassed, she stuttered an apology. "F-forgive me. I should not have—"

"Should not have told me that?" he queried gently. "Balderdash! We are friends and, as such, can tell each other anything."

If only that were true! Karla could not find it within herself to confess her deception, fearing she would completely lose his regard. "Until recently, I have not had a close friend in whom I could confide."

"But now you have at least one other?" It was half statement, half question.

"Yes, one other. And—"

Several people entered the room. Knowing the reel must be over, Karla stood, as did Elston. He offered his arm, then brushed a finger against the card dangling from her wrist. "Can an old friend claim a dance or have you already promised them all?"

Wordlessly, she handed him her card, all too aware of the many unclaimed sets.

"It would appear that few of my friends have made your acquaintance. I shall have to introduce some of them to you."

"You are very kind, my lord."

His brown eyes twinkled. "My gentlemen friends will certainly think so."

When they reached Lady Blackburn, Karla slid her hand

from his arm and curtsied. "Thank you for the lemonade, Elston."

"My pleasure, Miss Lane." He returned her card with a bow.

After exchanging a few words with the countess, he snagged her card and claimed a dance. Then, with another bow and smile for both of them, he left. Somehow the cozy little corner seemed quite empty in the wake of his departure.

As he continued his stroll around the room, Robert pondered which of his acquaintances might be persuaded to ask Karla to dance. The fops and dandies would not wish to partner a dowdily dressed girl, but most of the Corinthian set would not be deterred by an ugly gown. And if some of the leaders of Society danced with Karla, her success would be assured.

Blackburn, Ashton, Durwood, and Peyton had claimed dances. The earl was a prominent figure in government, but not in social circles, although the fact that he had claimed two of Karla's dances, including the supper dance, would not go unnoticed. After suggesting to Lord Howe, Mr. Radnor, and Mr. Brewster—all noted Corinthians—that they might wish to make the acquaintance of the Countess of Blackburn's protégée, the late Viscount Padbury's daughter, Robert dropped the same hint in the Duke of Fairfax's ear. Gentle, quiet, and rather plain of feature, Fairfax was not one of the leaders of the *ton*, but any lady who caught a duke's eye would garner attention. Robert knew Fairfax would enjoy Karla's company, and she would be comfortable in his.

Espying Dunnley coming off the dance floor, Robert wondered if he could make the same request of the viscount. As one of Society's leading lights, his notice would bring Karla to the *ton*'s attention. Robert did not know Dunnley all that well, despite the fact he was George's cousin, but the viscount settled the question by hailing him.

"Well met, Elston! Beth was looking for you before this dance."

"She was?" Robert did not partner her again until the supper dance.

"I believe she wanted to introduce you to a friend of hers. Miss Lane."

"I have known Karla—Miss Lane—since she was in the cradle."

The viscount's voice dropped to little more than a whisper. "Is it true that her stepmother has chosen a dowd's wardrobe for her?"

"Beth could answer your query better than I, but it is true that Karla is wearing an unflattering gown this evening. A gown selected by her stepmother."

One of the viscount's tawny eyebrows winged upward in question.

"I suspected Lady Padbury would attempt to puff off her daughter whilst trying to hide her stepdaughter's light under the proverbial bushel. As an old friend, I took the liberty of asking."

Dunnley glanced around the room. "I have not seen the Lanes this evening."

"They are in the far corner. Look for Lady Blackburn. Karla will be nearby."

"I met Miss Lane at a soiree at Castleton House last week. A charming young lady, far more worthy of the *ton*'s notice than her half-sister." A mischievous twinkle lit the viscount's gray eyes. "Wouldn't you say it is our duty as gentlemen to bring Miss Lane into fashion and, at the same time, show Lady Padbury the error of her ways?"

Smiling, Robert nodded. "Indeed I would. Which is why I have just suggested to several friends that they would enjoy making Miss Lane's acquaintance."

"Excellent. I shall do the same—after securing a dance with her."

As Dunnley strolled away, Robert consulted his mental list of partners. Lady Throckmorton's little cards provided advantages for the ladies, allowing them to promise their dances well in advance, but distinct disadvantages for the gentlemen, who had to remember their partners for the rest of the evening, not just for a set or two. Robert thought their hostess ought to have given the cards to the men: They had to be in the right place at the right time; the ladies need only stand next to their relatives or chaperones and wait for their partners to appear.

If he didn't want it known that he was seeking a wife—and Robert did not—then he ought to dance with a matron or two. And with young ladies not on the list. He didn't want his interest in the ladies of the codicil to be noticed lest he give rise to expectations he could not fulfill.

As he looked for a lady without a partner for the next dance, Robert saw Sir Christian and Lady Yates standing nearby. Attired in a very becoming emerald silk gown, her short dark curls like a halo around her head, Robin Yates was the picture of a young, fashionable Society matron. She was also very happily married and, therefore, an unexceptional partner for an honorable gentleman who believed in the sanctity of the marriage vows. After exchanging greetings and social pleasantries with the couple, Robert and Lady Yates joined a set for the next country dance.

Afterward, Sir Christian claimed his wife for the next dance—a waltz. Since Robert had just arrived in Town and did not know which young ladies (other than Beth) had permission from the patronesses to dance it, he had chosen Lady Blackburn as his partner. He had a number of questions for the countess, and a waltz would give him the opportunity to ask them.

Karla watched, a bit enviously, as her friend and mentor waltzed with Elston. *Lucky Lady B!* The countess had protested that he should partner a young girl, but he had merely smiled and reiterated his desire to dance with her. Karla hoped that someday she would twirl around a ballroom in his arms. Waltzing with the man one loved must be a heavenly experience.

Glancing around the room, she realized she was not the only member of The Six watching from the sidelines. Harriett, Deborah (and her catty twin), and Tina were also sitting out the dance. Since Harriett and Tina had been in Town for several weeks, Karla could not help but wonder if lack of permission or lack of a partner kept them from the floor. Both had vouchers for Almack's and had already attended at least one assembly.

Would she be granted a voucher? Karla wondered. During their afternoon calls last week, she had met two of the patronesses, Lady Sefton and Lady Cowper, but the Lanes had not received the coveted tickets. At least, not yet. If

Karla and Lydia were not granted admittance to what some wags called the Marriage Mart, the viscountess's displeasure would know no bounds. Shuddering at the thought, Karla returned her gaze to the graceful patterns of the waltz.

On the dance floor, Robert posed a similar question to Lady Blackburn. "Have Karla and Lydia received vouchers for Almack's?"

"Vouchers, if they are granted, will be given to Karla and Lady Padbury. Lydia will be permitted to attend, but only two ladies in a family can be on the list."

"*If* they are granted? Surely—"

"I have been told," the countess said, her voice barely audible above the music, "that some of the patronesses question Hortense's eligibility."

"Do they indeed? One wonders why."

"Among other things, her treatment of Karla has not gone unnoticed. And Hortense's family background is . . . less than distinguished."

Robert's left eyebrow arced upward, but Lady Blackburn did not elaborate. After several moments, he asked, "Is it possible for Karla to receive a voucher if her stepmother does not?"

"Yes, but I hope that won't happen. Relations between Karla and Hortense are already quite strained."

"Through no fault of Karla's, I am certain."

"You are right, of course, but . . ." The countess sighed deeply. "At Paddington Court, Hortense treated Karla little better than a servant. That is not the case here, I assure you, but Hortense resents her. Terribly."

Seeing the sheen of tears in Lady Blackburn's eyes, Robert held her a bit closer. "My deepest apologies, my lady. When I asked for your assistance, I did not realize how difficult this would be for you."

She looked down for several seconds, blinking rapidly. Just as she regained her composure, the musicians played the final chords of the dance, leaving the rest of Robert's questions unanswered for the nonce.

By the time he climbed into bed, Robert was exhausted. Not from the exertion of dancing—that was nothing to a man as physically active as he was—but mentally tired. Perhaps emotionally as well. Lying back, he clasped his hands behind his head and reviewed the day. The evening in particular.

In many respects, the ball had been a success. He had met Miss Broughton and Lady Sarah, the last two unknown eligible ladies on his father's list (Lady Mary having eliminated herself from consideration), spoken with the Woodhurst twins (and eliminated Lady Diana from *his* list), and renewed his acquaintance—and, he hoped, his friendship—with Karolina Lane.

The less than pleasant aspects of the ball arose from three sources: matchmaking mamas, astonishingly impertinent questions about his plans for the future, and an ugly rumor. It seemed that every woman trying to fire off a daughter or female relative this Season had introduced the young lady (or ladies) to him. That was an exaggeration, of course—he'd sought introductions to Harriett Broughton and Lady Sarah Mallory—but not much of one. His immediate plans were to find a bride and take his seat in Lords, but he had no wish for anyone other than Aunt Livvy, Beth, and George to know the former, and few females were interested in hearing about the latter.

The rumor was the cause of most of Robert's unease. It was particularly vicious, clearly intended to ruin a young lady's reputation. It was also a lie. Robert knew it was not true—he had accompanied Beth and George from Stranraer to Cumberland and they did not travel as husband and wife—but it would be devilishly hard to convince the gossip-loving *ton* that the rumor was false, especially in George's absence. But the difficulty of the task would not deter Robert. Nor his ally, Viscount Dunnley.

With a weary sigh, Robert closed his eyes. *Was quelling the rumor his fourth or fifth campaign this Season?*

Chapter Eleven

Karla was daydreaming over her breakfast, wondering if Elston would call today, when her stepmother and Lydia entered the dining room. Given that it was not yet ten o'clock and no excursions were planned this morning, their presence outside their bedchambers at this hour was not a good sign. No doubt the viscountess intended to ring a peal over Karla's head. Repressing a sigh, she hoped that, for once, it would be for a real misdeed, not an imagined one. Lydia's presence, however, made the latter more likely. And ensured there would be some sniping—probably a great deal of it—about the number of sets Karla had danced last night while her half-sister glared at her from the sidelines.

Lydia fired the first salvo, in a sickeningly sweet voice that did not conceal her envy. "Dreaming about the ball, sister dear?"

"No, I wasn't."

"I don't believe you!"

"I was wondering who might call this afternoon." Determined to be polite, Karla attempted to turn the conversation from herself to her half-sister. "Which of your partners would you like to call today, Lydia?"

"I don't have the vast number to choose from that you do." The remark was half sneer, half pout. "It is so unfair! You looked ugly and had hundreds of partners—"

Karla laughed at the gross exaggeration. "No one had hundreds of partners; there were only about twenty sets."

"Dozens, then," persisted Lydia. "You had dozens of partners even though you looked like a quiz. I wore a flattering gown and sat out most of the sets."

"I did not lie and tell a gentleman all my dances were promised, either."

"He was crippled! Besides, only you, Mama, and Lady Blackburn know I lied."

Karla prayed for patience, even as she wondered at her stepmother's silence. "Captain Ashton is not crippled. He is recovering from an injury and expects to be sent back to the Peninsula soon. As for your lie, do you think he did not notice that you sat out the next set?"

"He may have," Lydia conceded, "but no other gentlemen knew I lied."

"Perhaps others saw you refuse him and, therefore, did not ask you to dance."

"Or maybe he mentioned it to his friends," the viscountess said.

"That wasn't very gentlemanly of him!" Lydia retorted.

"Your lie was ladylike?" Karla refrained, barely, from rolling her eyes. "We don't know that he said anything to anyone. But even if he did and even if his words deterred a few gentlemen from asking you to dance, the fact remains that if you had not lied, it would not—could not—have happened."

"But—"

"Every action has consequences." Karla's reminder was gentle but firm. "Last night was a rather unfortunate demonstration of that principle, but you have learnt from your mistake, I think."

An emphatic nod was Lydia's only answer.

"So"—Karla smiled—"which gentlemen are you hoping will call today?"

"Lord Selwyn, Mr. Martin, and Sir Henry Smythe."

Karla remembered the first gentleman but did not recall meeting the others.

"And you, Caroline?" the viscountess asked. "Who do you think will call?"

It was a more difficult question. "I imagine it depends on whether or not the gentlemen are performing at Mrs. Broughton's musicale tonight."

Lydia's eyes widened. "Gentlemen will be performing?"

"Quite a few, I understand."

"Who?" The viscountess's question was blunt, her expression calculating. Lydia had argued against attending the musicale, and her mother had sided with her. They had accepted an invitation to a card party; Karla would attend the musicale with Lady Blackburn.

"Lord Howe, Lord Weymouth, and Lord Bellingham." Karla knew Tina was the baron's accompanist, and Beth was to play a duet with the earl and a trio with him and his father. "I think Harriett also mentioned Viscount Dunnley."

Lydia glanced uncertainly at her mother. Karla hoped they would not change their plans.

The viscountess motioned for a footman to pour her more coffee. "Who else?"

"I cannot recall the names of any other gentlemen."

"I meant," she said as if explaining the obvious to an idiot, "which ladies will perform?"

Karla ignored the unspoken barb. "Harriett, of course. Beth Castleton, Tina Fairchild, Deborah Woodhurst, Sarah Mallory." She frowned, trying to remember the other performers. "Miss Applegate, Mrs. Kincaid, Lady Sherworth—"

"So many?" Clearly, Lydia thought the evening would be a dead bore.

"There are a few more." Karla smiled slightly, almost certain she could predict her stepmother's decision.

Both girls looked at the viscountess. "Lydia and I will go to the card party. It will be much more lively. Caroline, you are already promised to the Broughtons."

Lydia clapped her hands in delight. Equally pleased, Karla merely nodded.

The viscountess smiled fondly at her daughter. "If you have finished your breakfast, go upstairs and decide which gown you will wear tonight." After Lydia left, the viscountess dismissed the servants. Karla braced herself for a thundering scold.

"Caroline, you must cut your connection with Beth Castleton immediately."

"*What?*" The words were so unexpected, Karla gaped at her stepmother.

"You must cut—"

"I heard what you said, ma'am. I do not understand why you said it."

"Miss Castleton is not the well-bred young lady she seems."

Karla shook her head. "I do not believe that."

"Last night at the ball, the gossip about her—"

"Gossip?" She arced a brow at her stepmother. "You know as well as I that such rumors are rarely truthful."

"It will not matter. True or false, this rumor will ruin Beth Castleton."

Her stepmother's certainty was daunting, but Karla did not believe Beth would ever behave so improperly as to cause her ruination. "What was said? And by whom?"

The viscountess leaned forward. "Lady Moreton told me that Miss Castleton and Lord Weymouth traveled from Scotland to London as husband and wife."

Karla laughed. "That is ridiculous."

"Lady Moreton had the tale from someone who stayed at the same inn."

"Beth attended a house party in Scotland." 'Twas there, if Karla remembered correctly, Beth met Elston. "Where was Lady Julia, or whoever was serving as Beth's chaperone, when she was supposedly consorting with the earl?"

The viscountess looked distinctly taken aback; she obviously had not considered Beth's very proper great-aunt. Karla seized the advantage. "Clearly, ma'am, the rumor cannot possibly be true. It must have been started by someone who is jealous of Beth."

"Perhaps. But, true or false, it will stain Miss Castleton's reputation."

"No one who knows Beth could believe such a thing," Karla averred. "Other members of the house party will be able to refute the gossip. No doubt some of them traveled together to London."

"Probably so."

Karla hid a smile at her stepmother's obvious reluctance to relinquish such a choice morsel of gossip. "The *ton* will quickly realize the rumor cannot be true." She devoutly hoped so, for Beth's sake.

"You should avoid associating with Miss Castleton until the gossip dies down."

Unspoken but nonetheless clear was "if it does." "How widespread was the rumor?" Karla feared the answer but felt compelled to ask.

The viscountess shrugged. "I do not know."

"Did anyone other than Lady Moreton mention it to you?"

"I don't recall. I heard several people discussing it."

"I wonder if the Castletons are aware of the gossip."

"How could they be, Caroline? Can you think of anyone bold-faced enough to tell Lady Julia?" The viscountess shuddered at the thought.

"Someone must tell them," Karla declared. "If they don't know the rumor is circulating, they cannot attempt to quell it."

"No one will believe Miss Castleton's denials."

"Why not? She certainly knows the truth of the matter."

"But she could lie to save her reputation."

Beth was too forthright ever to lie, but Karla did not argue the point with her stepmother. The *ton* would think just as the viscountess did. But something must be done to help Beth. "If you do not plan to use the carriage this morning, ma'am, I would like to call on Lady Blackburn."

"It is too early to pay a call, Caroline. And you will see Jane tonight."

"Lady Blackburn gave me leave to call on her any time—day or night. I would like to ask her advice about how best to apprise Lady Julia and Beth of the gossip."

"Caroline, I forbid—"

"I do wish," Karla interrupted, hoping to divert her stepmother, "you would either pronounce my name properly or call me Karla. The *ton* will think something is wrong with our family if my stepmother and half-sister so abuse my name."

"Very well, *Karla.*" The emphasis was sarcastic, but the pronunciation was correct. "You may use the carriage to call on Jane Blackburn, but you must send it back as soon as you arrive. Lydia and I will need it to pay calls this afternoon. And you are not to tell Lady Julia about the rumor."

"But—"

"You may tell Miss Castleton, but you will not risk losing Lady Julia's regard by telling her."

Karla doubted she would ever understand her stepmother's reasoning. "I am more likely to lose my good standing with Lady Julia if I do not tell her."

A thoughtful frown crossed the viscountess's brow. "If Miss Castleton insists, you may tell Lady Julia. But it would be better if an older woman told her."

"You, ma'am?"

"Certainly not! I don't want to lose Lady Julia's favor. Perhaps Jane . . ."

"Very well, ma'am." Karla rose from the table and walked to the door. "I must change my gown if I am going to call on Lady Blackburn and Beth." To forestall any arguments, she added, "I will send the carriage back as soon as I arrive. No doubt Lady B will see me home afterward."

Robert awoke confused—and aroused. Both states resulted from dreams of either Karla or Miss Lindquist. The confusion was because the woman in his rather fevered fantasies looked like Karla but called herself Catherine Lindquist; the arousal was due to the intimate activities in which he and the lady had engaged.

Flopping onto his back, willing his body to calm, he pondered the unprecedented occurrence. Never before had he dreamt of a woman. Or if he had, he hadn't remembered the dreams when he woke. He supposed it was not surprising that he had dreamt of Karla: After weeks of waiting, he had finally renewed his acquaintance with her last night. But in his nighttime reveries, they had done considerably more than resume their childhood friendship! Given that Karla and Miss Lindquist were cousins, it was quite possible they resembled each other. As best he recalled from his brief glimpses of the governess on the terrace at Paddington Court, they were similar in stature and coloring. *But why was he suddenly dreaming of her—and in such intimate detail?*

'Twas an unanswerable question for the nonce. And he had other problems to solve. Throwing back the covers, Robert rose, pulled on his dressing gown, and rang for his valet. He was meeting Dunnley at Bellingham House at eleven o'clock. Hopefully, George would have returned from his sojourn in Dorsetshire. If not, they would inform his father of the rumor, then attempt to trace the source of the gossip. Robert suspected the culprit's identity, but they needed proof.

*   *   *

Late in the afternoon, Karla and Lady Blackburn ascended the steps to Castleton House. Karla had wanted to come earlier, but the countess had pointed out that, even if Beth was practicing for the musicale, Lady Julia probably would be out making calls. Lady B felt that bad news was best told when loved ones were present to offer sympathy and advice. Unable to argue against such wise counsel, Karla had spent several pleasant hours with her mentor—while keeping one eye on the clock.

As she reached for the knocker, the door opened. Elston stepped back to allow the ladies to enter, then greeted them with a smile. "Good afternoon, Lady Blackburn, Miss Lane." The butler's welcome was an echo of the marquess's.

"Good afternoon, Elston." Karla returned the salutation and the smile. "North."

As the marquess bowed over the countess's hand, the butler deftly relieved him of what appeared to be a very large violin case. When her turn came, Karla quirked a brow at Elston. "I don't believe I knew you were a musician. Are you playing at the musicale tonight?"

"I am a violist. And yes, I will be performing tonight. Bellingham . . . ah, persuaded me to join them. Originally, as a substitute for Weymouth, so that Beth would play the same number of pieces. When George returned today, Bellingham decided to expand their program, since I had already agreed to perform."

Karla was delighted to know she would see Elston again this evening. "A quartet in addition to the duet and trio?"

"Originally there were two duets and a trio. Now there are three duets, a trio, and a quartet."

"Are you playing one of the duets as well as the quartet?"

"I am." Pride chased chagrin across the marquess's handsome face.

"I look forward to hearing all of you perform. Beth's talent is highly praised, as are Lord Weymouth's and Lord Bellingham's." Daringly, Karla added, "I daresay yours is equally deserving of compliments."

"I am not as talented as they are, but I have played with the Winterbrooks for years and thoroughly enjoyed it. I rarely perform in public"—Elston's smile was wry—"so it will be nice to have such a staunch friend in the audience tonight."

"Why—" Karla interrupted her question when she suddenly realized that if Elston had spent part of the afternoon with Beth and Weymouth, he might know if they were aware of the gossip. But she also conscious of the butler's presence a few feet away and didn't want to ask her question in front of him.

One of Elston's dark brows arced upward. "Why what, Miss Lane?"

"It is not important, my lord. But—" Uncertain how to proceed, Karla looked from one of her companions to the other.

The marquess solved her dilemma by saying, "North, I wonder if we might use the morning room for a few minutes?"

"Of course, my lord." The butler led them into the room, then closed the door.

When Karla and the countess were seated on a sofa, Elston took a nearby chair, so they could converse comfortably. "What was it you wanted to ask, Karla?"

Finding the subject much more difficult to address than she imagined, she glanced down at her hands for a moment before meeting the marquess's eyes. "At breakfast, my stepmother told me there was a nasty rumor about Beth being spread last night at the ball. About Beth and Weymouth," she amended. "I thought Beth and Lady Julia should know of it, so they can quell it. When I sought Lady Blackburn's advice, she very kindly agreed to accompany me here."

She gulped a breath. "I . . . When we were talking in the entry hall, it suddenly occurred to me that if you rehearsed with Beth and Weymouth this afternoon, you might know if they are aware of the gossip."

Elston scrutinized her features. "Did your stepmother tell you the rumor?"

"When I asked." Then, a second later, "How could anyone believe such a lie!"

"Regrettably, the *ton* doesn't concern itself with the veracity of gossip."

"Apparently not." Karla sighed. "I know that Beth attended a house party in Scotland. I told my stepmother that other members of the party probably traveled back to London with them and will be able to refute the tale, but I don't know who attended. Given the rumor's content, Weymouth must have, and I think I recall Beth telling me she met you at that party."

The marquess nodded. "You are correct on both counts. Weymouth was there, and that was, indeed, when I met Beth. I know the gossip is false because we traveled back to England in cavalcade."

"You have obviously heard the rumor, Elston," Lady Blackburn said, "but you did not answer Karla's question. Do the Castletons know of it?"

"They do now. Earlier this afternoon, Weymouth told Beth while Dunnley, Bellingham, and I informed Lady Julia. Dunnley planned to spend the afternoon tracking the gossip to its source."

Although the viscount's actions were laudable, Karla was more concerned about her friend. "Beth must be deeply distressed by such a vile rumor. I wish I could do something to help her!"

"How will Dunnley trace the source of the gossip?" The countess's words came on the heels of Karla's exclamation.

Elston addressed the latter question first. "Last night, I overheard Lady Cathcart telling it to Mrs. Phillips. When I confronted her, Lady Cathcart said she heard it from Lady Smithson. Later, my godmother questioned me about the validity of the tale. Lady Moreton told her. Dunnley will call on Lady Smithson and Lady Moreton and ask from whom they heard it. Then call on whomever they name, repeating the process until he discovers the rumor's originator."

He turned to Karla. "You can help Beth by supporting her during this difficult time—"

"Of course I will!"

Although she did not know what she had done to earn his smile, Karla savored it. "And by asking your stepmother from whom she heard the gossip."

"From Lady Moreton."

"Hopefully, the number of talebearers will be small and Dunnley can quickly determine the source of the rumor."

"For the Castletons' sake, I hope that proves to be the case," Lady Blackburn said. "If it is not, please let me know. I would like to help."

"Thank you, my lady." Elston rose. "I regret that I must leave. I require several hours of practice before this evening if I am not to disgrace my fellow performers—and myself. May I escort you home?"

Despite his less than successful attempts to quell the gossip with the truth at his club that morning, Robert was determined to support Beth and George in every possible way. Even performing in public without much rehearsal. He arrived at Mrs. Broughton's musicale in company with George and his father, the Castletons, and Dunnley.

Robert and George led the procession; Beth, on Bellingham's arm, walked behind them; Dunnley, Lady Julia, and the Earl of Castleton brought up the rear. Robert hoped that Beth's presence in his company, coupled with his refutations of the rumor, would cause the *ton* to question the validity of the tale.

Bellingham's plan was to bring Beth to Society's notice by making the musicale one of the Events of the Season. And, at the same time, to remind the *beau monde* that she was beautiful, intelligent, talented, honest, kindhearted, and as innocent as a babe.

Mrs. Broughton's greeting to Beth was civil but chill. Harriett's, however, was warm and welcoming. If she was aware of the gossip, she had dismissed it as the nonsense it was. Her loyalty to her friend was admirable. Nor had Robert failed to note Karla's this afternoon. The latter's was even more remarkable, since she had known Beth for only a week. With their loyalty and devotion—both essential traits in a wife—Harriett and Karla had moved up on his list of potential brides. Karla, in part because of his childhood friendship with her, was challenging Lady Deborah for the top spot; Harriett, despite his reservations about her shyness, was third; Lady Sarah was a more distant fourth, mostly because of her rather formidable reserve.

Wearing a white muslin gown with a pink sash and rosebuds embroidered on the skirt, Beth entered the Broughton's drawing room on Bellingham's arm, looking calm and composed. They joined Robert and George at the back of the room. After seating her, Bellingham announced, "Mrs. Broughton proclaims herself delighted at our expanded program. And for us to perform last. The grande finale, as it were."

"I only hope, sir," Beth said, "that I will not expire from a nervous disorder before then." Robert shared her sentiments.

The marquess patted her hand. " 'Tis natural to be nervous before you perform. Good, in fact. It gives your playing an extra brilliance."

"Then we shall dazzle the *ton* tonight."

"That's the spirit." Bellingham smiled and nodded approvingly.

As they waited for the musicale to begin, Robert and Beth's uncle escorted her around the room. Several people looked askance at her, but only two alluded to the gossip. With a haughty stare, Robert curtly denied the rumor with the truth: he had traveled from Scotland to England with Weymouth. Society did not need to know that Beth had been with them, or the reasons behind their rather irregular journey, only that the gossip was false.

All seven members of their party seemed to relax slightly during the first half of the musicale. Harriett Broughton started the program with excellent presentations of a Handel aria and a Scottish ballad. The hoydenish—or perhaps formerly hoydenish—Lady Christina Fairchild matched the caliber of Harriett's performance with a Mozart pianoforte sonata, but during her second piece, a much simpler folk song, she lost her place in the music and ended rather raggedly. Lady Deborah Woodhurst's brilliant rendition of a Beethoven pianoforte sonata contrasted sharply with Lady Sarah Mallory's technically excellent but seemingly emotionless harp performance.

When Mrs. Broughton announced the intermission, Robert rose with alacrity. "Miss Castleton, may I escort you to supper?"

"Thank you, Elston." As he tucked her trembling hand into the crook of his arm, she voiced a quiet request. "If possible, I would like to sit with Tina and Harriett."

Although he thought it unlikely those two young ladies, whose personalities were as different as night and day, would be seated together, Robert nodded and placed his hand over hers. *Lord, her fingers were like ice!* "Are you cold?" he whispered.

"No, only nervous."

He did not know if her nerves were due to their upcoming performance or to the prospect of facing everyone present, but their cause was not important. He kept his hand over hers, hoping to warm her. And to comfort her, if he could.

Beth knew her friends better than he did. When they reached the morning room, where supper was laid out, Harriett Broughton and Tina Fairchild were, indeed, sitting together—at a large table with Deborah Woodhurst, Karla Lane, and Sarah Mallory. After seating Beth, he filled plates for them both and joined the group, as did Dunnley.

At most of the *ton*'s entertainments, the majority of the supper tables would include an equal number of ladies and gentlemen. Musicales, however, were not a favorite of many male members of the *beau monde*, so the guests tonight were predominantly female: young ladies and their mothers or chaperones. From his seat between Beth and Karla, Robert looked around the room and counted only fourteen men, including himself and the other four gentlemen in his party.

When Beth praised her friends' performances, he added his own compliments. Lady Christina seemed determined to dwell on her faults until Beth said, "Tina, you played very well, even if not as faultlessly as you hoped. And you kept your head and finished the piece. I once turned a page of my music so hard"—she gestured wildly—"it flew off the stand and halfway across the room."

The image was so vivid, they all laughed. "I have done the same thing," Robert confessed, "although my music only traveled a few feet."

Lady Christina, obviously heartened, looked from Beth to him and back again. "Did you chase it down and finish the piece?"

Beth grinned. "Of course I did."

"I did as well," Robert said, "much to the dismay of the conductor. For weeks afterward, he scowled ferociously whenever he saw me." That provoked another bout of laughter.

As they finished eating, Harriett Broughton whispered

something to Tina Fairchild, who then whispered to Karla. In an instant, her smile was replaced by a strained expression.

Her obvious distress roused Robert's protectiveness. "Is something wrong?"

"Tina, Harriett, Deborah, and Sarah want to show our support of Beth by singing together. But we have only rehearsed once and I am afraid I will be too nervous to sing well, even in a group."

Her hands clenched into fists. "I want to help Beth, but . . ."

"She hasn't said anything about—"

"They haven't asked her yet. I am not certain they intended to." It was clear from her tone that Karla was not convinced this "surprise" would be good for Beth.

Knowing how nervous Beth already was, Robert thought any additional strain would be too much for her. Catching Dunnley's eye, he glanced down at Beth, seated between them, then nodded toward the drawing room.

The viscount stood. "Beth, may I escort you back to the drawing room?"

Robert felt her glance at him, but he kept his eyes on his plate and toyed with his dessert, hoping she would think he was still eating.

Apparently his ruse worked. Beth turned back to Dunnley. "You may, sir."

Tina Fairchild jumped up from her seat, hugged Beth, and whispered a fierce avowal of her belief in Beth's innocence. For a moment, Robert feared it was more than Beth's fragile composure could withstand, but she rallied and returned her friend's hug.

After Beth and Dunnley left the room and Lady Christina resumed her seat, Robert addressed Beth's friends. "Ladies, I commend your desire to support Beth during this difficult time, and to visibly demonstrate that support, but I believe your intended 'surprise' will be more of a strain than she can handle tonight."

"But she seems so calm," Harriett Broughton said.

"She may appear so, but she isn't," Lady Tina stated, her expression rueful. "My words and hug nearly had her in tears."

"I think she was . . . overwhelmed by your public demon-

stration of support." Robert looked from one young lady
to the next. "People under a great deal of stress react differently, but their emotions are always near the surface.
They run or fight or cry or wring their hands and do nothing. Beth, in her own quiet way, will fight."

"How can we"—Tina's sweeping gesture indicated herself and the other four girls—"help her?"

Robert pondered for several moments before answering.
"There are two things you can do. But first, I want to tell
you something. I suspect that you support Beth out of loyalty and friendship, not because she has denied the gossip.
I shall tell you that it is, indeed, a lie. A total fabrication.
Weymouth has been to Scotland only once in the past two
years, and I made the journey back to England with him.
Beth traveled with our group, staying at the same inns and
private residences he and I did. At no time did they travel
as husband and wife."

He met the gaze of each of the five young women, all of
whom seemed convinced the rumors were false. "As for
what you can do, first and most important, continue to support Beth in every way you can. Second, every time you
hear the rumor, refute it. Tell your families and friends and
everyone you call on that the rumor is a lie, and how and
why you know it is false."

Karla laid her hand on his coat sleeve. "Thank you,
Elston."

"Yes, thank you, my lord," Lady Deborah, Lady Christina, and Miss Broughton echoed. Lady Sarah merely
nodded.

"Now, we should return to the drawing room for the
second half of the program." He stood and pulled back
Karla's chair. "May I escort you to your seat?"

Delighted to be so honored, especially since most of the
other girls were prettier and of higher rank, Karla accepted.
When they were out of earshot of the others, she thanked
him again, adding, "We want to help Beth but didn't really
know what to do. Now, thanks to your excellent advice,
we do."

"I am glad I was able to help you."

After seating her and exchanging a few words with Lady
Blackburn, he returned to his chair at the back of the room.
Karla was looking forward to the rest of the program, espe-

cially to hearing him—and Beth and the Winterbrooks—
perform.

The second half was as good as the first. Tina accompanied Lord Howe in a stirring rendition of "Why Do the
Nations So Furious Rage Together?" from Handel's *Mes-
siah*. Viscount Dunnley, Lord Howe, and six other gentlemen sang two lovely madrigals. But the best performances
of all were at the end—a grande finale indeed.

Beth and Elston started off with a duet for violin and
viola; then she played a trio with Lord Weymouth and Lord
Bellingham, and a duet with the earl. The fourth selection,
a Beethoven quartet (Lord Bellingham announced the title
and composer of each piece before they played it), had the
audience on its feet cheering for more. Finally, Beth and
Lord Bellingham played a Bach violin duet that drew a
veritable storm of applause, far more than Karla would
have thought the relatively small audience could make, and
cries for an encore.

Judging by Beth's dismayed glance at Lord Bellingham,
they had not considered that possibility. After a short whispered conversation, he announced Beth would play a solo,
Bach's "Jesú, Joy of Man's Desiring." It was the most moving piece of music Karla had ever heard, and when Beth
finished, there was a moment of silence, then a deluge of
applause. Lord Bellingham stood quickly to escort her to
her seat, but before they had taken more than a couple
steps, the audience—with Tina and Harriett in the fore-
front, wiping away tears—was there to congratulate them.

Unwilling to fight her way through the crowd, Karla
smiled through her tears and led Lady B to the back of the
room where Beth's great-aunt and uncle were seated. Karla
hugged Beth and congratulated them all, as did Lady B. In
addition to Beth's hug and thanks, Karla was rewarded with
a warm smile and a whispered "Thank you, dear friend"
from Elston.

Chapter Twelve

*W*ednesday morning, Robert woke in the same state of confusion and arousal as the previous day—and for the same reason. Bothered by the intimacy of the dreams, still uncertain of the lady's identity, and bewildered as to why he was suddenly and repeatedly dreaming of Miss Lindquist, he hoped a bracing ride in Hyde Park would clear the cobwebs from his head. Hoped, too, that George, who generally rode with him, was less perceptive than usual this morning. Robert did not feel up to the task of airing his confused feelings, even to his best friend.

His worries proved groundless. When he reached the park, George was already there, as was his cousin. Robert joined them, riding on George's right, and Dunnley introduced the topic of their mutual concern: the gossip about Beth and George.

"I believe Elston's refutations of the rumor have helped to stem the spread of it. At White's last night, whenever the gossip was mentioned, so was his denouncement of it as a lie. The gentlemen of the *ton* are becoming convinced that Beth is being slandered. Her performance at the musicale will make the ladies question the tale."

"Do you think so?" In Robert's mind, there was no connection between Beth's exceptional talent and her innocence.

"I do. If she had not performed, or had played badly, they would think her poor showing was due to guilt. Since she was indisputably the best performer in a program that featured a number of excellent musicians, that won't be the case."

"That is not logical," George muttered.

"Since when are Society's whims governed by logic?" Dunnley countered.

Chuckling, Robert and George conceded the point. Unwilling to leave the restoration of Beth's reputation to chance, or to the fate of the fickle, gossip-loving *ton*, they planned their day as carefully as Wellington's commanders coordinated battle strategy.

Robert wanted to pay calls on Karla, Lady Deborah, Harriett Broughton, and Lady Sarah, but he knew he would probably spend the entire afternoon at Castleton House, refuting the gossip during Lady Julia's At Home. Although he was confident that he would be welcomed if he called at Padbury House and Kesteven House before proper visiting hours, he did not know the Broughtons or the Mallorys well enough for that. When he left the park, Robert sent bouquets—and messages conveying his respects—to all four ladies. Hopefully, that would keep him in their good graces.

He would see most of them tonight at Almack's. Lady Deborah and Lady Sarah undoubtedly had vouchers; Harriett Broughton probably did. Since Karla did not—yet—his first call this afternoon would be at Padbury House.

Elston's flowers brightened Karla's day considerably. She had received floral tributes before, of course, as recently as the previous day, but the pink, just blossoming roses he sent were prettier than any other admirer's posy. Even more lovely than the beautiful bouquet Blackburn sent after Lady Throckmorton's ball. Karla hoped Elston's roses indicated his desire to continue their childhood friendship, although deep in her heart she wished for more.

She was equally delighted when he called—nearly an hour earlier than the prescribed time—and glad she was wearing one of her favorite gowns, a sky blue muslin with lace trim at the collar and cuffs. Although she would have preferred not to be arguing with her stepmother about the gown when he was announced, Karla was too pleased by his presence to worry that he might have heard her stepmother's rantings. As she admired his handsome, elegantly clad form, she was torn between hope that his early visit denoted eagerness to see her and despair that he had come in advance of the normal hour because he had more important calls planned later.

"Good afternoon, Lady Padbury, Karla."

Karla smiled. It was a lovely afternoon now. "Good afternoon, Elston."

"Good afternoon, Lord Elston. How very kind of you to call." The viscountess motioned him to a chair. "I will run upstairs and see what is keeping Lydia. I know you want to see her."

When her stepmother left the room, Elston crossed to the sofa on which Karla was seated. "May I?" He pointed to the cushion beside her.

"Of course, my lord."

"I hope I won't put you to the blush if I say Lady Padbury is mistaken. You look lovely."

Although embarrassed that he had overheard part of the argument, his compliment thrilled her. "Thank you, Elston. You are very kind to say so."

"Telling the truth isn't always easy, nor always viewed as a kindness, but"—a smile curved his lips and lit his chocolate brown eyes—"in this case, it is both, as well as my pleasure."

"Th-thank you." She looked down at her hands to regain her composure, hoping he would think her stammer was due to his kind words. It was, however, the result of knowing that this honest man would scorn her—and reject her friendship—when he learned of her deception. "And thank you again for your help last night."

"I was happy to assist you." After a moment's hesitation, he added, "I hope you will always ask for my help, whenever you need it."

His voice and his expression conveyed his sincerity. Karla's heart beat faster. *Perhaps he wanted to be her champion.* "Thank you, Elston. You are a friend, indeed."

"Will you drive with me in the park tomorrow afternoon?"

Delighted by the invitation, she smiled. "I would like that. Very much. But I don't know my stepmother's plans."

"I will ask you again, when she returns."

"Are you a . . . a noted whip?"

A perplexed expression flashed across his face. "I am a member of the Four in Hand Club if that is what you are asking."

"It wasn't, but you have answered my question." That

seemed to bewilder him even more, so she explained. "Some gentlemen are admired for their prowess at boxing or shooting or . . ." She waved a hand, unable to think of any other sporting abilities. "I merely wondered if you were known for your driving expertise. Which you must be if you are a member of the Four in Hand Club."

"If I am known for anything," he said with uncharacteristic hesitancy, "I imagine it is for driving and fencing."

Karla wondered if he was uncomfortable discussing himself or merely modest. "And for your musical talent."

"Until last night, few people knew I was a musician."

"Why is that?"

Elston shifted in his seat. "I . . . er . . ."

The entrance of her stepmother and half-sister interrupted his halting reply. Karla wanted to know more about the man he had become, to compare him with the man in her dreams who had been her champion for so many years. Instead, the arrival of her relatives meant that she would, most likely, be forced to listen to her stepmother traduce her character and abilities. And also roused her fears that Elston would ask after "Miss Lindquist" in their hearing. She did not want to explain her deception to her family—or to him—but her conscience demanded the latter confession. Soon.

Elston left as soon as he could politely do so, but not before again inviting Karla to drive with him tomorrow during the fashionable hour. Much to her surprise, her stepmother agreed without demur—and without pushing to have Lydia included.

Thursday morning was no different than the previous two except that heavy rain prevented Robert's usual ride in the park. The inclement weather, however, did not deter the Earl of Weymouth, who arrived before Robert finished breakfast.

"George! What brings you out so early? And in such nasty weather?" Robert asked, although he felt certain he knew the reason. "Sit down and Baxter will pour you a cup of coffee."

Looking as if he had not slept well, if at all, Weymouth sat. Robert motioned for his butler to bring breakfast for his guest. After serving the earl, Baxter refilled both men's cups, placed a fresh pot of coffee on the table, and left the dining room.

Suddenly realizing that he had not yet received an answer to his question, Robert studied his friend, who seemed uncharacteristically despondent. Last night's events—Beth's voucher had been revoked almost as soon as she set foot in Almack's—undoubtedly formed a large part of his worries. "George?" When he received no response, Robert tried again, but this time it was the command of a brigade major. "George!"

Although he'd held the same rank in the same cavalry regiment, his friend jerked erect and looked at him rather quizzically. In a normal tone, Robert asked, "Are you going to sit in silence or would you like to talk about whatever is bothering you?"

George rubbed both hands over his face, then raked them back through his hair. After nearly twenty years of friendship, the gesture was a familiar one, denoting extreme agitation. Robert sipped his coffee while George gathered his thoughts.

"It is my fault that Beth's reputation is tarnished—because of Arabella's foul rumor and because she and her cousin came up with their stupid kidnapping scheme to force me into marriage. Beth was doing a good deed when she tried to save my niece from the kidnappers. She did another when she rescued me from Arabella's clutches. But the dear girl has suffered repeatedly because of her goodness. First a concussion. Then she was shot. Now her character and reputation are being shredded in drawing rooms all over London."

Robert nodded. He had heard all this before, in Stranraer and on the journey from Scotland to Brough.

"But"—George sighed—"Beth doesn't seem to realize the seriousness of the problem. I understood why she refused my marriage proposal when we arrived in Town. We had committed no impropriety and only you and our families knew we had traveled together with only her maid as chaperone."

Robert refrained from pointing out that, in the eyes of Society, their traveling together was scandalously improper since neither man was related to Beth. He knew, better than anyone, that expediency, not debauchery, was the reason for their rather irregular journey.

"And last night?" After leaving Almack's, the entire party (there had been eight of them, all save Robert related to Beth or George) had returned to Castleton House. When Lady Julia arranged a late supper in the morning room, George had stayed in the drawing room with Beth for a few minutes—and had, most certainly, proposed. "Did she refuse you again?"

"She did." George's tone was forlorn, like that of a child deprived of a treasured toy.

"Did she give you a reason?"

"The same one as before. She doesn't want me forced into a loveless marriage."

Robert wondered when his friend, an incredibly intelligent man and one of the leading lights of the Royal Mathematical Society, would realize he loved Beth. After seeing them together the past two days, Robert was quite certain she loved George. He, however, was burdened by a family tradition of love at first sight, and apparently no lightning bolts had struck when he was introduced to Beth.

Musing on the advantages of such a sign, Robert almost missed his friend's next statement. ". . . I am fond of Beth. I like and respect and admire her. We could have a happy marriage."

"I am sure you could, but it wouldn't be the love match you both want."

George crossed his arms over his chest, his chin jutting out pugnaciously. "In time it might become a love match."

"It might," Robert agreed, wondering which of them George was trying to convince.

"Damn it!" George shoved away from the table. "How can I convince Beth to marry me?"

"Do you really want to marry her?"

"I have to marry her. I *need* to marry her."

"Why, George?" Robert asked quietly. "Why do you feel that way?" He rose and left the room, leaving his friend to ponder—and, hopefully, understand—his feelings.

Aside from not knowing what to wear (she did not have a carriage dress since she had so adamantly refused the mustard bombazine) and her fears about Elston's reaction to her confession, Karla was looking forward to her drive with him. Standing in front of her wardrobe, scrutinizing the gowns within, she wished Lady Blackburn or Beth or another member of The Six were here to advise her. Karla did not feel she could trust the advice of her stepmother, her half-sister, or their maids, and Mary the chambermaid knew nothing about fashion. After dithering for nearly an hour, Karla finally decided on a pale pink ruffled morning gown, her rose sarcenet spencer, blush pink kid gloves, and a chipstraw bonnet with rose ribbons a few shades darker than the spencer.

When she was dressed, she studied herself in the cheval glass. Even though she wasn't fashionably attired for a drive in the park, she looked . . . quite nice. Karla hoped Elston would think so, too. And that he would not realize her ensemble wasn't quite what it should be. Then again, a show of disdain might make it easier to confess. *Why, oh, why had she been so foolish? How could she have allowed pride—false pride—to overrule her precepts and dictate her actions?*

By the time the knocker sounded, she had worked herself into quite a state. Her agitation increased when she entered the drawing room and saw her half-sister, very à la mode in a blue carriage dress with braided trim. At luncheon neither she nor her mother had mentioned an engagement to drive in the park—and such invitations were not the sort of thing about which either would keep silent. *Surely Lydia does not think she was included in Elston's invitation?*

Before Karla could question her half-sister, the marquess was announced. Wearing a bottle green superfine coat, a waistcoat of green-and-gray-striped silk, tan breeches, and gleaming Hessians, he looked even more handsome than usual. After greeting the viscountess and nodding to Lydia, he bowed over Karla's hand.

"Are you ready for our drive?"

"Indeed I am, my lord."

He tucked her hand (which he had retained after greeting her) in the crook of his arm, then escorted her toward the door. Karla held her breath, hoping she had misjudged her stepmother's intentions.

She had not. Just before they reached the portal, the viscountess said, "Elston, what about Lydia?"

He turned to face his interrogator, one dark brow rising. "Lydia, ma'am?"

"Yes. Surely you do not intend to take Caroline and leave her sister behind."

A muscle flexed in Elston's cheek, but his voice did not betray his ire. "I invited *Karolina* to drive with me. My curricle only seats two." After a moment's pause, he turned to Lydia. "I apologize if my invitation was unclear."

With a rather curt bow to the viscountess and her daughter, he escorted Karla from the room. He muttered something as they descended the stairs, but she couldn't quite hear his *sotto voce* comment. Mortified by her stepmother's behavior, she could think of nothing to say—and the air between them fair crackled with tension.

When they were outside, she managed to stutter, "I am s-sorry, Elston."

"Your stepmother can make her own apologies."

"But—"

He stopped abruptly but did not speak until she met his gaze. Although he was obviously irritated, his tone was kind. Firm but kind. "Karla, you are not responsible for your stepmother's actions. I know you had nothing to do with that . . . little charade."

With a mischievous grin, he added, "If Lady Padbury and your half-sister wish to make fools of themselves, let them."

Under other circumstances, Karla would have enjoyed his teasing, but she feared the consequences of just such an occurrence. After assisting her into his curricle and taking his place beside her, Elston turned to her, an expression of mock consternation on his face. "As my friend, you are supposed to laugh at my witticisms."

"I cannot on this subject." Karla looked down at her hands.

"What is wrong, my dear?"

The concern in his voice, coupled with the endearment, was almost her undoing. Blinking back tears, she choked out, "Later. I will explain later."

After several moments—rather uncomfortable moments during which she felt his gaze on her downturned face—he picked up the reins. By the time he turned onto South Audley Street, Karla had regained her composure. To change the subject, she admitted, "I have never ridden in a curricle before."

His eyebrows—at least the one she could see—rose, conveying his surprise, but he kept his eyes on the traffic. "I am honored that you chose to have your first curricle ride with me. What vehicle is favored by the young men around Selby? A phaeton?"

"Most drive gigs of some sort." She had never ridden in one with any man except the estate steward, but she was not about to confess that.

"Gigs are quite popular in Gloucestershire, too."

After several seconds of silence, Karla randomly chose a new topic of conversation. "Did you attend Almack's last night?"

He glanced at her. "You haven't spoken to Beth or your other friends today?"

The question seemed rhetorical, but she answered anyway. "No, I haven't."

Frowning a bit, he turned onto Upper Grosvenor Street. "It must have been the worst night in Almack's history. Beth had barely set foot in the door when Lady Jersey announced that her voucher had been revoked."

"What!"

"Beth was marvelous. She looked the countess in the eye and, more or less, chided her for believing lying gossip. Then, with the grace and dignity of a queen, Beth left, escorted by her uncle. Dunnley and I were quick to inform Lady Jersey of her error. Then he and Lady Julia, George and his aunts, and I walked out, too."

"Poor Beth! She must be devastated."

"At my club this morning, I learned there was a mass exodus," Elston said with some satisfaction. "Lady Blackburn called it a sad day when a patroness attempted to blacken a young lady's reputation. Then she and her son left. The Duchess of Greenwich declared that if a gracious, innocent, well-mannered young lady like Beth Castleton did not deserve a voucher, there wasn't a female present who did. Then she and Lady Christina departed. And the Marchioness of Kesteven said that if innocent girls were not being admitted, her daughters shouldn't be there, and she, the twins, and Lord Henry left."

"How wonderful of Lady B, the duchess, and Lady Kesteven to publicly show their support of Beth!" Karla wished she could do the same.

"After that, the mothers of several other young ladies took their daughters home. Perhaps as a show of support—or for fear their daughters' virtue would be questioned if they stayed after the marchioness's pronouncement. Or possibly because a number of the most popular, and eligible, bachelors left."

"Men other than Weymouth, Dunnley, you, Blackburn, and Lord Henry?"

Elston nodded. "I know Brummell, Howe, Ashton, Radnor, and Brewster left. Others may have, as well."

"Did they, too, declare their belief in Beth's innocence?"

"Brummell and Ashton did. I don't know about the rest."

When Elston halted his rig, Karla looked around, startled to realize they were in the park. The Greenwich landau was beside them, the duchess and Tina inside. As greetings were exchanged, the younger girl could barely contain her impatience.

"Karla! Where were you all day?"

"At home working on my costume for the masquerade."

"But—"

The duchess's explanation overrode her daughter's protest. "We called at Padbury House this morning, Miss Lane, and again this afternoon. Both times your stepmother told us you were not at home."

Robert watched Karla's hands writhe against her skirt. "I am s-sorry, Your Grace. I cannot imagine why she said that."

He could imagine all too well why the viscountess had done it. Judging by her expression, the duchess could, too. Lady Christina did not hesitate to voice her opinion. "Lady Padbury attempted to fob us off with Lydia"—she rolled her eyes dramatically—"but we declined, claiming the press of other calls."

Robert could not help but wonder if Lady Tina's disdain for Karla's half-sister was due to Lydia's behavior or loyalty to Karla. Tina and Lydia were the same age and, by all appearances, would seem the more likely pair of friends.

"Have you heard what happened at Almack's last night?" Lady Tina asked.

Karla nodded. "Elston just told me." Then, to the duchess, "Your Grace, you have my greatest respect and admiration for supporting Beth in such a . . ."

"In such a dramatic fashion?" The duchess's tone was wry, as was her smile. "That is how Greenwich described it."

"Well, I imagine it was rather dramatic, but I meant in such a pointed manner."

A phaeton attempting to pass almost scraped the wheels of the curricle. Robert steadied his horses, then said, "Ladies, much as I hate to interrupt your conversation, we are blocking the path."

"We are," the duchess agreed. "Miss Lane, I hope you will visit us soon."

"Thank you, Your Grace. I don't know my stepmother's plans for tomorrow afternoon, but I will see you at St. Ives House in the evening."

Lady Tina waved as the landau moved into traffic. "Until tomorrow, Karla."

Before Robert and Karla completed a circuit of the park, he was furious and she was on the verge of tears. Lady Deborah, Miss Broughton, and Lady Blackburn had also called today and been told Karla was not at home. To give her time to regain her composure, he turned off the main path, halting his rig beside the Serpentine.

"Shall we walk for a while?" At her nod, he stepped down, then turned to assist her. Hoping to draw a smile, he intended to grasp her waist and swing her down, turning in a circle as he did so.

The jolt of . . . something he felt when he wrapped his hands around her tiny waist was unexpected. And powerful. So strong that he nearly stumbled. After half a circle, he set Karla on her feet, wondering if her waist was tingling like his hands and arms were.

A becoming flush colored her cheeks. Robert would have given much to know if it was due to his unexpected maneuver or because she'd felt the same whatever-it-was he had. But he could not ask, and contented himself with tucking her hand in the crook of his arm.

As they strolled toward the river, she peeked up at him through her lashes. "You helped me dismount like that when I was little."

"Indeed I did." He smiled down at her. "I was hoping you would remember—and not slap me for being forward."

That drew the smile he'd hoped for earlier. "Elston, I cannot imagine you behaving in so ungentlemanly a manner as to deserve a slap."

Given the dreams he'd had the past three nights, Robert was not certain he deserved her trust. The intimate activities he'd enjoyed in those erotic fantasies were definitely ungentlemanly, unless they were married. That idea gained greater appeal by the day—and not only because it would remove her from the viscountess's sphere.

"I hope I shall always behave in a manner worthy of your regard, Karla."

They walked for several minutes in companionable silence, enjoying the lovely spring afternoon, before Robert introduced the topic he had brought her here to discuss. "I do not like hearing that your stepmother is up to her old tricks."

"I am not happy about it either, but I doubt I can do anything to change it."

"Would you like me to talk to her about it?"

Karla stopped and stared up at him. "You would do that for me?"

"Of course I would." Robert could not understand why that seemed to surprise her. Had he not indicated, more than once, that he would stand her friend?

"Since my father's death, no one has stood my champion against the viscountess except Lady Blackburn and, more recently, my brother. And I think you are responsible for Charles's efforts."

"What about your cousin?"

"My c-cousin?"

"Have you so many you cannot keep track of them?" he teased, resuming their stroll. "I was referring to Miss Lindquist."

"Sh-she has d-done what she can, b-but . . ."

"I am aware that her situation is similar to yours. And that Lady Padbury does not esteem Miss Lindquist as she should."

"N-no, she d-does not."

Uncertain whether Karla's stammering was because she was upset about her cousin's situation, or because she suddenly realized that no one else was nearby and was uncomfortable being alone with him, Robert resolved to change the topic. After a few more questions. "I don't believe you said whether or not you wish me to speak to your stepmother."

"I am n-not s-sure that would be wise, Elston."

"Oh? Why not?"

"The viscountess b-believes you are interested in Lydia—"

"I have absolutely no interest in your half-sister," he averred. "Unless her actions affect you."

"I still do n-not think it would be wise. But I thank you for your willingness to stand my champion in this."

"If you change your mind, let me know." He grinned. "I am quite willing to show your stepmother the error of her ways."

"Th-thank you."

"Now, tell me about your costume for the masquerade. Because of another engagement, I won't be there until late, but I hope you will save one of the dances after supper for me."

"I will be dressed as a lady of the last century. I found some of my mother's gowns in the attic and want to honor her memory by wearing one."

"She would be honored, and very happy, to know her daughter esteems her so highly."

Stopping again, she glanced up at him. "Do you really think so?"

"Most assuredly. What mother would not?"

"Lydia and the viscountess think I am stupidly sentimental."

"I do not." Robert vented his renewed anger at Lady Padbury with a silent string of curses. Karla, apparently reassured, resumed walking.

Several minutes passed before he felt sufficiently in control of his emotions to ask, his voice light and teasing, "Are you going to tell me what color your costume is?"

"It is blue. Light blue."

"And will you save me a dance?"

Karla's smile rivaled the sun for brilliance. "Of course. Which one would you like?"

"Shall we say the first minuet after supper?"

"The first minuet," she affirmed with a nod.

"And the first waltz."

"I—"

"I know you have not yet received permission to dance it, but I will enjoy sitting it out with you." And he would. Far more than he would enjoy dancing it with any other woman.

Chapter Thirteen

$\mathcal{F}$riday morning the Lanes had several callers. Karla's stepmother did not enjoy the visits. The first to arrive, Lady Blackburn, took the viscountess to task for denying Karla to her—and others—the previous day. Her Grace of Greenwich did the same when she and Lady Christina called. As did the Marchioness of Kesteven. Needless to say, the viscountess was not pleased to have her lies exposed to three ladies of such high rank. During luncheon, she made certain her stepdaughter was aware of her displeasure.

Karla, who had begun the day by berating herself for not confessing her deception to Elston during their drive yesterday, was in rather low spirits before the meal. She bore her stepmother's verbal barbs with as much fortitude as she could muster, but she had to bite her lip repeatedly to prevent herself from responding. Telling the viscountess that she was reaping the consequences of the lies she had sown would only make the situation worse. And it was difficult enough already.

After her stepmother's vicious tongue-lashing, Karla was eager to escape the house, even if the only means of doing so was to pay calls with the viscountess and Lydia. At least there would be other people, and different topics of conversation. Karla was pleased that their first visit was to Castleton House. Her stepmother's efforts to curry Lady Julia's favor were rather pathetic, and usually unsuccessful, but Karla always enjoyed talking with Beth. The American girl seemed hopeful that she had survived the worst of the rumor campaign, thanks to Weymouth, Elston, and Dunnley. She spoke fondly of all three men, but Karla believed (or, perhaps, hoped) that Beth had given her heart to the earl. After being introduced to Lady Sefton, who spoke fondly of the late viscountess, Karla spent several minutes in conversation with her.

Friday evening the *beau monde* flocked to the Duchess of St. Ives's masquerade. Karla was pleased with her costume—and delighted to see Lady Julia similarly, if a bit more elaborately, attired in a plum-colored gown. By the time the Earl of Blackburn led Karla onto the floor for the opening minuet, many of her dances had been bespoken. Lydia, too, had promised several and, for once, did not seem to begrudge her half-sister's greater popularity. The same, however, could not be said for the viscountess, despite the fact that a number of the gentlemen who requested dances with Karla also asked Lydia to stand up with them.

Blackburn, garbed as an Elizabethan courtier, looked even more distinguished than usual. Karla was a bit surprised that the serious, rather somber earl was in costume, especially since many of the men merely wore dominoes over their usual evening attire, and she could not help but wonder if he had a more lighthearted side she had never seen. She wondered, too, if he truly wanted to dance with her or if he asked only to please his mother. But those were not the kind of things a young lady could ask a gentleman, so she contented herself with the pleasure of his company—he was an excellent dancer—during the minuet. Perhaps she would learn the answers to her questions before the end of the Season.

As they promenaded after the dance, Karla pointed out a man whose attire was quite similar to the earl's. "Do you see the man, standing near Beth Castleton, whose costume is almost identical to yours?"

He looked in the direction she indicated, where several clusters of people stood chatting, then shook his head. "I don't see Miss Castleton, and I am not certain I would recognize her if I did. I have never met her."

"Would you like to? I will gladly introduce you." She smiled up at him. "Especially after your gallant support of her at Almack's two nights ago."

"I would be pleased to meet your friend, but I cannot

take credit for what happened at Almack's. That was mostly Mother's doing."

With a gentle tug on his arm, Karla steered him toward the group. "Beth is dressed as Euterpe, in a white Grecian robe with musical notes embroidered on it. She is standing next to Dunnley."

"The muse of music is an appropriate identity for her. I heard she dazzled the *ton* at Mrs. Broughton's musicale." Then, a moment later, "Ah, I see my fellow courtier now. That is Fairfax."

"Is it?" Karla peered at the duke, with whom she had danced at Lady Throckmorton's ball. "I did not recognize him." Lowering her voice, she confided, "I have been able to identify only a few people this evening."

"You have been in Town less than a fortnight, Karla. It would be surprising if you did recognize many of the guests." With colorful descriptions of their attire, Blackburn directed her attention to several people—mostly men—and named them.

A buxom blonde who almost overflowed the bodice of her shepherdess costume shoved past them, nearly knocking Karla over. With unexpected agility, the earl grasped her arms and pulled her close, steadying her. "Are you all right?"

Warmed by his concern—or, perhaps, by the near embrace—she stepped back and nodded. "Yes, thanks to you. Who was that?"

Blackburn studied the woman, who was talking to two older ladies standing nearby. "I don't know. She looks familiar, but I am not certain of her identity." Tucking Karla's hand in the crook of his arm, he resumed their stroll.

As they approached the group around Beth, Dunnley whispered something to her. After greetings were exchanged and introductions performed, the viscount said, "You look lovely, Miss Lane. I hope you have not promised all your dances?"

Delighted by the compliment and amazed that he thought her so popular, Karla smiled. "Thank you, my lord. I still have several sets unclaimed."

"The first waltz, perhaps?"

"I . . . I have not received permission to waltz." *Nor a voucher to Almack's.*

"I enjoy your company, dancing or not."

Dunnley's compliments could turn a girl's head. "You are very kind, my lord."

"May I also have the first country dance after supper?"

"I already claimed that one," Blackburn declared.

"The second one, then?" the viscount queried.

"I will look forward to it." Karla dipped a curtsy.

As Dunnley asked the earl his impression of a debate yesterday in Lords, she moved closer to Beth. "You look lovely. How are you this evening? No rumors swirling tonight, I hope."

"None that I know of." The American girl's smile was rather strained.

"Good." Inching closer, Karla murmured, "I have not seen Weymouth and Elston. Are they in costume? I expected one of them would be your escort tonight."

"They will be wearing unusual attire when they arrive, but that won't be until later. They are attending a regimental celebration."

Karla gaped at her friend. "They are in the army?"

"They served in the Queen's Light Dragoons for four or five years, but resigned their commissions in 'eleven, after both were injured."

"I did not know. 'Tis unusual for a peer's heir." Particularly for Elston, since he was his father's only son. Weymouth had a younger brother, although Karla had not met him since he preferred life in the country.

"It is, but they both felt strongly about serving, although for different reasons."

There were times—and this was one of them—when Karla wanted to shake her reticent, more knowledgeable friend. "They were not seriously injured, I hope?"

"I don't know, but I wouldn't think so. Both look hale and healthy to me," Beth quipped.

"Indeed they do."

Blackburn's appearance at Karla's side signaled the end of the interlude. She hugged her friend and whispered, "Everything will be fine tonight," then took his arm and allowed him to lead her back to her stepmother's—and his mother's—side.

Robert stood in front of the cheval glass, feeling quite unlike himself in his dress uniform. Even on the Peninsula, he had seldom worn it; he'd been out scouting enemy positions and meeting with Spanish guerrillas while his comrades-in-arms threw impromptu balls. Behind him, Higgins grumbled about the fit of his uniform, which was quite snug around the waist. When the knocker sounded, Robert placed his shako on his dark curls and left the room. Higgins, still muttering, trailed in his wake.

"Good evening, George." A quick glance showed that his friend's uniform fit as well as Robert's did.

"Good evening, Robert. Higgins." A chagrined expression on his face, the earl confessed, "I did not realize you were joining us tonight, Sergeant."

The erstwhile batman beamed at the use of his rank, which he had earned for carrying Weymouth and several other officers off the field in the midst of dense artillery fire. "O' course I am. Old Doc MacInnes patched the pair of ye up often enough to deserve my thanks."

"Yes, he does. But I didn't . . . I wasn't . . ." George raked a hand through his hair. "Thinking Elston would be my only passenger, I brought my curricle."

"As long as ye didn't bring your tiger, there's a seat for me. Or I can walk."

"I would be honored to have you as my ceremonial tiger this evening, Higgins."

"Ceremonial tiger. Sounds pretty naffy, don't it, Major?"

Since he and George had held the same rank, Robert did not realize Higgins was addressing him until both his companions turned to look at him. "It does, indeed." Pondering his uncharacteristic lapse of attention, Robert followed his companions outside. *Now Karla and Miss Lindquist were invading his thoughts during daylight hours!*

Despite his earlier request, Karla was surprised when Dunnley bowed before her promptly after the first waltz was announced. Some of her amazement must have shown on her face, for he smiled and asked, "Did you forget you promised me this dance, Miss Lane?"

Forget she'd agreed to sit out the waltz with one of the leaders of Society? Karla smiled at the impossibility of any young lady so easily dismissing the handsome, charming, extremely eligible viscount. "No, my lord, I did not forget. But . . ."

"But?" His gray eyes were kind, and clearly indicated interest in her response.

"But I find it hard to believe that you wish to sit out this waltz with me when you could dance it with any number of other ladies."

She could not interpret the expression that flashed across his face. Nor did his tone hint at his feelings. "Shall we stroll around the ballroom and watch the dancers?"

With a nod, Karla accepted both his invitation and his proffered arm.

When they were out of earshot of her stepmother and Lydia, he resumed their conversation. "I chose to sit out this waltz with you because I enjoy your company."

"Thank you, Dunnley. I enjoy yours, too."

He studied her for a long moment. "I hope I will not offend you with a bit of plain speaking. Your stepmother's attitude toward you does not *in any way* reflect Society's."

Feeling fiery color rise to her face, Karla directed her gaze at the floor.

"From all I have seen and heard, Miss Lane, you are well liked and respected by the *ton*. Your stepmother, however, is not. Mostly because of her disparaging actions and her belittlement of you."

This was plain speaking, indeed! How could she possibly respond to such statements?

Fortunately, the viscount did not require a reply. "You have earned my admiration and respect, and that of many other people, for the way you have risen above Lady Padbury's attempts to demean you."

"Thank you, my lord. You are very kind. . . ."

His smile rueful, he shook his head. "I wish I had been kind enough to say that without putting you to the blush."

"What," Karla said with feigned insouciance, "is a blush or two among friends?"

"I am honored to be counted among your friends, Miss Lane. And to count you among mine."

He adroitly changed the topic and soon had her at ease again. The time passed so quickly that she was startled when the waltz ended and other couples joined the promenade. Glancing around, she saw Beth and Fairfax strolling some distance ahead.

A few moments later, the trouble began.

*   *   *

An hour into the celebration, Robert had spoken with
all the men who had served under him, wished Dr. MacInnes well in his retirement, and was more than ready to
leave. The dinner, however, was far from over. Seated at
one end of a long table next to a nearly deaf colonel, and
thoroughly bored by the prolonged prosing of the windbag
currently at the podium, Robert leaned back in his chair
and allowed his attention to drift.

He wondered if George, who was at the next table, was
also suffering from boredom. Wondered, too, if he would
recognize Karla when he got to St. Ives House. If he ever
got there. *Had the* ton *greeted Beth kindly on her first appearance in Society after the debacle at Almack's? Was Lady
Padbury treating her stepdaughter well today?*

After yesterday's revelations, Robert's concern about the
latter was growing by leaps and bounds. He had stopped
at Blackburn House and discussed the matter with the
countess, but there was little that either of them could do.
Unless he married Karla.

The idea held great appeal. Not only would it free her
from her stepmother's tyranny, it should also end his
dreams, replacing them with a reality that might—or might
not—match his fantasies. But although his feelings for
Karla were much stronger, in every way, than for any of
the other young ladies, Robert was not quite ready to make
his decision. For one thing, her stammering yesterday might
be an indication that she was not comfortable alone with
him. She had never stuttered during any of their previous
conversations, but those had occurred when other people
were nearby.

Did she enjoy his company as much as he enjoyed hers?
She had been happy to resume their friendship, but perhaps
that was all she was willing to grant him. And he wanted
so much more.

Karla saw Beth smile at Mrs. Kincaid, then slip her hand
from Fairfax's arm and turn to confront the buxom blond
shepherdess who had nearly knocked Karla down earlier.
And it was clearly a confrontation, not a pleasant
conversation.

Still watching her friend, Karla whispered, "Dunnley, I

think the woman standing next to Mrs. Kincaid said something that upset Beth."

As the viscount searched for the pair, Beth pulled off her half mask and spoke to the blonde. A few moments later, the duke removed his mask. Dunnley muttered, "Dear God," and increased their pace. They reached the group just as Mrs. Kincaid placed a hand on the shepherdess's arm and said, "I told you it wasn't true, Arabella, but you refused to listen."

Beth stiffened. "Lady Arabella Smalley, perhaps? I can well believe you wish to discredit me. After all, I can expose your criminal actions—and your cousin's—to the full view of Society. And a court of law."

Dunnley forged a path to American girl's side, then placed his free hand at the small of her back, silently offering his support. Karla stood beside him, her hand still tucked in the crook of his arm, determined to help her friend in any way she could.

The blonde paled at the accusation but blustered on. "Criminal? You must be mistaken. I have done nothing wrong."

Beth arced an eyebrow. "You do not consider forgery, three abductions, and attempted murder wrongful acts? I daresay most people would disagree with you."

Karla had no idea what her friend was referring to. Judging from the murmurs of the gathering crowd, no one else did, either. Except Dunnley, who whispered something to Beth.

A few moments later, Beth enlightened them all. Lady Arabella and a cousin had concocted a plan to force Weymouth to marry her. The scheme began in early February with the kidnapping of the earl's niece—and of Beth when she tried to save the child. Less than a week later, the earl, too, was abducted. With the help of two servants, Beth foiled the plot and rescued both Winterbrooks, but was shot in the shoulder. After they escaped, Beth, Weymouth, his niece, and the servants stopped at a hunting lodge belonging to Elston so Beth's wound could be treated. The marquess, who was in residence when they arrived, traveled back to England with them and, thus, could refute the lies about Beth and Weymouth that Lady Arabella had been spreading.

Karla thought Beth deserved a medal for her courageous
and altruistic deeds. The *ton*, however, ignored the fact that
she had saved two lives. After the shocking revelation that
she had been kidnapped, then traveled hundreds of miles
in the company of two men with only a maid for chaperone,
Beth teetered on the brink of social ruin, her position even
more precarious than before. But Lady Arabella had fallen
over the precipice by publicly admitting her crimes. She
was escorted from the ballroom, kicking and screaming, by
one of the guests, who was a magistrate, and the Duke of
St. Ives.

After her departure, Fairfax turned to Beth and bowed
over her hand. In a voice that overrode the crowd's shouted
queries and carried to the farthest corners of the ballroom,
he asked, "Miss Castleton, may I have the privilege of
dancing with the most honest and honorable lady in all
of England?"

Karla was not surprised her friend chose to dance instead
of answer questions. As the musicians played the opening
bars of another waltz, Fairfax led Beth to the center of
the floor, where they danced alone. Twirling his partner in
elongated circles, the duke moved slowly but inexorably
toward the door. Watching them, Karla suddenly realized
that her partner was Beth's escort and needed to be at the
portal when the music ended. Karla wanted to be there,
too, to support her friend.

Apparently Dunnley experienced the same revelation.
"Thank you for the dance, Miss Lane, but I must leave."
Tucking her hand in the crook of his arm, he started for
the door, scanning the room for her stepmother.

"Do not worry about me, my lord. I will find my way
back to my stepmother or Lady Blackburn after I say good-
bye to Beth."

He glanced down at her. "Are you certain?"

"Yes. I won't get lost," Karla quipped, hoping to ease
his strained expression, which she knew was due to worry
about Beth.

A smile quirked his lips but did not reach his eyes. "You
are well aware that is not what I meant."

"Yes, I am, but it is true nonetheless. I want to support
Beth, and I can find my way back to my stepmother's
side unaided."

Their arrival at the doorway, where Beth was apologizing to Her Grace of St. Ives, prevented Dunnley from arguing further. As the duchess admonished Beth to leave before the crowd descended on her, Karla stepped forward and hugged her friend.

"Beth, I am so sorry you had to go through that . . . ordeal two months ago, and to relive it tonight."

"Thank you, Karla. You are a wonderful friend."

"I will come see you tomorrow, if I can."

"You are always welcome, Miss Lane," Lady Julia said. Beth curtsied again to the duchess. Dunnley, who had been talking quietly with Fairfax, offered one arm to Beth, the other to her great-aunt, then escorted the Castleton ladies from the ballroom.

Her heart aching for her friend, Karla watched them leave. Turning to make her way back to her stepmother or Lady Blackburn, she encountered a veritable wall of people, many of whom were still shouting questions at Beth. Thankful that her friend had escaped in the nick of time, Karla was about to take refuge with the duchess when Fairfax bowed in front of her.

"Miss Lane, may I escort you back to your stepmother?"

The duke was only of average height, and rather slender, but Karla appreciated the kindness—or good manners—behind his offer. "Thank you, Your Grace." As he forged a path through the crowd, she praised his gallantry. "It was wonderful of you to honor Beth as you did."

"Such courage and honesty should be rewarded."

"I agree, but I doubt the *ton* will. I fear Beth will again be the subject of gossip."

"That is inevitable. But for Miss Castleton's sake, I hope it dies quickly."

"A nine days' wonder, Your Grace?" Karla shuddered at the thought of being the subject of Society's speculations for nine very long days.

"Perhaps even less, if someone does something quite outrageous."

"Hmm." Karla peered up at him through her lashes. "Do you know of any young ladies on the verge of eloping with a groom or footman? If so, I will do my best to persuade them to leave for Gretna Green. Soon."

A moment later, they reached the viscountess, Lydia, and

Lady Blackburn. After greeting all three women, the duke bowed over Karla's hand. "I hope you will save a set for me later this evening, Miss Lane."

"I would be honored to dance with you, Your Grace. Thank you for your gallantry, and your kindness."

"It was my pleasure." Then, after a moment's pause, "I daresay you already have a partner for the supper dance. Perhaps the first set afterward?"

"I have not promised the supper dance, but you may have the first set after supper. Unless it is a country dance," she amended, remembering Blackburn's claim.

"Might I be your supper partner, Miss Lane?"

The duke's diffidence was unexpected, especially after his stalwart championship of Beth. "I would be honored, Your Grace."

Bestowing a boyishly charming smile upon her, he bowed again and departed. As soon as he was out of earshot, Lady Blackburn leaned close to Karla and whispered, "Geoffrey didn't ask you for the supper dance?"

"No, my lady. He asked for the first country dance after supper."

The countess's frown indicated that was not the answer she expected, but before she could reply, the viscountess grabbed her stepdaughter's arm.

"Idiot!" she hissed. "Are you trying to ruin yourself?"

Bewildered by her stepmother's ire, Karla countered with a question. "How could talking with the Duke of Fairfax and granting him the supper dance ruin me?"

"I am not talking about Fairfax!" The viscountess's grip tightened; Karla knew her arm would sport a bruise tomorrow. "How could you be so stupid as to take part in that Castleton chit's fall from grace?"

"First of all, I don't believe Beth fell from grace this evening. And—"

"Of course she did! She ruined herself past redemption by admitting she traveled hundreds of miles in the company of two men who aren't related to her."

"With a maid as chaperone," Karla pointed out.

"A maid isn't a proper chaperone. And—"

"Is Beth to be blamed because her abductors failed to take her great-aunt?" Sarcasm edged Karla's voice. "I can-

not believe anyone will fault her for doing her best to satisfy the conventions under such impossible circumstances.''

"Then you are a bigger fool than I thought!"

"You are the fool, Hortense.'' Lady Blackburn grasped
the viscountess's arm and squeezed—hard enough that she
released her stepdaughter's arm. "Karla's loyalty to her
friend should be commended. And her involvement could
not be avoided. She was promenading with Dunnley, who
is Beth's escort tonight.''

"Caroline didn't have to make a spectacle of herself by
hugging the chit!''

"Keep your voice down,'' the countess admonished.
"You are the one creating a spectacle.''

Glancing around, Karla realized the argument had drawn
attention. "We will discuss this later,'' her stepmother
hissed. Karla did not know if it was a threat or a promise,
but either way, it was sure to be unpleasant.

Before the applause from the last speech had died,
George appeared at Robert's side. "Let's get out of here.''

More than ready to depart, Robert stood. With haste and
less than their usual grace, they said their good-byes and
took their leave.

Observing George as he guided his curricle through the
crowded streets of Mayfair, Robert wondered if his friend
had experienced an epiphany during dinner. The earl's blue
eyes gleamed as if lit by a fire in his soul. Perhaps a question or two would reveal the reason—and explain his
friend's hurry.

"Did you enjoy the dinner?''

George shrugged. "It was pleasant enough, but far too
long. Especially the speeches. How did such prosing palav-
erers ever accomplish anything?''

"The same thought crossed my mind, about an hour into
the celebration.'' A few moments later, Robert prodded,
"Why were you in such a rush to leave?''

His friend shot him an incredulous glance. "To attend
the masquerade.''

"George, George,'' Robert chided, shaking his head in
feigned disbelief. "You might fool some people with that
answer, but not me. Now, why the haste? Are you worried

about Beth's reception by the *ton* after the debacle at Almack's?"

"A bit, although I think the worst of the scandal is past."

"If you are only a bit concerned, then why are you in such a hurry?"

George hunched his shoulders, ducking his head slightly. "There is something I need to tell Beth," he mumbled.

Had George finally realized he loved Beth? "Oh? Something you forgot to tell her this afternoon?" Robert didn't know if his friend had called at Castleton House this afternoon, but it was more likely than not.

"No. Something I didn't realize until later that I need to tell her."

Wonderful! Delighted for his friends and the joyful future awaiting them, Robert grinned. "So, you finally realized you love her?"

George's eyes slewed to his. "You knew?"

"I, my friend, knew you were falling in love with her before we left Stranraer."

"Why didn't you say something?"

"Would you have believed me?" Robert crossed his arms over his chest. "No. You would have told me all you felt for her was gratitude. Or friendship." Relenting a bit, he added, "She loves you, too."

"I realized that as well."

"Tell her and propose again. Then the two of you will live happily ever after." Robert stifled a sigh, wondering if he would be as fortunate.

Robert and George arrived at St. Ives House shortly after midnight. The receiving line had long since dispersed, so they stood side by side in the ballroom doorway and looked for their hostess. The duchess spotted them and hurried toward them as fast as her rheumatic knees would allow. When they met her near the edge of the dance floor, she extended a hand to George and spoke before they could greet her.

"Weymouth, you should have been here earlier."

George bowed. "I regret that I had a previous commitment, Your Grace."

"As did I." Robert captured the duchess's ring-bedecked hand and made his obeisance.

"I don't mean the ball. You should have been here to support Miss Castleton when she confronted Lady Arabella."

George swore. Robert offered his arm to their hostess. "Allow us to escort you to a seat, Your Grace. Then you can tell us what happened."

When they were seated in a quiet alcove with the diminutive duchess between them, George requested, "Please tell us what happened, Your Grace."

The duchess did not know how it had begun—Fairfax or Mrs. Kincaid could tell them that, she said—but she rejoiced in the ending: Beth honored by Fairfax after Arabella was carried off by Sir Thomas Hodge to be charged for her crimes.

George propped his elbows on his thighs and covered his face with his hands. "Why did she do it? Castleton, my brother, and I chose not to prosecute Arabella and her cousin because we feared a public recounting of the events would damage Beth's reputation. Why—"

The duchess poked his arm with a bony finger. "What else was she to do, Weymouth? Stand there and allow the Smalley chit to spew her lies?"

"No, but—"

"There are times when one cannot back down, nor stand silent. This was one of them."

Robert agreed. Concern for his friends compelled his next question, which was, he suspected, what George really wanted to know. "How badly has Miss Castleton's confession damaged her reputation?"

The duchess thought for several moments before replying. "I don't know. Beth made it clear that Weymouth's behavior was honorable, and that he offered for her but she declined. There may be some high sticklers who look down on her for traveling such a distance with two men, and staying at inns with only a maid for chaperone, but what else could the dear girl have done?"

She stood. "Come, you will want to talk with Fairfax and Mrs. Kincaid."

When they stepped out of the alcove, they were greeted by a swarm of people, all of whom, it seemed, were shouting questions at George. He sighed and crossed his arms over his chest, waiting for a chance to speak. Robert, standing beside him, did the same, determined to do everything in his power to help his friends.

When the crowd quieted, George explained Arabella's scheme and its consequences. Robert searched the crowd for Fairfax and Mrs. Kincaid. And for Karla. The duke and Karla appeared to be working their way through the throng to a spot between Robert and George and the doorway.

After an eloquent plea asking the *ton* to consider how they would want their daughters and sisters to behave if they found themselves in the same situation as Beth, George muttered, "I favor a hasty retreat. Preferably with Fairfax. What say you?"

"Lead on, O Fearless One. Fairfax and Miss Lane are about halfway between here and the door. The duchess and her son are with them."

With military precision, Robert and George turned on their heels and strode toward the foursome. A quintet now, with the addition of a man in the flowing robes of an Eastern prince. Recognizing the man, Robert corrected himself: not an Eastern prince, but the Persian ambassador, Farhad Booeshaghi.

After taking leave of their host and hostess, Robert turned to Karla. "I hope you will forgive me for not staying to claim the dances I requested, but—"

"You need not beg forgiveness, Elston. Weymouth needs your support tonight."

"May I call on you tomorrow?"

Her smile rivaled the sun. "You are always welcome at Padbury House."

As he bowed over her hand, Robert heard the ambassador tell George, "Miss Castleton has the heart of a lion. And Miss Lane, the fierceness of a lioness guarding her cubs."

Karla blushed. Robert arced an inquiring eyebrow, but the crowd, once again shouting questions, was almost upon them. "Until tomorrow," he murmured. Then, after another bow to the duchess, he, George, and Fairfax departed.

The happily-ever-after ending Robert envisioned for his friends had not yet been achieved. But it began to seem possible he might attain one himself.

Chapter Fourteen

Well before the church bells chimed noon on Saturday, Karla longed for the day to end. Last night after the ball, her stepmother had been too tired to rake her over the coals, but the viscountess had more than made up for it this morning. According to her stepmother, Karla was a stupid idiot with more hair than wit whose behavior was foolish beyond permission. There had been more, of course—the viscountess's harangue had gone on for half an hour—but that was the essence of it. Karla had battled tears through most of it, determined not to allow her stepmother that victory, but it was a near run thing. They had streamed down her face as she'd fled the viscountess's chamber.

After indulging in a good, long cry and bathing her eyes, Karla wrote a note to Lady Blackburn, asking her mentor's opinion of her behavior last night, then went downstairs to the morning room. A few minutes later, the butler appeared in the doorway.

"Miss Karla, are you at home to the Duchess of Greenwich and Lady Christina?"

"Of course, Harris. I am always happy to see them."

"Will you receive them here or in the drawing room?"

Karla glanced quickly around the room, which was neat as a pin. Although less formal than the drawing room, it was her favorite of all the salons. "Here, please."

With a nod and a "Very good, miss" he departed, returning a few moments later with her visitors.

As soon as greetings were exchanged and her guests were seated, Tina asked, "Did you know anything about Beth being kidnapped and shot and . . . all of that?"

"No. I doubt anyone there knew, other than Beth, Lady Arabella, Lady Julia, and, perhaps, Dunnley."

"But—"

"Imagine how horrible it must have been for Beth to suffer such an ordeal." Karla shuddered at the thought. "To confess it to the *ton* requires even more courage. Certainly more than I have."

"More than most young ladies possess," the duchess said, "since doing so might destroy their reputations. But you do not give yourself enough credit, Miss Lane. I think, in the same circumstances, you would have behaved just as Miss Castleton did."

Karla thought for several moments before replying. "I would have tried to rescue the little girl. And I would have agreed to help Weymouth. I would have traveled back to London with him, too, probably even without a maid to serve as a chaperone, since the only other choice would have been waiting in Scotland while a letter was sent to my family and they came to get me. But to confront Lady Arabella at the ball? No. I don't believe I could have done that."

The duchess shook her head but did not dispute Karla's assessment. Possibly because Harris appeared in the doorway. "Miss Karla, the Marchioness of Kesteven and her daughters have called."

"Please show them in."

Deborah and the marchioness proclaimed their delight in finding Karla at home, and Tina and the duchess present. Diana, however, appeared to wish she were somewhere else. Karla could not help but wonder why Deborah's twin had come.

Beth's ordeal—both in Scotland and at the ball—was discussed at length, although Diana contributed little. In an attempt to draw her into the conversation, Karla asked the twins, "If you had been in Beth's situation, would you have confronted Lady Arabella at the ball?"

"I don't know," Deborah said. "I thought about it last night, but I am not sure I have the courage for such a public confrontation."

"I would never have gotten myself into such a situation," Diana declared.

Karla thought Diana was far more likely to cause a scandal than her twin.

"You would not have rescued the little girl?" Tina's tone expressed disbelief that anyone could be so unfeeling.

"Perhaps," Diana shrugged. "If I knew the child, I might have."

The marchioness looked askance at her daughter. "Lord David Winterbrook must be grateful that it was Beth Castleton, not you, who saw his daughter kidnapped."

"If she hadn't rescued the child, she would not be embroiled in a scandal."

All five ladies gaped at Diana. The duchess was the first to recover her voice. "Miss Castleton could not have known that her good deed would have such unfortunate consequences. But even if she had, I don't believe she would have acted differently."

Karla, Tina, Deborah, and Lady Kesteven nodded their agreement.

"If Lady Arabella was so determined to marry Weymouth that she would resort to kidnapping, she might well have circulated lying gossip about Beth anyway," Karla pointed out.

"Very true, Miss Lane," the duchess said. "He is seen in her company more often than any other young lady's."

"It might be his way of expressing gratitude for her assistance," Diana argued.

"Possibly," the duchess allowed, "but I do not think so."

"Nor do I," the marchioness declared.

Believing, as she did, that the earl had captured Beth's heart, Karla hoped the older ladies were correct.

"Beth Castleton is seen as often in Lord Dunnley's company. And the Marquess of Elston has been almost constantly at her side this week."

Lud, was Diana always so argumentative? "Elston is the only person, other than Beth and Weymouth, who can refute the gossip. As an honorable man, he would not remain silent while his friends are being slandered."

To forestall the argument she imagined was forming on Diana's lips, Karla added, "Although often in Beth's company this week, Elston has favored other young ladies with his attention, including your sister."

"And you," Tina and Deborah said, almost in chorus.

"Certainly Elston and Dunnley have supported Miss Castleton this week," the duchess agreed. "And Dunnley has escorted her and Lady Julia to several social events this

Season. My point, Lady Diana, was not that Beth Castleton has demonstrated a partiality for Weymouth's company, but that he has shown one for hers."

"Just as well, since he will have to marry her."

Diana's spiteful remark brought Lady Kesteven to her feet. "It is past time for us to leave." She and Deborah wore strained smiles as they made their adieus, but Diana showed no remorse.

Silence reigned for several moments after the Woodhurst ladies departed. Not surprisingly, it was Tina who broke it. "Well, that was certainly interesting. I wonder if Diana would argue that the sky is not blue."

"Tina!" the duchess admonished.

"I am sorry. That must have sounded as catty as Diana's last comment, which was not my intent. I just find it hard to believe that two girls identical in appearance have such different personalities."

"I, too, find it difficult to credit," Karla admitted.

"That is often the case with twins—identical appearances but personalities as different as night and day." The duchess stood, then turned to her daughter. "It is time we were leaving, too."

Karla linked her arm with Tina's and escorted the Fairchild ladies out. As the duchess adjusted her bonnet in front of the mirror, a packet on a silver salver on the table caught her eye. "It appears you have had other callers this morning, Miss Lane."

Karla darted a questioning glance at the butler. "Lady Sefton's footman delivered it, Miss Karla," Harris explained, "with her ladyship's compliments."

"Your voucher! I just know it is your voucher." Tina bounced on her toes, as excited as a child on Christmas morning. "Oh, do open it."

"Please forgive my daughter's unladylike curiosity, Miss Lane. And for my sake"— smiling wryly, the duchess settled gracefully onto a chair—"please satisfy it. Otherwise Tina will be in a fidget all afternoon."

Returning the duchess's smile, Karla picked up the packet, then sat beside her. Although she hoped Tina's prediction was correct, Karla thought it unlikely. Surely vouchers would be sent to the viscountess, not to her.

When she opened the missive, the coveted tickets fell

into her lap. Visions of waltzing with Elston danced in her head as she began reading Lady Sefton's note.

"Oh, no!" The images in Karla's head now were of acrimony and discord.

The duchess's gloved hand covered hers. "What is wrong, my dear?"

Wordlessly, Karla smoothed out the crumpled letter and handed it to the duchess, who read it quickly. Then, with an arm around Karla's shoulders, Her Grace rose, bringing Karla to her feet. "Let's go back to the morning room and discuss this. Perhaps I can help."

Karla mustered a wobbly smile. "Thank you, Your Grace. I appreciate your kind offer, but this is a battle I must fight myself."

Robert was restless all morning. He wandered from room to room, unable to find a task that could hold his interest. Reaching the music room, he picked up his viola, hoping he could lose himself in music as he waited to hear the result of George's early-morning visit at Castleton House, and for afternoon, when he himself had several calls planned. The one to Karla was the most important, but Robert would call on Lady Deborah and Harriett Broughton, too. Only a fool put all his eggs in one basket.

Although he was not ready to propose, as George intended, Robert wanted to ask Karla to drive with him in the park this afternoon. If she seemed more comfortable in his company than she had been on Thursday, then he would find out who the Lanes' guardian was. Lady Blackburn probably knew, but Robert was not certain he wanted her to know his intentions—and she was far too astute not to realize the import of such a question. Her son might know, but asking Charles would be better. Robert had not yet determined if Blackburn's attentions to Karla were those of a suitor or of a kindhearted neighbor.

By one o'clock, Robert could wait no longer. Closing the book he'd been attempting to read, he stood. "Aunt Livvy, I am going to Padbury House to pay a call on Miss Lane, then on several other young ladies. Would you like to come with me?"

She glanced at the clock, then back at him. "A bit early for visiting, isn't it?"

"Perhaps, but Miss Lane will not object."

"Her stepmother might."

Robert shook his head. "She didn't when I called at this time a few days ago."

"I met the Lanes last night. Lady Blackburn introduced them to me." Livvy had attended the St. Ives with Blackburn and the countess. Robert was supposed to escort his aunt home, but he had forgotten all about her after the duchess told George and him about Beth's confrontation with Lady Arabella. He had apologized profusely at breakfast this morning, feeling like the veriest cad, and was heartened when Livvy said he had done the right thing by supporting, and leaving with, Weymouth.

"Do you wish to pursue the acquaintance?" Although he wanted to know his aunt's impression of the Lanes, Robert was not yet ready to reveal his interest in Karla. Not even to his beloved aunt.

"Miss Lane—Karolina Lane—is the only one worth knowing, and she cannot wish to further her acquaintance with an old spinster."

"You give yourself too little credit. And Miss Lane as well, I think."

"Perhaps." Livvy shrugged. "She seems rather reserved, yet she was the only young lady to bid Miss Castleton farewell last night. Hugged her, in fact. Miss Lane must have known that her stepmother—such an irritating, encroaching woman!—would not like it, but that did not stop her from supporting her friend."

"Karla's loyalty to her friends cannot be questioned." Robert felt certain that Karla's public show of support had earned a scold from her stepmother. No doubt the atmosphere at Padbury House was a bit strained today.

"If I cannot entice you to come with me, darling Livvy, I would ask a favor. If Weymouth calls, would you please receive him and find out his news?" Smiling, he added, "George finally realized last night during the dinner that he loves Beth. He intended to call at Castleton House this morning and offer her his hand and heart."

"Of course I will receive him, dear. I hope his news is good, they are well suited."

"I agree." Bending, Robert kissed his aunt's cheek. "I will be back before dinner."

After donning his hat and gloves, he picked up his cane and headed out the door, only to turn back on the threshold. "Baxter, if Lord Weymouth calls, Lady Lavinia will receive him. Even if he asks for me, show him into the drawing room."

The butler nodded. "Yes, my lord. Is Lady Lavinia at home to other callers?"

"You will have to ask her. My instructions only included Weymouth."

"Very good, my lord."

The drive from Upper Brook Street to Curzon Street was a short one, but with every turn of the curricle's wheels, Robert's trepidation increased. *Would Karla be less nervous in his company today? Had Lady Padbury raised a fuss over Karla's championship of Beth last night?* But his concern did not in any way prepare him for the scene he witnessed at Padbury House.

The moment the butler cracked open the door, Robert could hear Lady Padbury shouting. He pushed against the panel until the opening was wide enough to enter, then strode inside.

"What the devil is going on, Harris?"

The butler scrutinized him for several moments before answering. "Lady Padbury is angry at Miss Karla again." The man's concern for his late master's daughter was almost palpable. "This morning was not so bad, but this . . ."

Apparently there were no words to describe the current infamy. As he teased off his gloves, Robert asked, "Would I be correct in assuming that Karla received this morning's scold for her support of Miss Castleton last night?"

"That is my understanding."

"And this one?" Removing his hat, he dropped his gloves inside and handed it and his cane to the butler. After several seconds passed without a reply, Robert added, "I cannot help Karla if I do not understand the problem."

"Do you intend to help her, Lord Elston?"

"Yes, Harris, I do. And if the matter is beyond my abilities, I will not hesitate to enlist the aid of others."

The butler nodded, clearly relieved. "Miss Karla received a voucher for Almack's this morning. Lady Padbury and Miss Lydia did not."

Robert remembered his conversation with Lady Black-

burn at the Throckmorton ball. At the time, he had thought
her concern exaggerated, but that was clearly not the case.
"Karla is to attend with Lady Blackburn?"

"Yes, my lord. The Duchess of Greenwich seemed willing to help also."

"I will have powerful allies if I cannot resolve the
problem."

As the viscountess's tirade escalated—in volume and in
viciousness—he headed for the stairs. "It will be best if you
do not announce me, Harris."

From the doorway, Robert studied the scene in the drawing room. Lady Padbury stood in the center of the room,
her color high and her features distorted with rage as she
delivered a harangue that would have put a Billingsgate
fishwife to the blush. Lydia was curled up in a chair on the
far side of the room; her posture and expression conveyed
her distress. Ashen-faced, Karla sat on the sofa with her
head bent, unwilling or, perhaps, unable to speak a word
in her defense. When the viscountess moved toward Karla,
Robert stepped into the room.

"What the devil is going on here?"

At the sound of his voice—the brigade major at his
best—Lady Padbury whirled to confront the intruder.
When she recognized him, and realized he had overheard
part of her diatribe, some of the color drained from her
face, leaving her complexion mottled. She stared at him for
several seconds before finding her voice—and an explanation. "Nothing of concern, Elston, just a little family
disagreement."

"I think not, madam," he retorted, striding toward her.
"Your 'little family disagreement' can be heard in the
street."

Most women would have been mortified; the viscountess
didn't even blink. "Why are you here, anyway?"

"I came to take Karla for a drive." He glanced over at
her and smiled, hoping she would agree to his hastily con-
ceived plan to remove her from the house for a while, then
glared down at Lady Padbury. "But I will hear your explanation first."

"I need not explain my behavior to you."

"Perhaps not." Steel edged his voice as he informed her

of her choices. "You can either explain this contretemps to me or I will regale the *ton* with the tale of what I have just seen and heard."

One of the girls gasped. The viscountess flushed, then countered, "No honorable man—"

"My honor compels it. If this is an example of your dealings with your stepdaughter, the *beau monde* should know. It will help them understand your behavior toward her."

Lady Padbury debated the merits of the two courses open to her for several seconds, then flounced to a chair and dropped heavily into it. Although he had not been invited to sit, Robert joined Karla on the sofa.

Surprisingly, it was Lydia who offered an explanation. "Mama is angry because Caroline—er, Karla—received a voucher for Almack's and I did not."

In a far gentler tone than he had used with the viscountess, Robert explained, "You could not have received one, Lydia. The patronesses have a rule that only two ladies of a family can be on the subscription list."

"I did not know that. I daresay Mama doesn't, either."

"Possibly not, but she would have known if she'd had a voucher when she made her come-out, or after her marriage to your father."

Lydia's shoulders slumped when she realized the implications of his statement. If her mother had never been on the patronesses' lists, her own name was unlikely to appear there. She darted a wary glance at her mother, who appeared lost in thought and completely unaware of their conversation, then asked, "It is Mama's fault, not Karla's, isn't it?"

There was no gentlemanly answer to that question. Robert shrugged, then turned to study Karla's downcast face. Her delicate features were taut with strain. "If your stepmother is likely to take her anger at me out on you, I think you should stay with Lady Blackburn for a few days."

"I would like that above all things, but I have not been invited. And the viscountess would never agree."

"We will call at Blackburn House on our way back from the park," he improvised. "The countess will take one look at you and welcome you with open arms. As for your stepmother, I do not intend to give her a choice."

"I will have Mary—no, Collins—pack a bag for you," Lydia offered. "Harris will have it delivered to Blackburn House."

Overwhelmed, or exhausted, Karla capitulated. "Very well."

Lydia jumped up, forcing Robert to his feet, then leaned over to hug her half-sister. "I will fetch your spencer and bonnet." She turned to leave, then stopped and glanced back at him. "May I ask you a question, Lord Elston?"

"You may, Miss Lydia."

"Would you really have told the *ton*?"

"Yes. But I would not have involved you or Karla."

With obvious reluctance, Lydia pointed out, "Mama didn't explain; I did."

"That is why she has no choice but to agree to Karla's visit with Lady Blackburn."

A few minutes later, when Lydia returned with Karla's spencer, bonnet, gloves, and reticule, Lady Padbury still had not moved or spoken. Although he wondered what occupied her thoughts, Robert was far more concerned with removing Karla from the house—and protecting her from other such tirades. Even so, it did not seem right for her to leave without her stepmother's knowledge. Suppressing a sigh, he crossed to the viscountess's chair.

Before he reached it, Lydia said, "My lord, it will be better if I explain to Mama."

"Are you certain you want to take on that task?"

"Yes." Her tone and the accompanying nod were decisive.

"Very well, but if you change your mind and wish my assistance, send a message to Symington House. Lady Blackburn will undoubtedly send a note to your mother. You—"

"I will ask Harris not to give it to her until after I have explained."

Although Lydia had never demonstrated the character or backbone her brother and half-sister possessed, Robert had little choice but to trust her. He hoped he would not regret his decision.

Mortified that Elston had overheard part of her stepmother's tirade, Karla kept her head down as he escorted her downstairs and informed Harris that she would be staying with Lady Blackburn for a few days. Once they were seated in Elston's curricle, it was more difficult—as well as extremely rude—to avoid his gaze. She gathered her courage to face him, but before she was quite ready, he turned to her.

"Does your stepmother often enact such scenes?"

With a small sigh, Karla succumbed to the inevitable. "Too often for my taste."

"Once is too much," he retorted. "How often are you subjected to such vituperation?"

"Here in London or at home?"

His dark brows soared skyward. "There is a difference?"

"Yes. It wasn't as bad at home. At least, not after she banished me upstairs."

He muttered a curse. "How often, Karla?"

"The first time in Town was after I ran out of the modiste's shop. There was a . . . a scene before Beth's singing party, and another yesterday morning after Lady B, the Duchess of Greenwich, and Lady Kesteven took the viscountess to task for denying me their calls on Thursday. Then one this morning for my support of Beth at the ball last night, and the one you interrupted."

"Good God!"

Cringing at his harsh tone, she stammered, "I-I do not believe any were deserved, except the first one."

He rubbed the back of one gloved finger against her cheek. The gentle touch radiated all the way to her toes, curling them in her slippers. "I doubt that one was, either."

He truly was her champion! And he had rescued her this afternoon, just as he'd always done in her dreams. "Thank you, Elston."

"For what?"

"For believing in me. And for rescuing me this afternoon. I . . . I don't know how much longer I could have borne the viscountess's accusations."

"How long had that tirade been going on when I arrived?"

"I am not certain. It seemed like forever, but probably not above an hour."

Scowling, he picked up the reins and, after nodding to his tiger, set the horses in motion. "Do you think your stepmother will agree to let you spend the rest of the Season with Lady Blackburn?"

"No. Much as I might wish it, I know she will not."

"You sound quite certain of that."

"I am. Before we arrived in London, Lady B made the same request. The viscountess flatly refused."

"Hmm" was his only comment as he turned onto South Audley Street. They were halfway down the street before he voiced his next question. "Does Lydia ever defend you?"

"She has a few times, but it only makes her mother angrier. I was surprised she did today. She must be disappointed that she didn't receive a voucher."

"Despite her disappointment, Lydia is intelligent enough to know that you are not to blame. Although I cannot help but wonder if she will give a proper accounting of this afternoon's events to your stepmother."

"Lydia is not always strictly honest, but she was shocked by her mother's ire—and accusations—today."

Elston muttered something that sounded like "And so she should be."

Glancing over at him, Karla wondered how much of the viscountess's harangue he had heard. "I think she will give an accurate explanation."

Her voice wobbled on the last few words, drawing his eyes from the road to hers. "But you are not certain?"

"No, not entirely, but it is to her advantage to be truthful."

"How so?"

"Lydia did not prevent me from leaving. Her mother will be angry unless there was a compelling reason."

A smile twitched at the corner of his mouth. "And I am a compelling reason?"

"Of course. According to the viscountess, eligible gentlemen can do no wrong."

"You cannot possibly believe that!"

"I don't, but I think the viscountess does."

Frowning—and not at the traffic—he asked, "You said your stepmother would blame Lydia, but what about herself? She sat there and didn't say a word when you left. Didn't even seem to realize we were leaving."

"She finds it much easier to blame others than herself."

"And how often have you been blamed for thing were not your fault?"

Karla shifted on the seat, wishing he would discuss something—anything—else. "Often enough."

"How often, Karla?" It sounded as if he spoke through clenched teeth.

"Quite frequently." Blinking back tears, she requested, "Please, may we talk about something, or someone, else?"

He shifted the reins to one hand and laid the other over hers, which were fisted in her lap. "I am sorry, sweetheart. I did not mean to distress you."

The concern and contrition in his voice were almost her undoing. She bit her lip and nodded, unwilling to trust her voice.

"Perhaps it would be best if I took you to Blackburn House now. We can drive in the park later this afternoon."

"Yes," she choked out, before the tears spilled over. She groped for her handkerchief but was unable to unknot the strings of her reticule. Once again Elston came to her rescue, dropping his handkerchief onto her lap before taking the reins in both hands again. When the curricle stopped a few minutes later in front of Blackburn House, she sighed in relief and mopped her tears.

"Karla."

"Yes?" She kept her head down, not wanting him to see her red-rimmed eyes.

"I did not reach the age of thirty without seeing a woman cry. And Lord knows you had far more provocation than most."

Hoping to divert Elston's attention from her tearstained face, she challenged him. "Thirty? I thought you were nine-and-twenty."

Karla did not hear his sigh, but she felt it—and marveled at his patience. "I am. My birthday is not until the end of the month." With gentle fingers, he grasped her chin and lifted her face to his. "Do you see the house with the green door and shutters on the other side of the street, halfway between here and Grosvenor Square?"

"Yes." It was one of the larger houses on the street.

"That is Symington House. If you need my assistance reasoning with your stepmother, or in any other matter, send a message to me."

He wanted to be her champion! Closing her eyes against the tears that once again threatened, she nodded, too over-whelmed to speak. She had loved him for so many years. Even though his feelings did not match hers, he obviously cared about her. That was enough. For now.

"My great-aunt is here for the Season. I understand you met her last night."

Karla nodded, fighting to gain control of her emotions—and her voice. "Yes. She seems very nice."

"She thought the same of you." He hesitated a moment, then added, "In fact, she said you were the only member of your family worth knowing."

Wide-eyed, she stared up him. He must have thought she questioned his word, for he said, "She was very impressed by your staunch support of Beth."

"Do you suppose Lady Lavinia could persuade my step-mother to that view?"

He smiled wryly. "If we asked, Livvy would try, but your stepmother seems quite intractable."

"She is." Karla's shoulders slumped in defeat.

"If Lady Blackburn is not at home, we will go to Syming-ton House. You can take tea with my aunt while I write a note to the countess, explaining what has happened."

Although Karla did not feel up to conversing with a near stranger, it was far preferable to returning to Padbury House. "Very well."

Elston stepped down from the curricle, then came around to assist her. Fortunately, Lady Blackburn was at home. Parks, Blackburn's rather starchy London butler, took one look at Karla, then led them up to the drawing room. A few minutes later, the countess joined them.

Lady Blackburn glanced from Karla's tearstained face to Elston's rather grim one. "What happened?"

After Elston explained the scene he had witnessed, the countess said, in a tone that brooked no refusal, "Karla, you will spend the rest of the Season with me."

It was her fondest wish, but she felt obliged to point out, "The viscountess is not likely to agree."

"Yes, she will." Lady Blackburn's certainty was heartening.

Elston's smile dawned as bright and warming as the sun. "You do not intend to give her a choice, do you, my lady?"

"I do not."

"Good. I didn't allow her one, either."

Exhausted, Karla leaned back against the sofa and closed her eyes. A few minutes later, Elston bowed over her hand.

"Karla, you have been through a great deal today. I hope you will feel better tomorrow and will drive in the park with me then."

She mustered a smile. "Thank you, Elston, for everything you have done today. I will look forward to driving with you tomorrow."

After leaving Blackburn House, Robert returned home. When Aunt Livvy informed him that George had not called, Robert's concern for his friends drew him back to the stable, then across Mayfair to Bellingham House. After being greeted at the door by Hargrave, whose normally impassive countenance bore an expression of relief, Robert was escorted to the study. The whispered admonishment "do something" followed him into the room.

George, his features taut with strain, sat in a wing chair in front of the fireplace, staring at a piece of paper clutched in his hand.

Robert's unease grew as he crossed the room. "George."

His friend roused, glancing around as if dazed.

"I have been waiting all day for you to call."

"Did we have an appointment? My apologies, Robert. I forgot."

Without waiting for an invitation, Robert sat in a nearby chair, wondering what bad news the letter had brought. "You said you would call after your visit to Castleton House, so I could be the first to wish you happy."

George buried his face in his hands. "She's gone."

"Who is gone?"

"Beth."

"Gone where?"

"I don't know. No one does."

Robert leaned forward. "Are you telling me that Beth left London without a word to anyone?"

"She left a note for her uncle and Lady Julia, and one for me, but neither says where she is going. Only that she is leaving." George lifted his head, looked down at the letter, and quoted, " 'Having destroyed my reputation beyond repair with my confession, I am leaving London for a time in the hope that my absence will minimize the repercussions of my foolishness for you, Uncle Charles, and Aunt Julia.' "

"She just left?" Robert asked, incredulous. "Alone?"

"Not alone. Her maid is with her."

He slumped back in his chair, totally flummoxed by such uncharacteristic behavior. "Is Castleton, or are you, searching for her?"

"He has men checking all of his estates. I sent my father's grooms and footmen to check the posting inns, and then the docks, but there is no word of her yet, and all the men have reported back except one. I am hoping he found the inn Beth left from and followed her, but I don't know that for certain yet. And won't until morning."

Robert nodded. "When you know, you can send men after them both."

"Yes. And pray to God we find her."

"Do Castleton and Lady Julia have any idea where Beth might have gone?"

"Castleton thinks, and I agree, that Beth will not go to Castleton Abbey. Buckinghamshire is too close to Town. The gossip would reach there in a day or two."

Beth was, usually, an intelligent, logical woman. If she had chosen her destination rationally, not emotionally—an assumption Robert was not certain they could make—distance would have been a determinant. "One of his other estates, then. Which is farthest from London?"

"He said she has never been to any of the others."

That was a facer. "Perhaps she has gone to visit a friend?"

George shook his head. "All her friends are in Town for the Season."

"Perhaps she told one of them what she was planning."

"When? She left the ball early, and she was gone from Castleton House before six o'clock this morning."

Time—or the lack thereof—was undeniably a factor. Even so, Robert thought Beth's friends an avenue worth pursuing. "Did she leave letters for anyone else?"

"I didn't think to ask this morning, but I will send a note to Castleton."

"If Beth told anyone, it would be Miss Lane. She didn't

mention Beth when I saw her earlier, but she had other things on her mind. I will call on my way home and inquire." Doing so would allow him to ascertain if Karla were feeling better now that the confrontations with her stepmother were a few hours in the past.

"Thank you, Robert. Send me word if Miss Lane knows anything."

"I will do better than that. I will come back and tell you what I learn. Then, over dinner we can plot a strategy, like we used to do on the Peninsula."

Chapter Fifteen

*R*obert felt a bit foolish returning to Blackburn House so soon, but he would willingly endure much worse to ensure his friends' happiness. Apparently he had been decreed a welcome caller; the butler escorted him to the morning room and announced him without taking his card to the countess first.

Setting aside the book she was reading, Lady Blackburn rose to greet him. "Two calls in one day, Elston?" she quizzed. "I feel certain it is not my charms that draw you."

"Your assumption is both wrong and right." He bowed over her hand. "In my opinion, you are one of the most charming ladies of the *ton*. But it is concern for a friend's happiness that brings me back this afternoon, not your charms. Or Karla's," he added, alluding to her teasing.

The countess waved him to a chair, then resumed her seat on the camelback sofa. "Karla is resting now, but she seems to have . . . accepted the day's events. When I showed her to her chamber, she was happier than she has been all week."

"I am very pleased to hear that. But it is not concern for her that brings me here now. Well," he amended, "mostly not."

"Has something happened?"

Robert cursed himself for having alarmed the countess. "Nothing that directly affects Karla, although it will concern her."

"Tell me, please."

"First, I must ask that you not tell anyone what I am about to tell you." Robert did not believe the Castletons or George would object to Lady Blackburn and Karla knowing that Beth had left London. Neither woman was a gossip, and both liked Beth.

Robert fought the urge to squirm as Lady Blackburn studied his face, feature by feature. "Not even Karla? You said the matter will concern her."

"I think Karla already has more than enough to worry about, but you may tell her if you deem it necessary."

"Very well. You have my word that I will not tell anyone, except possibly Karla, what you are about to tell me."

"Thank you, my lady. When you hear my tale, you will understand why I asked for your pledge."

Parks entered with a tea tray. When the butler left, Lady Blackburn lifted the teapot, then placed it back on the tray. "Would you prefer a glass of wine?"

Smiling at her kindness—many gentlemen disliked tea, considering the delicate beverage fit only for women—Robert shook his head. "No, thank you, my lady."

As his hostess poured out, then served him a selection of cakes, he gathered his thoughts. "I just learned from Weymouth that Beth Castleton left London early this morning. He is anxious to find her, as are her great-aunt and uncle, but her letters to them gave no hint of her destination. I was hoping Beth sent a message to Karla."

"Lady Julia and Castleton must be frantic! Why did Beth leave?"

"Her letter to Weymouth indicated that she believes her reputation tarnished beyond hope of salvaging after last night's confrontation with Lady Arabella."

"The poor girl!" A frown pleated Lady Blackburn's brow. "No one knows where she went?"

"Not unless she told a friend. I thought Karla her most likely confidante."

"I will inquire—discreetly—when she wakes up, and send a message to you if she knows anything. I intend to keep this news to myself for a few days. Karla is already overburdened with worries."

"Whatever you think best, my lady."

Robert set his cup and saucer on the tea tray and rose. "I hope you will forgive my precipitous arrival and departure, ma'am. Weymouth is expecting me."

"You are always welcome here, Elston."

"Thank you." He bowed over her hand. "Until tomorrow, my lady."

Sunday morning, Robert awoke with both head and loins throbbing. The latter had been a daily occurrence since he met Karolina Lane Monday evening, although he still was not certain if the woman in his dreams was Karla or her cousin. The headache was an unusual—and unwelcome— variation in routine, the result of having consumed too much brandy last night while attempting to divert George's thoughts from Beth's disappearance. With his eyes closed against the sunlight pouring into the room, Robert groped for the bellpull, hoping his friend was equally afflicted this morning.

When Higgins entered the room several minutes later, he took one look at his master, then turned on his heel. "I will be back in a few minutes, my lord, with The Cure and coffee."

The Cure, a vile-tasting concoction brewed by the butler from his grandfather's recipe, was extremely effective in reducing the effects of overindulgence. When Robert was younger, he had tested its curative powers with some frequency, but he had not been forced to do so for years. Grimacing, he settled back against the carved headboard and cradled his head in his hands. If the world were just, George, who had drunk at least twice as much, would be feeling twice as miserable. With that cheerful thought in mind, Robert planned his day.

An hour later, Cure'd, bathed, shaved, and dressed, he went downstairs. Breakfast held no allure, but he sat in the dining room with Aunt Livvy and drank several cups of coffee. Fortunately for the state of his head, his great-aunt was not one for chitchat, especially at breakfast. After accepting his apology for not dining with her last night, she said very little, allowing Robert to read the *Times* and his mail.

When he reached his book room, intent on working on his maiden speech for Lords, the letter lying in the center of his desk shattered his carefully laid plans.

"Baxter!"

The butler arrived on the run. "Yes, my lord?"

"When did this"—Robert waved the missive—"arrive?"

Baxter's eyes followed the letter, attempting to identify it. "In yesterday afternoon's post, my lord."

Robert gritted his teeth in an effort to curb his ill temper. His servants did not deserve his ire, nor were they its target. "Is there some reason no one mentioned it to me yesterday?"

"Did you not see the letter last night when you came in here, my lord?"

"I was not in the book room last night. When I got home, I went upstairs to bed."

The butler gaped. "But you always have a brandy here before retiring."

Was he so habit-bound that his every action was predictable? "Last night I did not, since I was already awash in brandy."

"My lord, I am sorry if the delay in receiving this letter has unduly inconvenienced you. From now on, I will give the night footman strict instructions to inform you of any messages that arrive after you leave the house."

Robert rubbed his temples, where the headache, although much less severe, still throbbed. "It is I who owe you an apology, Baxter. Much as I might wish otherwise, I could not have acted on this letter last night."

"What can I do to help now, my lord?"

Gathering his thoughts, he replanned his day. And the next fortnight. "Tell the grooms to have the blacks harnessed to my traveling coach and at the door in a hour. And send Higgins in here so he can start packing."

"Yes, my lord." Turning to leave, Baxter muttered, "Packing. Black team on heavy coach."

They were not questions, but the butler might have to deal with queries about Robert's absence, so he explained. "I must go . . . solve a problem at one of the northern estates. I will be away for about a fortnight, perhaps a bit longer if the weather, and the roads, are bad."

The butler nodded. "Lady Lavinia will be disappointed that you must leave so soon after arriving in Town."

Damnation! Robert had not considered how his departure would affect his great-aunt. "Before I leave, I will give you several letters that must be delivered today."

"Yes, my lord."

After giving instructions to his valet, Robert paced in front of the fireplace as he mentally composed several notes. Given the constraints of the letter he had received, the messages had to be carefully worded to conceal the purpose of his journey. He was seated at his desk, writing the fourth and final missive, when the butler knocked and entered.

"My lord, this was just delivered from Bellingham House."

Lord, what now? "Thank you, Baxter."

It was, of course, from George. He now knew the inn from which Beth had departed London yesterday and was preparing to give chase, but her trail disappeared at Biggleswade. Weymouth asked Robert to meet him there, with as many men as he could spare, so they could fan out and search the countryside.

He rose, reaching for the bellpull, then realized Baxter was there, waiting to see if a reply would be sent. "I need half a dozen men, grooms and footmen who can ride, to accompany me as far as Biggleswade, where they will stay and assist Lord Weymouth. They will need clothing for several days. I will supply funds for their bed and board."

"I will have them pack their things and meet you in the entry hall, my lord."

As he gathered the books and papers he needed to take with him, Robert's eye fell on the half-written letter on the blotter. With an oath, he crumpled it into a ball and tossed it in the fire. He would give George its message when he saw him this evening. After tucking the missive he had received that morning into his coat pocket, Robert picked up the three notes he'd written and carried them into the hallway. Baxter would have them delivered to Karla, Lady Blackburn, and Lady Julia.

Karla was enjoying her visit at Blackburn House. The countess's kindness, and her delight in sponsoring her protégée, were a balm to Karla's sadly battered esteem, and vastly different from the viscountess's callousness and petty cruelties. Blackburn, too, seemed pleased by Karla's presence, and had expressed the hope that she would remain with them until the Season ended and his mother returned to Yorkshire.

She had been a bit disconcerted to encounter the earl

at the breakfast table this morning, but he had folded his newspaper as soon as she entered the room and engaged her in conversation on topics ranging from literature to current events. When it became evident that she knew little about politics, he had explained the workings of Parliament and described some of the bills currently being debated in Lords. She also learned that Elston had taken his seat and attended regularly, but had not yet given his maiden speech.

Now, sitting in the morning room with Lady B, who was sorting through invitations for the coming week, Karla was not thinking about social events, but of the man who had made her Season possible. She was determined to make her long-overdue confession to Elston today, but her mental rehearsal of it was interspersed with frequent prayers that he would understand both the reasons for her deception and her reluctance to reveal it.

Although not at all certain he would forgive her, Karla was going to confess. Elston deserved her honesty. And her trust.

She started rather violently when Parks entered the room. Spying the silver salver he carried in his gloved hand, she returned to her musing as he offered the tray's contents to Lady Blackburn. When he suddenly bowed beside Karla's chair, she jerked as if stung by a bee, causing the butler to react in much the same manner.

"I did not mean to startle you, Parks, but you startled me."

"I beg your pardon, Miss Lane." He bent over and picked up a letter that had fallen to the floor, replaced it on the salver, then offered it to her. Hesitantly, she reached for the note, wondering if seeing her stepmother's scolding in black and white would be more, or less, bearable than listening to it.

Expecting the viscountess's looping scrawl, Karla was surprised to see her name inscribed in a bold, masculine hand. She turned the missive over and studied the seal. Elston. *Why is he writing to me when he will see me this afternoon?* Reluctant to open his message, convinced she would not like the news it bore, she put off the moment by pursuing her previous thought.

"Lady B, don't you think it strange that we have heard nothing from my stepmother? Or from Lydia?"

The letter the countess was reading dropped to her lap as she considered the question. Or her answer. "I am not quite certain what to think, my dear. I am surprised that Hortense has not called, either to give the appearance of granting me your company or to take us both to task, but Lydia did send two trunks of your clothing."

"I cannot help but wonder if she is spreading the worst sort of gossip about me."

"Lydia?" the countess asked, incredulous. "Why would she do that?"

"I meant the viscountess."

"Oh, my dear." Lady Blackburn crossed the room, then sat beside Karla on the sofa and embraced her. After several moments of silent comfort, the countess offered verbal assurance as well. "From what you have told me, and what Elston said yesterday, Hortense dare not test his promise. If he were to tell the *ton* what he saw and heard, she might not be ruined outright, but most people would deny any acquaintance with her. Since the *beau monde* has not welcomed her with open arms, I don't believe she will risk it."

"I am not certain she realized he was serious."

"Perhaps I misunderstood, but I thought you—and Elston, too—told me she didn't appear oblivious of what was being said and done until *after* he vowed he would tell the *ton* what he saw and heard yesterday."

Karla lifted her head from the countess's shoulder. "That is true, but what if—"

"Do not torment yourself with 'what if.' There is enough trouble in this world without worrying about things that might not happen. Or things we cannot change."

It was good advice, but not so easily accomplished. "Yes, my lady."

"Read your letter. Then we will make our plans for the week." Lady Blackburn returned to her escritoire.

Still assailed by misgivings, Karla picked up Elston's message, broke the seal, and began to read.

Dear Karla,
Much to my regret, I will not be able to take you driving in the park this afternoon. I received word this morning of a problem that re-

quires my attention, so I am leaving London immediately to deal with it.

I hope that my absence will not create problems for you with your stepmother. If she becomes troublesome, I recommend that you ask Lady Blackburn, her son, the Duchess of Greenwich, and Lady Kesteven for assistance in dealing with her. The ladies are aware of some of what you have endured from the viscountess, and I believe all would gladly help you in any way they can. Also, Weymouth and Dunnley would readily assist you.

I have asked Lady Blackburn if she would be kind enough to allow my great-aunt to accompany you to social events. I hope you will not object to sharing your mentor with Aunt Livvy. Few of her friends are in Town.

I apologize for canceling our outing, and for not calling in person to do so, but time is of the essence. I hope to be back in London in a fortnight, and I shall look forward to seeing you, and driving in the park with you, then.

Elston
11 April 1813

The letter dropped from Karla's suddenly boneless fingers as she struggled to contain a moan. *Elston would be gone for a fortnight.* Not only was she unable to confess her deception to him today, but she would not have his support in dealing with her stepmother. She slumped against the sofa cushions, wondering how she would manage the viscountess without him.

What will I do if my stepmother causes trouble? After considering that worrisome possibility for several minutes, Karla picked up Elston's note and read it again, hoping she had mistaken the length of his absence. Unfortunately, she had not.

He had, however, given considerable thought to her plight. And his suggestions were good ones. Lady B would certainly help if the viscountess tried to cause problems. So, Karla believed, would the duchess. Lady Kesteven had not expressed a willingness to do so, although she had chastised the viscountess for denying her stepdaughter to callers.

With luck, there would be no trouble. But Karla was not feeling very lucky.

Chapter Sixteen

Robert abhorred lying and liars. Even social fibs, such as agreeing that a lady wearing an unflattering gown looked lovely, made him uncomfortable. All the way from London to Biggleswade, his honor fought his conscience, but neither achieved victory. Since his choices were to break the vow of silence requested by one friend or to lie to his best friend, the battle was doomed from the start.

By the time his coachman halted at the inn George chose as their meeting place, Robert was miserable. And he still didn't know what to do. Both alternatives seemed equally dishonorable.

Dunnley's curricle was just ahead, the ostlers removing his pair of grays from the traces, six men in his livery leading their mounts toward the stable. Much as Robert would have preferred not to have an audience for his deceit—in whatever form it took—he waited for the viscount just outside the door to the inn.

"Well met, Elston. George was not shy about asking for help, was he?"

Robert shook the viscount's outstretched hand. "I will be very surprised if he requested it from anyone else."

"I don't imagine he did. Neither would I in his situation."

They entered the inn and were greeted by the landlord. After bespeaking rooms for themselves and their men, they—and their servants—entered the private parlor Weymouth had hired.

The earl was sitting at a table covered with maps and issuing instructions to a score of men. He did not notice their arrival until Robert spoke.

"What news, George?"

"Count me in as a searcher" was Dunnley's greeting to his cousin.

After thanking them both, George drew them to the table. And its maps. "Theo, search between here and Cambridge. Robert, you take the area toward Wolverton. Beth's uncle sent word that she was not at Castleton Abbey last night, but she may be headed in that direction."

"I regret that I cannot stay to assist in the search; urgent business calls me north." Grabbing a pen and paper, Robert wrote a short note. "If you have need of additional men, sent this to Elston Abbey and my steward will provide as many as you need."

Pleased with his explanation, which was entirely truthful, if not the entire truth, he hoped George would be satisfied and not demand details. Robert saw the angry retort hovering on his friend's lips, but after several tense seconds' scrutiny, George nodded. "Thank you, Robert."

"I will be traveling the Great North Road as far as Darlington and will inquire after Beth at every stop. If I find her, or hear news of her, I will send Higgins back with a message."

"That will help a great deal."

When Weymouth was satisfied that all the men knew their tasks for the morrow, he dismissed them. Then the three friends settled in for a comfortable coze.

The next morning, after an early breakfast with Weymouth and Dunnley, Robert continued his journey north. At every town with a posting house, he made inquiries about Beth and her maid, but there was no trace of the two women after Biggleswade. When he arrived in Darlington, Robert hired a courier to carry that news back to his friend. Then, his mission for George completed and his honor and conscience no longer at war, Robert set off for Hawthorn Lodge in Stranraer, Scotland. It was the start of yet another campaign.

As his traveling coach bowled along, Robert tapped the note in his coat pocket, wondering why Beth had chosen Stranraer as her retreat. It was, of course, quite remote. And hundreds of miles from London. If there were gossip about her, it might never reach the small town, and even if it did, the townspeople were unlikely to be interested in the tale.

The real question, however, was what he would do when he found Beth. Convincing her to return to Town, so George could propose, might prove difficult. She was determined to marry for love, and equally determined not to force Weymouth into wedlock. Although Robert was certain she loved George, she did not believe the earl returned her regard. Robert hoped he could persuade her that marriage to George would fulfill her wish—and his—for a love match.

Robert also would have to convince Beth that her reputation was not irrevocably ruined. It was, perhaps, a bit tarnished, but marrying George would restore it.

Marriage to Robert would have almost the same effect, since he had traveled with them from Scotland to England. But it would not be the love match Beth wanted. Nor the one he had begun to hope he could attain. She was a wonderful friend, and he was fond of her, but his feelings were platonic, not passionate. Even so, if he could not persuade Beth that George loved her, Robert's honor would compel him to propose.

It was almost enough to make him hope he did not find her.

Almost.

The letter she had sent him unequivocally stated that she was going to Stranraer, swore him to secrecy, and begged his pardon for trespassing on their friendship by trespassing on his property. Hawthorn Lodge was clearly her destination. Her fate was, or soon would be, in his hands. And his fate might well rest with her—even though she was not listed in the codicil.

Monday morning, Karla called at Castleton House. She wanted to see Beth, not only to ascertain that she had recovered from the contretemps at the St. Ives masquerade, but also to inform her friend that she was now living at Blackburn House. Although it was unusual for two days to pass without the two friends seeing each other, Karla had not attended any social events since Friday. Saturday night, she was still too shaken by her stepmother's venomous harangues to go anywhere, and she, Lady B, and Blackburn had spent Sunday quietly.

North answered the door almost as soon as Karla released the knocker. "Good morning, Miss Lane."

"Good morning, North. Is Miss Castleton at home?"

After a moment's hesitation, the butler showed her into the morning room.

"I will tell the Castletons that you are here, Miss Lane."

Karla did not especially want to see Lady Julia and the earl—the presence of Beth's relatives might inhibit her conversation—but visitors who called before the proper hour could not be too particular. Beth's great-aunt had always been kind to Karla, and she enjoyed Lady Julia's informal lessons on manners and deportment, often presented allegorically in tales of social gaffes in past Seasons.

It was not, however, Beth or her great-aunt who entered the room several minutes later. Karla jumped to her feet when Beth's uncle crossed the threshold, his limp more pronounced than usual, and seated himself in a nearby chair.

"Miss Lane, I know I am not the person you came to see, but I am afraid you will have to make do with my company this morning. Lady Julia is not feeling well."

In Karla's opinion, the earl did not look well, either. "Is Beth also not feeling quite the thing?"

"She certainly has not been her usual calm and logical self." Castleton sighed deeply. "The truth, Miss Lane, is that I do not know the exact state of Beth's health. She left London Saturday morning."

Beth left Town without saying good-bye? Stunned, Karla stared at the earl for several seconds. "She . . . she didn't tell me she was leaving." Gathering her reticule—and her wits—she stood. "I am sorry to have troubled you this morning, my lord."

Her curtsy wobbled precariously when Castleton said, "Beth did not tell anyone she was leaving. She ran away, fearing her confrontation with Lady Arabella destroyed her reputation."

Hearing the anguish underlying his words, Karla sank to her knees in front of the earl's chair. "What can I do to help, my lord? Would Lady Julia be cheered by a visit?"

*   *   *

Monday evening, Karla, Lady Blackburn, Lady Lavinia, and Blackburn joined the throng at the Italian Opera House to hear the acclaimed new soprano, Theresa Nardo, sing Mozart's *Le Nozze di Figaro*. On Tuesday, Lady Lavinia accompanied them to the Woodhurst twins' come-out ball. Karla enjoyed herself, and did not lack for partners, but the ball seemed sadly flat without Elston. And without Dunnley's gallantries. Blackburn and the Duke of Fairfax vied for the honor of taking her into supper, and one or the other was almost constantly at her side, but even so, she missed her old friend. Missed, as well, the boost to her confidence the viscount always provided.

Beth's absence was noticed—and commented on by everyone from gossipy dowagers to the other members of The Six, especially Deborah, who worried that she had offended Beth in some way. Although she wanted to ease Deb's concern, Karla could not without betraying Lord Castleton's confidence, and her vague reassurances had little effect.

Lydia and the viscountess were also absent. Conspicuously so, in Karla's opinion, although no one else seemed to notice. As the evening progressed and her fears of a confrontation with her stepmother eased, she could not help but wonder if their invitation had been rescinded or if they had chosen not to attend.

Both possibilities seemed equally unlikely. Although Lady Kesteven might not hold the viscountess in esteem, she would not punish Lydia for her mother's sins by rescinding the invitation. On the other hand, given Deborah and Diana's popularity, their father's high rank in the peerage, and her mother's reputation as one of Society's premier hostesses, Karla could not imagine her stepmother choosing not to attend the ball. Especially since there were certain to be an abundance of gentlemen, some of whom would not have the opportunity to dance with the twins and, therefore, might wish to dance with Lydia.

Since she could not put the question to her hostess, Karla resolved to call upon her stepmother and half-sister tomorrow and ask them. Hopefully, a private meeting would also dispel her fears about any retribution the viscountess might be planning.

*   *   *

Wednesday evening at Almack's, amidst more speculation about Beth's absence, an overheard conversation turned Karla's thoughts from her family to Elston. And to Beth. *Was it possible that he had followed her in order to propose?* His note had not specified the nature of the business that compelled his departure from Town, although he had mentioned its urgency. *Since he had traveled with Beth and Weymouth, did Elston feel honor bound to offer for her?* She had refused the earl, and marrying Elston would, Karla supposed, restore her friend's reputation as well as marriage to Weymouth.

But if the Castletons and Weymouth did not know where Beth had gone, how could Elston? Was it possible that she had confided her destination to him? Or that she had met him somewhere and they were even now racing toward Gretna Green? When she was thinking rationally, Karla knew that Beth had left London more than a day before Elston, and that there was no reason for them to go to Scotland to marry, but the heart is not governed by logic.

The Season lost its sparkle as Karla alternated between worrying that the man she loved would marry another and fretting about her stepmother's possible reprisals for her departure from Padbury House.

After seven very long days of driving, and seven even longer (or so it seemed) nights of haunting dreams, Robert arrived at Stranraer. Beth, however, was not there. Although it was possible that he had traveled more quickly than she, despite her earlier start, no one at any of the posting inns had seen her. Not since Biggleswade. Since he did not know if George had located her, nor if he'd found any trace of her route, Robert decided to wait a day or so to see if she arrived.

Feeling reprieved, and rather chagrined that he was experiencing such an unworthy emotion, he turned his attention to the other women dominating his thoughts: Karla and Miss Lindquist. He resolved to detour through Selby on the way back to Town and call at Paddington Court. Seeing Catherine Lindquist in the light of day should allow him to determine the identity of the woman in his dreams.

Two days later, Beth still had not arrived at Hawthorn

Lodge. Although he worried what had become of her, Robert had no way of knowing if she had changed her plans or if George had found her. After leaving instructions with his housekeeper to welcome Miss Castleton if she appeared, and to notify him immediately, Robert departed for London. Via Selby.

Robert arrived at Paddington Court four days later. Although the journey, both to and from Stranraer, had been blessed by good weather, allowing them to drive fourteen or more hours each day, Robert was tired of traveling. He had put the hours he'd spent sitting inside the coach to good use, studying estate papers, agricultural treatises, and the information he had collected on the plight of children working in mines and factories. He'd even written the first draft of his maiden speech for Lords, although that had been penned late last night in a private parlor at the inn where they had stopped, not in the coach. But although the trip had allowed him to catch up on his studies, it had not accomplished its intended purpose. And it seemed interminable. He missed the gaiety of Town, and his friends and activities there.

When he stepped down from the coach, Robert was greeted by Briggs, underbutler during his previous visit, but elevated to butler in Harris's absence.

"Good afternoon, my lord. I regret to inform you that the family is not here."

"I am aware that Lady Padbury, Miss Lane, and Miss Lydia are in London." Robert turned toward the open front door. "I am calling today to speak with the governess."

Mouth agape, the servant trailed behind, not speaking until they were inside. "You wish to see Miss Langhurst?"

Langhurst? For a moment, Robert questioned his memory—and his hearing. Then, remembering that the woman on the terrace was related to the late viscount's first wife and was, therefore, a Lindquist, Robert reiterated, "I wish to speak with the governess." The lady herself would answer the question of her name.

After sending a footman to notify the teacher of her visitor, Briggs conducted Robert to the drawing room and offered refreshments. He accepted a glass of sherry, then stood at the mantel, awaiting the arrival of the lady who might—or might not—be the object of his fantasies.

The woman who entered the room a few minutes later was definitely not the subject of Robert's dreams. Tall, spare, and on the far side of forty, she looked brisk and competent—and rather puzzled by his request.

"I am Sophia Langhurst." She curtsied. "You wished to speak to me, my lord?"

"You are the governess?"

"Yes, my lord." She motioned him to a chair, then seated herself.

"How long have you held your position?"

"About six weeks. Since the fifteenth of March."

Robert had visited Paddington Court earlier in the month, nearly a week before Miss Langhurst's arrival. "Do you know the current whereabouts of Miss Lindquist?" At the woman's blank look, he added, "Your predecessor."

"The previous governess was a Miss Meadows, my lord. She was dismissed last fall—October or November. I don't know where she is currently employed, but the house-keeper may know."

Remembering Catherine Lindquist's claim that she was not required to be useful until Lydia began appearing in local Society, Robert said, "Miss Lindquist taught the chil-dren between Miss Meadows's dismissal and your arrival."

"That may well be true, my lord, but when I arrived, the eldest Miss Lane was teaching them."

"Karolina was teaching them?" Robert asked, incredulous.

"I believe her name is Caroline. That is name the family used, except for the viscount. He called her Karla."

"Have your charges mentioned a Miss Lindquist? Cath-erine Lindquist."

"No, my lord, they have not."

She could not have vanished into the air. Perplexed, Rob-ert sat in silence for several moments. "Miss Langhurst, did Miss Lane mention a relative of hers who taught the chil-dren earlier this year?"

"No, my lord." After a short pause, she added, "Al-though she didn't explicitly say so, it was my impression that Miss Lane had been teaching them for some time."

More baffled than before, Robert thanked the governess and dismissed her.

Several minutes later, when Briggs entered the room, Robert asked to be shown to the library. His immediate objective was to find a copy of Burke's *Peerage*—and to read the section on the Earls of Maitland. Karla's mother, Ingrid Lindquist, was the daughter of the late earl and a sister of the present one. If Catherine Lindquist was a relative, her name was almost certain to be listed.

It was not.

His frustration mounting, Robert went in search of the butler. "Briggs, when I visited here last month, who was the children's governess?"

The servant shifted from foot to foot, avoiding Robert's gaze. "They didn't really have a governess, my lord. Not until Miss Langhurst came."

"Who was teaching the children when I was here last month?"

"Miss Karolina was, my lord."

Stunned, Robert nodded in acknowledgment and thanks. Then, his teeth gritted to keep from cursing the air blue, he turned on his heel and stormed outside. *Karla had deceived him! And she had compounded the crime by not confessing her deception.*

Chapter Seventeen

$\mathcal{A}$ determined man, riding hard and changing horses frequently, can travel quite quickly. Robert was angry, and very determined. At the first inn, he abandoned his traveling chaise in favor of a horse, leaving his coachman and Higgins to bring the rig back to Town. Twenty-seven hours and approximately one hundred eighty miles later, Robert arrived in London. And he was still furious.

But a man with only his thoughts for company can do a lot of thinking in twenty-seven hours. Robert certainly had. As a result, most of his anger was not directed at Karla. He still intended to confront her about her deception and the reasons for it, but he had realized that what she'd told him of "Catherine Lindquist" and her situation had been a truthful account of Karla's own plight.

Now his fury was aimed at Lady Padbury, for treating her stepdaughter like a unpaid servant and isolating her from her friends. And at himself, for not fully comprehending Karla's circumstances when he visited Paddington Court last month and for not immediately realizing that, with all that had happened in the week preceding his departure, she'd had little time and less opportunity to confess her masquerade. He was quite certain that she would do so. Whether he had the patience to wait until she did was much less likely.

He loved her. He wanted to wrest her from her stepmother's household, and to love and cherish her as she deserved.

Before leaving Town, he had accomplished the first. Karla was happily settled at Blackburn House with the countess now. At least, he hoped she still was. Lady Padbury might have assumed that his absence was a sign he had forgotten his vow. He had not. If the viscountess had been up to her old tricks while he was away, she would soon regret her folly.

Achieving his second objective would be more difficult. Karla's deception was a formidable obstacle for a man who prized honor and honesty above all else to overcome. Or overlook. Then there was the fact that he did not know if she returned his regard. She had been happy to resume their friendship, but he wanted more. Much, much more.

He wanted her love. He wanted her to be the sunshine in his life. He wanted his dreams to become reality. And he feared that in the fifteen days since he had last seen her, she might have given her heart, or her hand, to another.

His first impulse was to ride directly to Blackburn House and confront Karla. First, with her deception, and then, if he could accept her reasons for it, with his heart. But he would not dishonor Karla or scandalize Lady Blackburn by appearing in her drawing room weary, disheveled, and travel-stained, so he went home instead. Aunt Livvy greeted his return with cries of delight—then informed him that they were hosting a small dinner party that evening. Robert stifled a sigh and, after a few minutes, excused himself. He desperately needed a nap and a bath. In that order.

Two and a half hours later, clad in evening attire and slightly less weary, Robert descended the stairs. He had no idea who his aunt's guests were and could, perhaps, be forgiven for hoping they all had other commitments after dinner. With any luck, there would be a ball or rout the fashionable world felt they *must* attend. If he was truly fortunate, Aunt Livvy would know Karla and Lady Blackburn's plans for the evening.

He reached the drawing room just as the knocker banged against the front door. Before he had a chance to ask his great-aunt who their dinner guests were, Baxter escorted a trio of them up the stairs and into the room: Blackburn, his mother, and Karla. His smile one of genuine pleasure, Robert greeted them—and felt his fatigue evaporate like the morning mist. Karla's eyes widened when she saw him.

"Elston! How very nice to see you again. I didn't know you were back in Town."

He bowed over her hand. "I returned a few hours ago, but too late to pay a call. Will you drive with me in the park tomorrow?"

"I would like that, very much, but I am promised to Fairfax." A rueful smile accompanied the words.

"Wednesday, perhaps? Or are you already committed for the entire week?"

She laughed, as if such a thing were impossible. "Of course not."

When she turned toward Lady Blackburn for permission, Robert whispered urgently, "Karla, I need to speak with you alone."

She looked askance at him, no doubt wondering what he had to say that required privacy—and such a breech of social custom. "I need to speak with you, too." Then, in a normal tone, "I would be honored to drive with you Wednesday, my lord."

Why did she want to speak with him? "May I call for you at four o'clock?"

"That will be fine, Elston," Lady Blackburn replied.

After escorting Karla to a sofa, he sat beside her. He did not want to wait until Wednesday to talk with her, damn it, but he might not have a choice. Her whispered suggestion, "Perhaps, after dinner, you could show me the garden . . . or a portrait of your father?" surprised and delighted him. He nodded in agreement as she continued the unexceptional—and unwhispered—portion of their conversation.

"Was your trip successful, Elston?"

"I did not accomplish what I hoped to, but there were unexpected benefits."

She raised a brow, inviting him to expand upon his answer. Instead, he asked quietly, "Who else has my aunt invited this evening?"

"I do not know." After a moment's hesitation, she added, "It is a party to celebrate your birthday."

"Heaven help me," he muttered. Aunt Livvy had always made much of his birthdays. "But my birthday is not until the twenty-sixth."

"Today is the twenty-sixth, my lord Hard Work. And a Monday."

Her teasing comment drew his smile. No doubt a sheepish one. "It was all the traveling, not the work, that made me lose track."

The arrival of another group of guests interrupted their interlude. Although he was pleased to see Dunnley, Fairfax, Howe, Radnor, and Brewster, Robert wanted to talk more with Karla. Perhaps after dinner they could continue their conversation.

In a few moments aside with Dunnley, Robert learned the viscount had returned to Town last week, as had Weymouth for a day or so. But they had not yet found Beth, and George and the Castletons were frantic, so he had not stayed long.

Dinner was a pleasant, and rather jovial, affair. Although he enjoyed his friends' company, and that of the Blackburns and Karla, Robert was not displeased when all the men pleaded other engagements and left about an hour after the meal.

His aunt proposed a game of whist, but Robert countered with, "Perhaps a bit later, Aunt Livvy. I would like to show Karla the portraits of my parents."

Both older women's brows rose, but Karla's "Oh, you remembered my request!" settled them back into place. Smiling, Lady Blackburn granted permission.

"Of course I remembered." Robert offered his hand to help Karla from her chair.

When they reached his study, he pointed out the portraits, then seated Karla in a wing chair in front of the glowing embers of the fire. After adding another log, he sat in a matching chair. A piecrust table covered with books and papers separated the pair.

"You said earlier that you needed to speak with me. Has your stepmother been causing trouble?"

"No." Karla looked down at her hands. "At least, none that I am aware of."

"I am glad to hear it."

"Elston, I have not seen my stepmother or Lydia since the day you took me to Blackburn House! Every time I call, even if I go in the morning, they are out."

"That is unusual?"

She nodded. "Very unusual. The viscountess and Lydia are rarely seen outside their bedchambers before noon, even in the country."

"And at social events?"

"I have not seen them at all. Harris said they go out every evening, but . . ." Her shrug conveyed puzzlement, and a bit of helplessness.

"I will call tomorrow. If they are not home, I will ask Harris what social events they are planning to attend."

"I didn't even think to ask that. I always expect to find them home the next day."

"A reasonable expectation, if you call in the morning."

"I suppose so, but . . ."

"But it bothers you that you have not seen them." It bothered him, too.

"Yes." She sighed. "Perhaps it is foolish, but I would feel better if I saw them. I have a terrible fear that when the viscountess sees me, she will ring a peal over my head, no matter where we are. I would prefer that it occur at Padbury House."

"Hopefully, it will not happen at all. My visit should remind your stepmother of the folly of pursuing such a course."

Karla looked so unhappy that Robert could not bring himself to add to her distress by taking her to task for her deception. Stifling a sigh, he resigned himself to at least another day's wait. Then, after another look at her downcast head, he asked, "What else is troubling you, my dear?"

"Elston, I did something very foolish. And very stupid."

Alarmed, he leaned forward slightly. "What did you do?"

"I foolishly allowed pride—false pride—to overrule common sense and manners and . . . everything. When you visited Paddington Court last month, I pretended to be Catherine Lindquist the governess. So you would not know that my stepmother treated me little better than a servant."

Although elated by Karla's confession, Robert was not certain how best to react to her disclosure. "You are Catherine Lindquist?" He hoped he sounded as surprised as he had felt the previous day when he'd learned the truth.

Clearly miserable, she nodded. "I regretted the lie almost as soon as I uttered it, but I did not know how to admit it without revealing the reason for it."

After several moments of silence, he asked, gently but

with real curiosity, "Why didn't you want me to know your circumstances?"

"Because . . ." Her hands writhed in her lap. "Because ever since I was a little girl, whenever things were difficult at home, I dreamt that you would rescue me. Like a knight in a fairy tale, you always came and saved me." Averting her face, she added, "A lady does not want to be pitied by the man who is the hero of her dreams."

Stunned, Robert sank back into his chair. Her soft-voiced disclosure touched him in more ways than he could count. Or name. After a silence that grew almost long enough to be awkward, he said, "You set your knight a difficult task, my lady, expecting rescue but refusing to admit to him you need it."

"Yes, I realize that now."

"I would have thought our friendship sufficient to guarantee my compassion."

She glanced at him, then away. "How could it when we had not seen each other for seventeen years?"

"Must friends see each other in order for friendship to endure?" he countered, rising to his feet. "You did not forget me during the intervening years, nor I, you."

"But—" Karla sputtered in confusion when Elston grasped her hands and drew her to her feet.

"I was delighted to resume our friendship when I arrived in Town. Had, in fact, been looking forward to it since I visited Paddington Court. I thought you were as pleased."

"Oh, I was, Elston. That was part of the reason it was so difficult for me to confess I had deceived you. You are known as an honest, honorable man, and I feared I would lose your regard."

"You still have my friendship, and my regard." He raised her hands to his lips, brushed a kiss against the knuckles of both.

The warmth in his voice, as well as the unprecedented salute, gladdened Karla's heart—and set her insides aquiver.

"What else made it difficult to tell me?"

"I wanted a degree of privacy for my confession, so no one else would know I had lied, but I always saw you in company. It was quite a conundrum. I could not tell you

when you called at Padbury House, but I was terrified you
would ask about Miss Lindquist in my family's hearing."

"Poor girl. No wonder you stammer during my visits."
He wrapped an arm around her shoulders and steered her
toward a nearby sofa. "And on the one occasion I mentioned her name."

Frowning in concentration, she sat. "When was that?"

"The day we drove in Hyde Park."

"I do not recall a mention of Miss Lindquist."

He sat beside her, holding her hand. "We were walking
by the Serpentine."

"I only remember being upset because my stepmother
denied me to callers."

"That was a more urgent problem."

Curious, she looked up at him. "How can you recall a
mention of Miss Lindquist weeks ago?"

"I remember because you began stuttering." She must
have looked as confused as she felt because he explained.
"I feared it was an indication that you were uncomfortable
alone with me."

"No, Elston. Never that."

"Is there anything else you wish to tell me? Other secrets
you wish to confess?"

"No." Then with great daring, she added, "Only that I
missed you while you were gone."

"I missed you, too, sweetheart."

Pleased by his admission, and the endearment, she
leaned her head against his arm. And was startled erect by
his next words.

"I have something to tell you. Several things. And something to ask."

He took a deep breath and let it out slowly, as if steeling
himself for a difficult task. "Who is your guardian?"

"My uncle James, the Earl of Maitland." Although she
wondered why he wanted to know, a glance at Elston's face
indicated it would be best not to ask now. With his next
statement, the question flew out of her mind.

"I have dreamt of you, too, Karla. Every single night
since we met at the Throckmortons' ball. The dreams confused me because the lady in them looked like you but
called herself Catherine Lindquist. Perhaps I should have
realized you were one and the same, but I did not. On my

way back to Town, I detoured through Selby so I could stop at Paddington Court and see Miss Lindquist again."

"You already knew, didn't you?" It was a statement, not a question.

He nodded. "Yes, but it is better—for both of us—that you confessed your deception."

"I know the advantages for me. That lie has weighed on me for weeks. But I don't understand how you benefit from my disclosure. Unless . . ." She peeked up at him through her lashes. "Did it mitigate your anger? I expected you would be furious."

"I was very angry when I left Paddington Court yesterday afternoon—"

"You could not have traveled from Selby to London in one day!"

"It is possible, if one rides hard and fast. And late into the night," he added rather wryly. "But all those solitary hours gave me time to think, and when I did, I realized that 'Catherine Lindquist' gave an accurate description of your situation."

"Yes, she did . . . I did."

"Once I understood that, I redirected my anger to the proper targets."

"'The proper targets'?" she echoed, bewildered. "I was the one who lied."

"Yes, you did. But if your stepmother treated you as she ought, you would not have felt the need to conceal your circumstances."

There was no arguing with that, but it seemed beside the point.

"I was also angry at myself, for not having fully comprehended your situation when I visited Paddington Court. And for taking so long to realize it here."

"At the Court, you understood more than you realize, and did much to alleviate my circumstances by convincing my stepmother to present me this Season. And here in Town, you rescued me from Padbury House." Turning to face her champion, Karla laid her hand on his coat sleeve. "Blame me, and the viscountess, but not yourself."

He caught her gaze and smiled into her eyes. "Then let us blame your stepmother, since her actions caused yours. And mine."

With great trepidation, Karla asked the question that had tormented her for weeks. "In time, will you be able to forgive me for deceiving you?"

"I believe I already have."

Elston had considered his reply before voicing it, but even so, Karla was not convinced she was exonerated. At least, not completely. And perhaps she did not deserve to be until she had shown him, by word and deed, that she was worthy of his trust. And his regard.

"Karla, I want to ask your uncle for permission to pay my addresses to you." A note of uncertainty entered Elston's voice. "If you do not object."

Her heart racing, she stared at him, fearing she had misunderstood. "What?"

"I want his blessing before I ask you to marry me."

One of them was suffering from obtuseness, but Karla was not certain who was afflicted. Perhaps they both were. "Why do you want to marry me? Is it because—"

"Because I love you, sweetheart." He raised her hands to his lips, then brushed a kiss across her knuckles, the second more lingering than the first. "And because I like and admire and respect you."

It was the answer she hoped for, but even so, she felt . . . unsettled. And uncertain. "I love you, too, Elston. I have for years. But . . ." She bit her lip, and sought the courage to make her dreams come true.

Robert's heart leapt when she professed her love for him, but now his muscles tensed. "What, my dear?"

"I know you are fond of me as a friend, but I want my husband to love me as a woman, too."

"I love you as a friend and as a woman, Karla." She looked so lovely in her rosy pink crepe gown with blond lace at the neckline that it was difficult to refrain from pulling her into his arms and showing exactly how he felt— and what he'd dreamt.

She scrutinized his features for several seconds, as if seeking the truth behind his words. "I have no objection to you asking my uncle for permission to pay your addresses. I would be honored, and very proud, to be your wife."

Robert's muscles began to relax . . . until he sensed an imminent "but."

"Will you do something for me?"

"Of course, sweetheart. If it is within my power."

"Even if you speak with my uncle tomorrow, I would ask that you not propose for a fortnight."

She placed a finger against his lips, stilling his objection. "You need to be certain that you can forgive me for deceiving you. I need to be sure that your offer is not prompted by pity or a sense of obligation, but by love.

"Will you grant us both that time, Elston?"

Although disappointed, Robert could not dismiss the validity, or the importance, of her concerns. "Yes, my dear, I will. But I hope you do not mean that we should not see each other for a fortnight. That would resolve nothing."

"I did not mean you should not call, but . . . but you ought to spend time with other young ladies, so you are certain of your heart."

He stood, then pulled Karla to her feet—and into a loose embrace. "I have known my heart for weeks, but I will do as you ask, so you may be equally certain."

Bending his head, he brushed a soft, quick kiss against her rosy lips. If her heart was uncertain, perhaps that would help to persuade her.

Chapter Eighteen

Tuesday morning, after sending a bouquet of pink rose-buds to Karla, Robert called on her uncle, the Earl of Maitland, and received permission to pay his addresses to her. Although impatient to make Karla his wife, Robert would grant her request for time. He did not need it; he had forgiven her for deceiving him once he'd understood why she had done so. Her remorse, and the fact that she had always spoken truthfully since they'd met in Town, even when it cast her or her family in a less than favorable light, was enough to convince him that lies and deceit were not part of her character.

Against all odds, he had found love. If Karla accepted his proposal, he would also honor his father's final request. Having begun the Season fearing he would end up married to a woman who admired his title and fortune more than him, he understood Karla's need to be certain it was love, not pity, that inspired his proposal.

So he would wait. And while he did, he would do everything in his power to ease her fears and prove his love for her.

Early in the afternoon, he drove to Padbury House to call on Karla's stepmother and half-sister, but the ladies were not at home. According to Harris, they rarely were. Since the viscountess had few acquaintances among the *beau monde*, Robert could not help but wonder how, and where, they spent their days. After expressing Karla's concern for her half-sister, and alluding to her wish to avoid a public confrontation with the viscountess, he was invited to the butler's pantry to share a glass of wine with that worthy. When he left the house half an hour later, Robert was in possession of a list, scrawled in Harris's rather crabbed hand, of Lady Padbury's engagements for the week. And a warning that the viscountess was "up to something"— something that would *not* benefit her stepdaughter.

He called at Blackburn House to give Karla the news, and to suggest that they attend one or two of the social events on Harris's list, but neither she nor Lady Blackburn were at home. Robert's disappointment must have shown in his face, for after placing his card on a silver salver on the hall table, Parks informed him that he could see them tonight at the Greenwich musicale. Robert hoped that Aunt Livvy had accepted the invitation, and that she did not have an escort.

Next, he went to Castleton House, although Tuesday was not one of Lady Julia's At Home days. Beth's great-aunt was not in, but the earl was happy to receive him. After thanking Robert profusely for his assistance in scotching the rumors about Beth, Castleton informed him that she was still missing, but they had received a letter from her last week, sent from Northumberland, stating that she was safe and well. Robert was happy to hear good news about Beth and not at all surprised to learn that Weymouth had departed for the distant shire the day after the missive arrived.

Feeling his luck was out, but determined to pay three more calls and thereby honor Karla's request that he spend time in the company of other young ladies, Robert drove to Broughton House, simply because it was closest. Mrs. Broughton and her daughter were not at home, so Robert left his card, but as he was stepping into his curricle, they returned. He waved the footman aside, then handed them down from their carriage.

A shy smile and a "Good afternoon, my lord" were Miss Broughton's greeting, but her mother was more voluble. "Lord Elston, how nice of you to call. Will you join us for a cup of tea?"

"It would be my pleasure, ma'am." He escorted them inside, a lady on each arm.

In the drawing room, after refreshments had been served and social pleasantries exchanged, Miss Broughton asked, "Will you be performing at the Duchess of Greenwich's musicale tonight, my lord?"

"No." With a wry smile he added, "Not unless Bellingham and Weymouth planned something and neglected to inform me."

"I believe Lord Weymouth is out of town." Harriett Broughton's speaking glance indicated Robert would know why.

"My daughter is correct," Mrs. Broughton said, "although we might be mistaken. I understood from your great-aunt that you, too, were away."

"I was, until late yesterday." He turned to Miss Broughton. "Shall I have the pleasure of hearing you perform tonight?"

"Yes." A rosy flush colored her cheeks. "I hope it will be pleasurable."

"You will do splendidly, just as you did at your mother's musicale."

"Thank you, my lord."

After several more minutes of conversation, Robert took his leave. But not before bespeaking a dance with Miss Broughton the following night at Almack's, and inviting her to drive in the park with him on Friday.

At Kesteven House, the drawing room was so thronged with callers, both male and female, that Robert feared he would be able to do little more than greet the ladies of the household. But by extending his call slightly longer than was proper, he was able to talk with Lady Deborah long enough to reserve a dance with her Wednesday night at Almack's and to invite her to drive in the park with him on Thursday. Both requests received her mother's smile of approval. Lady Diana was so surrounded by admirers vying for her attention that he was unable to speak with her, but the marchioness agreed to convey to her younger daughter his request for a set at Almack's. Robert had no real wish to dance with Lady Diana, but it would be rude to ask one twin and not the other.

His final call, at Tregaron House, was as unsuccessful as the first; Lady Sarah and her mother were not at home. They would surely be at Almack's tomorrow—young ladies making their come-outs rarely missed the assemblies—and Lady Sarah might well be performing at tonight's musicale. As he drove away from the house, he wondered if the beauteous Sarah's reserve had melted a bit as she became more familiar with the *ton* and its denizens.

Returning home to Upper Brook Street, Robert considered calling again at Blackburn House but decided against it. He did not want Karla to feel hounded, or pressured to make a decision. Harriett Broughton had said that she, Karla, and three other young ladies would be singing at the musicale tonight, so he would hope for an opportunity to talk with her then.

Despite the fact that he was unable to claim Karla as his supper partner (Blackburn having asked in advance), Robert enjoyed the Greenwich musicale. He did manage a few minutes of conversation with her, as well as with Miss Broughton, Lady Deborah, and Lady Sarah. The four, and Lady Christina, gave an excellent performance of a Purcell quintet. He later learned they had planned to sing two sextets, but were forced to change their program after Beth Castleton's sudden departure from London.

The rest of the week passed in much the same way. He paid calls early in the afternoon, drove in the park at the fashionable hour with various young ladies (Karla on Wednesday and Sunday, Lady Deborah on Thursday, Harriett Broughton on Friday, and with Lady Sarah, whose reserve was still formidable, on Saturday), attended Parliament, and appeared at a number of social events. Wednesday night at Almack's, he danced with Karla (a minuet and a waltz), Lady Deborah (another waltz, much to his surprise given her popularity) and her twin (a country dance), Miss Broughton, Lady Sarah, Lady Christina, and a number of others. Thursday evening, he spent some time in conversation with all five young ladies and their parents (or, in Karla's case, her chaperone) at Lady Moreton's soiree. On Friday, Robert gave his maiden speech in Lords to great acclaim. That night, he danced with all five young ladies at the Sherworth ball, and escorted Karla to supper. They shared a table with Lady Deborah and Dunnley, and Robert was astounded (and extremely flattered) to learn that both young ladies, as well as Miss Broughton, had been in the galley to hear his speech, which they deemed powerful and very moving.

Saturday afternoon, his daily calls to Padbury House finally paid off. He was so accustomed to being told the viscountess and her daughter were not at home that he was surprised when Harris informed him they were in, then escorted him upstairs to the drawing room.

"Good afternoon, Elston," Lady Padbury gushed. "I am sorry we were not here earlier in the week when you called, but we have been very busy planning Lydia's come-out ball. We do hope you will be able to attend."

Hoping the viscountess had misspoken, but fearing she had not, Robert arced an eyebrow and said, evenly, "Lydia's come-out ball? Surely you mean a ball for Karla and Lydia."

"No. Caroline chose to leave this house. If she wants a ball, she must look to Jane Blackburn to give her one."

"Mama," Lydia protested, "I have told you and told you that I want to share my ball with Karla."

The viscountess frowned at her daughter. "We will discuss this later."

"I think," Robert said, "we should discuss it now. I remember well why Karolina left this house, Lady Padbury. It was not her choice, but yours."

"Mine?" The viscountess shook her head. "No, Elston, you are mistaken."

"Do you so easily forget the deplorable scene I witnessed, madam? Or my promise to you?"

"Scene?" Lady Padbury sounded as if she had no idea what he meant.

He glanced at Lydia, hoping for an explanation, but her only response was an unenlightening shrug. Choosing to ignore, at least for the moment, the viscountess's faulty memory, Robert returned to the subject of the ball. "I realize, Lady Padbury, that you spent most of the years of your marriage in Yorkshire and, therefore, may not be as familiar with Society's rules as the mothers of other young ladies being presented this year."

The viscountess agreed that might be the case.

"If you give a ball for Lydia and ignore Karolina, who should be equally honored, the *beau monde* will not attend. In fact, such an unprecedented occurrence will most likely result in you and your daughter being shunned. Or ostracized."

"But—"

"Lady Blackburn and Karla have made it generally known that the countess has long wanted to sponsor a young lady in Society, and that you were kind enough to give her the opportunity to chaperone Karla for a few weeks. If the *ton* learns the real reason for Karla's stay at Blackburn House, you—and, by extension, Lydia—will become social pariahs. Since that will not suit your plans, I suggest you make haste to reconcile with your stepdaughter, and to include her in the ball."

"But the invitations have already been printed! Most have been addressed and are ready to be delivered on Monday."

"I would think it better to have the invitations reprinted, so the *ton* will attend the ball, but . . ." Robert shrugged. When Lady Padbury did not respond, he turned on his heel and strode quickly from the room.

On the evening of the tenth of May, Karla entered Padbury House on Elston's arm. The occasion was, ostensibly, her and Lydia's come-out ball, but Karla felt more like a condemned man approaching the gallows than a young lady about to be feted by Society. This night ought to be one of the highlights of her Season, but she, as well as Elston and Lady Blackburn, feared the viscountess would use the occasion to puff off her daughter while demeaning her stepdaughter. Or worse.

Karla stole a glance at her escort. She had fallen even deeper in love with Elston in the past thirteen days, and she believed—no, she *knew*—he loved her, too. He had honored every aspect of her request, and she wished, desperately, that she had not asked him to wait a fortnight before proposing. Were she his betrothed, she could face her stepmother with equanimity. Instead, because of her foolishness (or, more accurately, her lack of self-esteem), she was quaking in her slippers.

Elston handed his hat and cane to Harris, who whispered something to him. The marquess frowned, then exchanged a few quiet words with Lady B. Karla's trepidation increased. When he returned to her side, Elston placed his hand at the small of her back. "Do you want to speak with your stepmother before the ball? Lydia asked Harris to tell us she thinks you should."

"I don't know." The circumstances were extraordinary, if not bizarre. Karla had known nothing about the ball until she received the invitation. The viscountess had had new invitations printed, but she'd made no attempt to reconcile with, or even visit, her stepdaughter. Lydia had called at Blackburn House two mornings last week, but Karla had not seen her stepmother since the day she'd received her voucher for Almack's, exactly one month ago.

Elston must have sensed her confusion, for he steered her and Lady Blackburn into the morning room, closing the door behind them. After seating the countess in a chair by the portal, he led Karla to a sofa at the far end of the room. He paced for a minute or two, his coattails flaring out with each turn, then perched sideways on the cushion beside her and captured her gloved hands between his. His legs, clad in white satin knee breeches and white silk stockings, brushed the skirts of her ivory silk ball gown.

"Sweetheart, I know this will be a difficult evening for you. I wish I could do something to make it easier for you."

You can. You can propose to me now. In the security of your love, I can face the viscountess, and anyone—or anything—else. But a young lady cannot say such things, not even to the man she loves with all her heart. Instead, Karla leaned forward and rested her head against Elston's velvet-clad shoulder.

In a moment, his arms encircled her. She thought he brushed a kiss against her hair, but the touch was so light, and so fleeting, she could not be certain. She did not know how long they sat thus, but after a time he lifted her head with a gentle finger under her chin and caught her gaze.

"I love you, Karla. I will be by your side tonight, a knight to stand your champion against all opponents." After a moment's pause, he added, "And if you make me the happiest of men, I will be beside you every day for the rest of our lives."

"I love you, too, Elston."

He grasped her hands and raised them to his lips. Karla wished her gloves would melt away, so she could feel his kiss against her knuckles, but the tingling heat that radiated from her fingers down to her toes, although scorching, was not sufficient to melt the thin ivory kidskin.

At the sound of voices in the hall, he stood and pulled

her to her feet. Then, still holding her hands in his, he kissed her, the soft, gentle caress of his lips against hers as much a declaration of his love as the words he'd spoken earlier.

"Ahem."

Elston raised his head and darted a glance at Lady Blackburn. When he looked back at Karla, a smile quirked the corners of his mouth. "I think your wonderful chaperone is trying to tell us it is time to adjourn to the ballroom."

Karla smiled. "I think you are right."

His hands tightened their clasp on hers. "The fortnight I promised you, my love? Do we count from the night you requested it or from the day I received your uncle's permission to offer for you?"

"From the night I requested it," she said, knowing it to be the shorter time.

Smiling, he brushed a quick kiss against her lips. "In that case, I have a very important question to ask you later."

"Ask me now."

Karla did not realize she had spoken the words aloud until Elston knelt at her feet, his hands still holding hers. "I love you, Karolina. Will you accept my hand and heart and do me the very great honor of becoming my wife?"

"The honor is mine, Lord Elston," she said formally, freeing one hand to touch his dark curls. "I would be very happy, and very proud, to be your wife."

In one lithe movement, he rose to his feet and pulled her into his arms. Karla would have been content to stay there forever, enjoying his kisses, but after a time, a knock at the door and the murmur of conversation recalled them to their surroundings.

Lady Blackburn, Lady Lavinia, Charles, and Lydia greeted them with beaming smiles, and Charles's "Finally!" drew a round of laughter. Of the ball itself, Karla remembered nothing, save waltzing twice with Robert.

Epilogue

*O*n the anniversary of his father's death, and six months
to the day after Robert and Karla had been married
at St. George's in Hanover Square with their families and
friends and most of the *ton* as witnesses, Robert met with
his solicitor in the library at Elston Abbey. Mr. Waring
discharged his last duty to the late marquess by delivering
a letter to the man's son, the current marquess. Robert,
reading the letter a second time, was not aware of the solicitor's departure until Karla entered the room.

"Is everything all right? Mr. Waring did not stay very
long."

"Everything is fine," Robert replied, pulling her onto his
lap. "Better than fine." He handed her the letter.

> *My dear son,*
>   *I hope that in the past year you have not found*
> *the duties of the marquessate too onerous or*
> *overwhelming, and that you have found a young*
> *lady with whom you can share all of the joys*
> *and burdens of your life. I wish for you and*
> *your wife all the love and laughter, and all*
> *the joys and blessings, your mother and I shared.*
> *You were the greatest blessing of all, Rob, a*
> *living, breathing, and wholly wonderful testa-*
> *ment to my love for your mother, and of hers*